THE MARSHAL & MRS. MORGAN

MATCHMAKER MISCHIEF

MATCHMAKER MISCHIEF

MARIE PATRICK

OLIVERHEBERBOOKS

The Marshal & Mrs. Morgan 2025 © Marie Patrick

Cover art by Dar Albert, Wicked Smart Designs

Published by Oliver-Heber Books

0 9 8 7 6 5 4 3 2 1

CHAPTER 1

SERENITY, NEW MEXICO—SPRING, 1891

*T*resia Morgan placed the last bar of fancy soap all the way from Paris, France on the display table and took a step back to admire her handiwork—or more truthfully, critique her work. It wasn't perfect, but then, it rarely was, no matter how hard she tried.

She tilted her head to the side, pulled her bottom lip between her teeth, then reached out and made an adjustment. Better, but still not perfect.

And it didn't matter. Nothing ever seemed to please her cousin, Arnold, who now owned Sullivan's Emporium though it should have belonged to her. She'd had such plans for the store but that all ended at the reading of her father's Last Will and Testament, which left everything to Arnold, including the apartment over the store she'd grown up in. Yes, she still worked here, but that was only because her father had made that a provision in his will. Arnold wasn't happy with that arrangement. Neither was Arnold's wife, Willetta, and they both let her know that with unceasing regularity.

She put up with their attitudes. She had to until she could either buy the store back from him—if he would consider selling, which she doubted at the moment—or save enough money to start her own, either here in Serenity or somewhere else. That was The Plan anyway.

She made one more adjustment to the cakes of soap, then took another step back, still unsatisfied. The bell at the front door jingled, letting her know she had a customer. She pasted a smile of welcome on her face and whirled around to see who had entered the shop. The smile disappeared as quickly as it had come.

"Oh no! You stay away from me, Lucy Hart! I know that look on your face!" She held up her hand in a stopping motion. "I am not interested in any of your matchmaking shenanigans today! Once was enough!" She dropped her hand once Lucy stopped in her tracks, still at the entrance to the store. "And don't give me that innocent look either!"

Lucy, her best friend, had the audacity to giggle, before she swept into the store like she hadn't a care in the world and drew her into a big hug.

"Believe it or not, Tresia, I'm not here for that." Lucy released her from her embrace, then took a step away, her gaze roaming over the display of soaps before focusing once more on the matter at hand. "You told me the last time when I suggested you and Jameson Hicks should get to know each other better that you aren't interested in finding a match. I understand and I respect your wishes."

Hmmm, there was something about the way Lucy said those words that had the fine hair on the back of her neck rising. "Now why don't I believe you?"

Lucy shrugged, giving off an air of innocence, her eyes wide, her smile still in place...a secretive grin that gave Tresia pause. "I've met the new marshal, Devlin Goodrich."

And there it was. Despite Lucy knowing she wasn't interested in 'finding' someone, the woman just couldn't help herself. As a matchmaker—not to mention the town busybody and founder of the Serenity Ladies' Society—she believed everyone should be happy like she was.

"Oh, let me guess. He'd be the perfect match for me." She couldn't keep the sarcasm from her voice. "Even though I'm not interested. Getting married again is not part of my Plan."

Lucy shrugged again, an elegant lifting of her shoulders. "Actually, I don't think he would be. He seems nice enough, I suppose, and very serious, but he isn't very handsome."

She took umbrage at the statement. "What a terrible thing to say! As if a person's looks has anything to do with who and what they are. You can be the most beautiful or handsome person in the world but if your heart is ugly, it doesn't matter."

"Is that right?"

"You know it is. My Brett wasn't the handsomest man I'd ever known, but he was kind and sweet and funny and I loved him, so much so that I married him." She stopped speaking and stared at her friend. "You know what?"

Lucy just continued to smile at her. "What?"

"You're a terrible person, Lucy Hart. I don't even know why I'm friends with you."

"Because you love me, despite me being such a terrible person?" A sparkle of mischief lit the woman's mocha brown eyes.

Tresia thought about the truth of those words before she responded. "Yes, I do love you." She shrugged. "Can't seem to help myself." She snaked her arm around her friend's waist. "Come on in the back. I think Arnold just made a pot of coffee. Maybe we can drink it all before he notices."

"And you say I'm a terrible person," Lucy laughed as they walked through the store to the storage room in the back, a place made comfortable with old furnishings that never sold. Tresia opened the back door to let some air circulate into the room, which was stuffy.

She chose two coffee cups from a wide selection on the shelf and placed them on the ornate table then grabbed the coffeepot from the little Ben Franklin stove that warmed the area. "So why are you here, if not to match me up with Marshal Goodrich?"

"I have a job for you," Lucy said.

Tresia spread her arms wide to encompass the storage room of Sullivan's Emporium, almost splashing the rich brew from the pot. "I have a job."

"And you hate it. Hate working for your cousin and his wife. And they hate that they have to give you a job because your father's will demanded it." Lucy held out her cup and allowed her to pour coffee, then took a sip. "Admit it, Tresia, there is no love lost between you and Arnold. Or Willetta." She added a little bit of sugar from the bowl on the table and stirred.

"No, there isn't." She poured coffee for herself as well. "It would be a different story if I owned this store, but the chances of that happening aren't very good right now." She bit at her bottom lip, still upset that her father, the late, great Lyle Sullivan —the man she'd taken care of for two years after he suffered a stroke—decided she wasn't smart enough or worthy enough to inherit Sullivan's Emporium. The knowledge broke her heart.

Lucy smiled at her and tilted her head to the side. "How would you like to tell Arnold you quit?"

"Oh, I'd love that, but I couldn't." She put the coffeepot back on the stove, then slid into one of the comfortable chairs. "I need a job to support myself. You know that. You know that Brett didn't leave me much when he passed, and I won't touch the money Daddy left me. That's for the new store—or buying this one back."

"What if I told you Marshal Goodrich needs someone to keep house and take care of his daughter?"

"I don't know, Lucy." She paused, thinking it over, then admitted, "That's the last thing I want to do. I'm thirty-one—"

"I know how old you are."

Tresia continued, ignoring the interruption. "—and I've taken care of people since I was thirteen. First Mama, then Brett when he became ill—which was an honor, don't get me wrong—then Daddy after he had his stroke." She shook her head and glanced at her friend. "It's my time…to just live for myself, to follow my dreams."

"And how is that plan working for you? Have you saved enough money to buy this store back from your nasty cousin and his equally nasty wife? Can you afford any of the stores you've found in the newspapers you get from all over the country?"

She hung her head. "No." She put her coffee cup on the table, then twisted her hands in her lap to keep them still. "It just isn't right, Lucy! I worked hard, keeping the store open and taking care of Daddy."

"You did. No one worked harder than you." Sympathy flashed in Lucy's eyes.

"And I was good at it. Efficient. Smart about my decisions. I made a steady profit, just like Daddy did." She twisted her fingers a little tighter, until they hurt, then untwisted them and rubbed her palms against the material of her skirt. "To have it all taken away after Daddy died is sometimes more than I can bear. It makes me angry, too, at the unfairness of it all."

"I, more than anyone, know what you've been through, Tresia, and I know that working for the marshal is not what you want. Not right now anyway, but here's the difference." Lucy studied her over the rim of her coffee cup, her eyes crinkling at the corners with both concern and something else she couldn't identify. "Neither Devlin Goodrich nor his daughter are ill. He's a widower. He just needs someone to take care of Avery during the day and make sure his house is clean and there's healthy food on the table."

"What would happen to Sullivan's if I'm not here?"

Lucy shrugged. "Arnold would continue to run it into the ground, despite your efforts. Or maybe in spite of them."

She let out a sigh. "I would hate to see that happen. Sullivan's has been in Serenity for over thirty-five years. It's a staple in the community. Everyone comes here." She let out another sigh. "At least, they used to."

"You can't stop what he's doing." Lucy lowered her voice. "Your father should have known better."

Still reeling with the pain and regret that her father had done this, she stiffened. "Yes, he should have known better." She paused before saying what she suspected. "Arnold manipulated him, I think. Took advantage of him because he couldn't think as clearly as he did before the stroke. That stroke took more from him than his voice and his ability to move freely." She laughed a little. "Except when it came to playing chess. His mind was definitely sharp then."

"Taking the job with the marshal would pay so much more than what you're currently making here. The hours would be steady. Just think, more savings toward The Plan."

"I don't know, Lucy." She shook her head. "It's not what I want."

"And you'll never get what you want with Arnold running things and cutting your hours. If he had his way, you'd only be working one hour a week, and we both know that wouldn't go far. You'd have to dip into your savings just to pay your room and board." Lucy leaned forward, took her hand, and squeezed gently before releasing her. "I so wish you would have moved in with Ben and me."

Tresia shook her head. "No, that wouldn't have been right, Lucy, and you know that. You and Ben have only been married two years. Neither one of you needs me making a nuisance of myself."

"Be that as it may, let me tell you about this job. Or rather, the marshal's daughter. Her name is Avery. She's almost five and she's just adorable!" Lucy smiled a big Cheshire cat grin. "Just meet them, Tresia. What could it hurt?"

What could it hurt, indeed? Actually, it couldn't hurt at all.

She'd love to tell Arnold she quit. Maybe then, he and his wife would actually have to work, which they didn't now because she did everything from ordering supplies and keeping the books to making sure all their displays were attractive, despite the meager hours he gave her. Oh, Arnold came in every day, strolling in whenever he pleased, but he stayed in his office. What he did in there, she had no clue. And Willetta? She only came in when she wanted something or to berate her for some imagined slight.

And the extra money? Yes, she could use that, save it all for the day when she could take the store back from right under Arnold's nose...or buy another one somewhere else and make it her own. "All right. I'll meet them, but I'm not making any promises."

A knowing smile crossed Lucy's face before she lifted the coffee cup to her lips as if to hide that smile. "I can guarantee you'll love little Avery as soon as you meet her. I know I did. She doesn't speak much, but that's all right. She's as cute as a button!"

Half an hour later, coffee and Lucy gone, she removed the white apron she wore, pulled on the jacket that matched her skirt, and knocked on Arnold's office door. She didn't wait for him to respond, simply pushed it open to see him sitting there, cigar in his mouth, feet up on the desk, hands folded across his big belly. He didn't move except for his eyebrows, which lowered into a frown.

She ignored the cigar ashes that littered the floor and the desk, because he couldn't even be bothered to use the glass ashtray that was sitting right there. "I'm taking my lunch, Arnold."

She didn't give him a chance to respond as she closed the door as quickly as she'd opened it and hurried from the store. Walking across the town square, she felt the first jitter of anticipation flooding her belly. It had been a long time since she'd felt that and she had to admit, it was good. Her life, since losing Brett, then losing her father and the Emporium, had been a series of disappointments. Maybe this was the opportunity she'd been waiting for.

Stopping in front of the house all the Marshals of Serenity had lived in for as long as she could remember, Tresia smoothed her hair back into the chignon at the nape of her neck, tugged down the hem of her jacket, and stepped up to the porch. Her heart was in her throat. This was crazy. How'd she ever let Lucy talk her into this!

She knocked and waited. It wasn't long before she heard little footsteps scampering across the floor from inside the house. A moment later, the door swung open, and she came face to face with a tiny cherub of a girl, clutching a carved wooden horse in her hand. In an instant, she was smitten. Lucy hadn't lied. Avery Goodrich was the most adorable little girl she'd ever seen—short, light-brown curls that looked like she'd brushed them herself, if at all, sparkling, big blue-gray eyes, pert little nose, cupid's bow mouth. She was a petite little thing, too.

The girl fidgeted in the doorway, eyes wide, shifting her weight from one foot to the other as if anxious to be moving—or perhaps, a little frightened. She did not speak, nor did she move out of the doorway. Peeking past her into the parlor, Tresia noticed two more horses on the rug in front of the cold fireplace.

She brought her attention back to the little girl. "You must be Miss Avery."

The girl stopped moving and nodded, those curls surrounding her head like a halo bouncing as she did so.

"Who is it, sweet pea?" A hoarse, rather gravelly voice called out from further inside the house.

"A lady," Avery responded then lapsed into silence, her eyes still wide, her hand still clutching the horse, but a little tighter now.

A moment later, she heard heavier footsteps then a big, strong hand grasped the edge of the door and opened it wider.

Tresia froze. So did he, stunned for a moment that seemed to last forever.

She inhaled an involuntary gasp. Lucy lied. Straight up lied. The man standing before her was an Adonis. Tall and muscular with almost midnight black hair touched with a hint of silver and smoky blue-gray eyes the color of storm clouds that seemed to see right into her soul.

He recovered first as a slight smile appeared on his face—his devastatingly handsome face—revealing dimples in his cheeks. "You must be Mrs. Morgan. Lucy said you'd be stopping by."

Oh, that voice! Warm and raspy, it touched her all the way to her toes and made her mouth dry. She stared at him, looking for her voice, her composure, both of which seemed to have deserted her. Beyond surprised, she could do nothing but nod.

"I'm Devlin Goodrich, but you already know that." He moved out of the way, opening the door even wider. "Please come in."

Tresia took a step forward. The next thing she knew, she was falling...right into his arms, her hands pressing against his hard chest to keep herself from tumbling at his feet. Her first impression had been correct as she felt the tight band of his muscular arms wrap around her to steady her. The subtle fragrance of sandalwood coming from the open collar of his shirt tickled her nose.

"Are you all right?" His voice in her ear was gruff with concern even as his body stiffened.

"Yes, I'm all right." Her face hot with embarrassment, she nodded and stepped away, cursing herself for being so clumsy when she'd never been clumsy a day in her life. Lucy was going to pay for this! "I'm sorry, I don't know how that happened."

"No harm done." He bent down and inspected the doorway. "The threshold is loose. I didn't notice that before." He turned his head to look at her, still crouched down on his haunches then rose slowly to his full height, which had to be well over six feet, concern for her reflecting in those stormy eyes of his. "Are you certain you're all right?"

"Yes, perfectly fine," she lied. She wasn't fine. Her heart beat much too fast. She concentrated on trying to salvage her equilibrium…and her pride.

"Let's chat in the kitchen." He led the way, then pulled out a chair at the table and gestured for her to sit. Grateful, as her knees were still a little weak, she slid into her seat. Avery followed and crawled into her lap almost immediately—and without hesitation—though she didn't say a word.

Tresia didn't mind. She loved children, and they seemed to love her, though she'd never had any of her own. She glanced at the marshal, still a little taken aback by his appearance and the fact that Lucy had straight up lied to her.

He seemed surprised that his daughter sat on her lap but didn't make a comment. He blinked several times though and cleared his throat. "I'd offer you something to drink, but I don't know where anything is yet. We arrived late last night and stayed at the hotel. I didn't pick up the key to the house from Lucy until about an hour ago."

"Glasses are in the cabinet to the right of the sink," she offered.

Startled, his dark brows rose. "How do you know that?"

She laughed, slowly gaining her poise. "I've been in this house many times. I was friends with the last marshal's daughter. And I helped Lucy clean in anticipation of your arrival." She adjusted Avery in her lap and pointed to a door to his left. "There are foodstuffs in the pantry but nothing in the ice box. We didn't know exactly when you'd be arriving and we didn't want anything to spoil, but if I know Lucy—and I do—she's already arranged to have ice delivered. She probably also let Mr. Shaeffer —he owns the dairy just outside town—know that he can start bringing milk, butter, and cream, beginning tomorrow morning. He delivers between six-thirty and eight on Wednesdays and

Saturdays, but since you just arrived, he'll make an exception for you."

She watched him, her eyes roaming over his broad shoulders, slim waist and long legs before he turned and pulled a glass from the cabinet, giving her a view of his backside, which was perfect, in her opinion, though she had no business looking at it. He filled the glass from the pump at the sink then turned once again to hand it to her. She took a sip to relieve the persistent dryness in her throat.

Pulling out the chair opposite her, he sat, then folded his hands on the table. "Uh, I'm not sure how to do this. I've never hired anyone to take care of Avery before."

"Not to worry, Marshal." She smiled at him. He definitely needed her help and though it wasn't what she wanted, she'd do it anyway—for him and for the little girl sitting on her lap. "We'll figure it out. Ask me anything."

"Can you cook?"

"Yes, of course. Nothing fancy, mind you, but tasty and filling."

"I already know you can clean." He waved his hand, encompassing the room. "Avery and I haven't explored much, but everything looks spotless." He turned his attention back to her, tilting his head to the side. "Will Sunday and Wednesday afternoon off be acceptable?"

She couldn't concentrate on what he was saying. Not one bit. All she could hear was her heart beating rapidly, like it had suddenly sprung to life three years after she laid Brett to rest. She couldn't see beyond the warm glow of his eyes, either, or the slight smile that made his mouth fuller. Tongue-tied, she finally just nodded.

"I'm not sure of the hours but I was thinking something like seven to seven. Will your husband mind if you're here and not at home?"

"I'm a widow, Marshal. There is no one at home waiting for

me." She glanced at the girl in her lap then turned her attention back to him. "I can work whatever hours you need."

Sympathy appeared in his eyes and a slight flush colored his cheeks. "I'm sorry. I just assumed—Lucy didn't mention that when I met with her this morning." He recovered from his embarrassment rather quickly, but the empathy remained. "Did she tell you how much the salary would be?"

"No, she didn't."

He named a figure that was much more than she earned at the Emporium, considering that Cousin Arnold kept decreasing the hours she worked. With that much money every week, she'd be able to save a good deal toward The Plan. Excitement bubbled inside her that her dream was much closer now, but that feeling was overpowered by the warmth of his gaze. "Yes, that will be fine."

"There might be occasions where you'll have to stay late. Is that all right with you?"

"Of course." She shifted Avery's slight weight as the girl sat on her lap and tightened her hold on her. "I would never leave Avery alone. I'll just wait for you to come home. I have a room at Mrs. McMurty's boarding house so I'm close by. Actually, you can see her place from your back porch."

He visibly relaxed, the tension easing from his stiff posture. "You're hired. Can you start tomorrow?"

"I'd like nothing better." She removed Avery from her lap, then rose from her chair as he did the same. "I'll see you both in the morning."

"By the way, the rest of our belongings should be arriving tomorrow. Will you take care of Avery's things when they do?"

She watched as Avery slipped her little hand into his big one. She really was smitten with the girl. "I'd be happy to."

He walked her to the front door, then pulled a key from his pocket. There was a look in his eye as he handed it to her, as if he was saying he trusted her with his most prized treasure—his daughter. She understood better than he might think. She slipped the key into her drawstring purse, then pulled the strings tight. "Everything will be fine, Marshal. Avery and I will have a wonderful time together." She tried to reassure him but wasn't certain if he believed her. She'd just have to prove it to him.

He said nothing as he opened the door, simply nodded in response to her statement.

She turned her attention to Avery. "I'll see you tomorrow, all right?"

The little girl nodded with enthusiasm, those bright eyes of hers gleaming, but she remained silent.

As she stepped off the porch and into the street, she was aware of the marshal's gaze on her and felt the thrill of it settle in her stomach. Despite that feeling, the next time she saw Lucy, she'd have a word or two to say to her!

CHAPTER 2

*D*evlin watched the woman walk away, the scent of her honeysuckle perfume lingering in the air. Mrs. Morgan was not what he expected. Not at all. When he met with Lucy Hart earlier, as he'd been instructed to do, and let her know he needed someone to watch over Avery, he had expected an older lady—one with gray hair twisted into a tight bun at the top of her head and a face full of wrinkles. He had not anticipated the tall, slender, vibrant young woman with rich auburn hair and kind violet eyes who just left his house.

He admitted, if only to himself, he'd been surprised to see her standing at his front door, but thought he recovered his shock fairly well. She had appeared startled, too, given the widening of her eyes and her sudden gasp. And then she'd fallen into his arms. She was all kinds of soft and warm and his body's reaction to her touch made him question his own sanity.

He made the decision to hire her not on the fact that she could cook and clean but based solely on his daughter's reaction to her. Avery never took to a person that quickly. In fact, he'd never seen her sit on a person's lap aside from his or her mother's, not even with her grandmother, but after what she'd been through—what they'd both been through—over the last eleven months, if Avery felt comfortable with a complete stranger, then so be it.

"What do you think, Avery? Did you like Mrs. Morgan?"

The little girl nodded, making her light brown curls bounce, though she didn't speak, which still worried him. The passing of her mother had affected her in so many ways, but it was the propensity to talk as little as possible that hurt him to his soul. Before Hannah died, Avery was a regular little chatterbox. Maybe spending time with Mrs. Morgan would help in that regard.

He tore his gaze away from his daughter and glanced down at the loose threshold. "Do you suppose there might be a hammer somewhere in this house?"

Avery shrugged.

They'd only been in the fully furnished house, the one provided for them by the town, for less than an hour before Mrs. Morgan had shown up. He hadn't had time to explore everything as he'd mentioned to her, but what he'd seen so far, he liked—it would suit his and Avery's needs perfectly. And that was more than he could ask for at the moment. Already, he felt a comfort here, a solace that had been missing from his life for an extraordinarily long time.

Now, to get settled, and start their new life, one without Hannah. The pain in his heart made his breath seize in his lungs and he paused for a moment to let the ache subside, though it never truly went away. He didn't suppose it ever would.

He looked down at his daughter. "Will you help me?"

She nodded once again then scampered off to the kitchen. He could hear drawers opening and closing, her little feet going from one cabinet to another. He looked in the hutch in the formal dining room and anywhere else tools might be hiding. He came up with nothing and walked back to the open door and the offending threshold.

Avery joined him after a few moments, empty-handed.

"You didn't find one?"

She shook her head.

"Me, either." He grinned at her. "Well, I guess there's no help for it." He took off his boot then bent down.

The boot heel, as far as he was concerned, made a terrible hammer. Didn't matter how much he pounded, the nail that protruded and made the threshold loose wouldn't stay down. Every time he thought it would, he was mistaken. He even tried pulling the loose nail out and moving it to another place, but that didn't work either.

He heard chuckling, but it was deeper, richer, and certainly not coming from Avery. Standing on the top step of his porch, a huge smile on his face, a cowboy hat shading his face, was an older man dressed in a gaudy plaid jacket and matching trousers that might have been better suited to a horse blanket.

"That ain't gonna work," the man said, his voice—and his twinkling eyes—full of humor, "although I've seen my wife use a book as a hammer. Didn't work for her either."

"Well, they say necessity is the mother of invention." His face heated as he rose to his feet, boot dropping to the floor. "Can I help you?"

"You can if you're Marshal Goodrich."

"I am."

The man pointed to a horse-drawn wagon in the street. Painted white with red trim, the words 'Jennings' Ice' was emblazoned on the side. The horse that pulled the wagon wore a flowered hat, which was unusual...or maybe it wasn't in Serenity, New Mexico. "I'm Paul Jennings." His grin widened and his bushy gray eyebrows wiggled a bit. "The Ice Man. Lucy Hart let me know you were here and needed ice."

Devlin stuck out his hand. "Nice to meet you, Mr. Jennings." He turned toward his daughter, who hadn't said a word. In fact, she had moved to stand away from the door, almost hiding behind the small, ornate table against the wall. He held out his hand toward her. "This is my daughter, Avery."

She came forward, a bit reluctantly, but forward none-the-less and dropped a curtsy, as she'd been taught.

"A pleasure, Miss Avery." The big man bent down to be eye-level with her. "I got a couple granddaughters just about your age. Maybe you'd like to come and visit once you and your father get settled. Would you like that?"

His daughter nodded and murmured out a 'yes', which seemed to make the old man happy, not to mention what it did for his own heart. Maybe this move, this chance to start over somewhere that didn't hold so many memories, was the best decision he could have made—for both of them.

"I might have a hammer in my wagon, if that'll help."

Mr. Jennings interrupted his thoughts and drew his attention. "That would be great."

The older man ran down the steps as agile as a man fifty years younger, searched the wagon, but apparently didn't find what he needed before he jogged back to the porch empty-handed. "Looks like I was wrong, but you might want to head over to Sullivan's Emporium. It's on the other side of the town square. Can't miss it. Takes up half the street. They should have a hammer." He grinned. "And anything else you want. Old Lyle Sullivan always said, 'if we don't have it, you don't need it'." He touched the brim of his hat. "I'll get your ice now."

He stepped toward his wagon, rummaged around for a bit in the back then returned, holding a big block of ice with a pair of iron tongs. He took the path that led toward the back of the house and the kitchen without a word but with a happy little whistle, as if he enjoyed his job...or better yet, enjoyed his life.

For a moment, Devlin envied him and wondered if he'd ever feel that way again. He had once, but that had all changed in the space of a heartbeat.

"I'll come by next Tuesday, see if you need another block of ice."

He jumped, not realizing the man had returned, startling him from his thoughts.

"My sons and I deliver in town on Tuesdays, Thursdays, and Saturdays depending on your schedule, but if you need it sooner, just let me know." He jerked his thumb toward the east. "I'm just outside of town on the main road. Can't miss me." He smiled. "Or the icehouse. Stop by any time. My wife, Bettina, would love to meet you." He glanced at Avery. "Bring the little one. We always got the grandkids running around."

"Thank you, Mr. Jennings."

"Paul, please."

Devlin nodded. "It was a pleasure to meet you."

"The pleasure was all mine, Marshal. Welcome to Serenity."

He watched the man climb into his wagon, grab the reins, and shake them. The horse, wearing its silly little flowered hat, responded immediately and pulled the wagon down the street.

"Now what, Avery? What should we do? Maybe walk around town?" He bent down and removed the threshold, which came off easily in his hand. "Go over to Sullivan's Emporium and get that hammer and some nails, like Mr. Jennings suggested, and then maybe meet my deputies?"

She nodded enthusiastically to that though he wished she would say the words. In Albuquerque, she had always loved going to the office with him and loved the deputies who reported to him, though that had never made Frances Emerson Comstock, his mother-in-law, happy. She hadn't thought it seemly that her granddaughter, scion of Albuquerque's elite, should be with those less than her. God knows, she hadn't thought he was good enough for Hannah and let him know that whenever possible.

He pushed all thoughts of his former mother-in-law from his head, placed the piece of wood on the little table beside the door, then pulled on his boot.

"You ready?"

She nodded and placed her hand in his. He closed the door behind them though he didn't lock it. Didn't seem like he had to —and headed across the street, following the same path Tresia Morgan had just a short time ago.

Two streets over, they entered the town square with its random paths and little benches where one could sit and relax among the flowers growing there. It was a peaceful place, filled with young couples and their children, relaxing on a perfect afternoon. The fountain in the middle of the square gurgled water into the air, a haven for the birds that swooped by to take a drink. Apple and pear trees, their fragrant blossoms scenting the air, provided shade and would, when the time was right, fruit.

People waved as he and Avery passed them. He nodded in return but didn't stop to speak as they left the town square and stepped into the dirt road. There were people here, too, going about their daily business, carrying baskets filled with the things needed to run their homes efficiently—from fresh fruit and vegetables to paper-wrapped packages, chatting as they walked along the raised wooden sidewalk.

He looked up...and chuckled.

Mr. Jennings was right. He couldn't have missed Sullivan's Emporium if he tried. The store did take up half the block. Cloth awnings, forest green in color, shaded the big picture windows along the front of the building. Gold lettering on those windows proclaimed some of the items for sale within. There was sign above that extended half the edifice. He laughed as he read the words written in big block letters. 'Sullivan's Emporium. If we don't have it, you don't need it.'

With Avery's hand in his, he crossed the street and tugged on the door to the building. A little bell jingled as he opened it and stepped through. His eyes opened wide and a grin settled on his mouth as he glanced around. The store was huge and filled with everything a person could ever need—or want—from magazines and books to an overstuffed chair and ottoman and a kitchen table, complete with six chairs, all looking like they'd been hand carved. There was even an eight-foot stuffed bear, its paws outstretched, its mouth opened in a snarl that showed all its teeth, that hovered over a glass and wood counter where not one, but two, cash registers resided, one at either end. In between, beneath the glass, on beds of velvet, were pocket watches, rings, necklaces, and other assorted pieces of jewelry, all shimmering beneath the glow of a crystal chandelier, one of several, suspended from the ceiling.

He glanced down at Avery and his smile widened. It seemed she was just as impressed, her gaze moving from one thing to the next until stopping on a display of dolls—some porcelain, some rag. She slipped her hand from his and scampered in that direction without a backward glance.

Despite appearing to have everything, the store was empty, except for one woman. She stood at a display of soaps with her back toward him, just standing there, looking at it, her head tilted to the side, as if deep in concentration. The big bow of the apron she wore, the ends extending almost to the floor, was crooked, as if she'd hastily tied it and made a sharp contrast to the dark plum skirt she wore. "I'll be right with you."

He recognized the voice. Or at least, he thought he did and moved closer to stand directly behind her.

"Mrs. Morgan?"

She jumped, startled, and backed up a step, her shoe coming in direct contact with his boot then she turned quickly with a muffled 'oh' and slammed right into him. He held out his arms and wrapped them around her so neither one of them would fall. This close, he saw that her eyes were much more beautiful than he'd originally thought. Not just violet, but a deep pansy purple with tiny flecks of black and gold, all framed by thick, sooty lashes.

Her cheeks blossomed with color as she quickly pulled out of his embrace. "Marshal Goodrich! I'm terribly sorry." She gave him a tremulous smile, then took a few steps back so there was space between them. She looked rather frazzled and seemed to struggle for composure. "Are you all right? I didn't hurt you, did I?"

He shoved his hands in his pockets, a little embarrassed himself—not because he'd startled her, which he obviously had, but because this was the second instance within a short period of time that she ended up in his arms. And he didn't mind, which made him question his sanity once again. "Not at all." He purposely made himself look away from her. "I didn't know you worked here."

"I do...until six o'clock tonight." She nodded, her cheeks still rosy with color. "That's when I'll tell Cousin Arnold I quit."

Startled by her statement, he stiffened, suspicion filling him even though there was nothing even remotely suspicious about this woman. "Why would you do that? Why would you take a job with me when you already had one?"

She shrugged, the action bringing attention to her long, slim neck as the fabric of her white blouse moved against her throat. "It's a long story and I won't bore you with it." She took a step toward him and he thought, for a moment, she would reach out to touch him, but he was mistaken. She adjusted a display of lotions and creams just behind him instead. "What can I do for you?"

"I need a hammer," he said and smiled. "To fix that threshold. And some nails."

"There isn't one at the house?"

He shook his head. "Not that I could find."

"Not even in the shed?"

"Shed? What shed?"

She chuckled and the sound vibrated all the way to his soul. Why it should do that, he hadn't a clue, but he liked it. There was a warmth to this woman, a friendliness apparent in her vibrant violet eyes and ready smile. "You really haven't had time to explore everything, have you?"

"No, I haven't."

"There's a shed on the porch just outside the kitchen. I'm certain you'll find all the tools you'll need in there."

Now why would she tell him that and miss the opportunity to sell him something?

"Well, then, I should be heading back to find that hammer."

She chuckled again. "Do you know how to fix it?"

"Not really." He hated admitting that. Yes, he was handy with a gun and arrested criminals, but simple household repairs had never been his forte. "I figured I could just bang the darned thing in place."

She laughed this time, a full-throated explosion from deep in her chest. "No need for that, Marshal. Mr. Langston does handyman work. He can fix just about anything. He's got a small house right around the corner. Just knock on his door and let him know what you need to have done. He's reasonable, too." She smiled at him and her eyes widened just a bit as, once again, a blush stole over cheeks. "Or I could stop by after work and fix it for you."

Surprised by her offer, he blurted out, "You can do that?"

She waved her hand, encompassing the entire store. "I built all the displays you see. Well, my father and I did."

He glanced around, looking at all the wood and glass shelves and cabinets, admiring the work that went into them. If she—and her father—could build these, then she certainly could fix his threshold, much better than he could. "I think I would like that."

"Good. I'll come over after six and get that threshold fixed right up."

He nodded. "I'll see you then, I guess." He looked down, fully expecting to see Avery standing next to him or right behind him, but she wasn't there. He glanced around the store, panic beginning to set in. He'd always kept an eye on his daughter, knowing exactly where she was at all times. He'd been distracted, not only by everything in the store, but by the woman standing in front of him. "Where's Avery?"

"Right over there."

He looked in the direction she pointed and sighed with relief. Avery was cuddled up in the cushions of a soft leather chair, fast asleep, two of the dolls from the display nestled in her arms. He hated to wake her. She hadn't been sleeping well and it had been a long trip from Albuquerque to Serenity.

"Don't wake her." She did touch him then, resting her hand on his forearm, the warmth of her fingers seeping through the fabric of his shirt. "I'll bring her with me when I come to fix your threshold."

Her gaze stayed on his daughter, a softness stealing into her eyes, making the pansy color seem more pronounced. The woman appeared to like children and Avery certainly liked her. He didn't hesitate long before agreeing to her suggestion. After all, this was the woman he'd hired. She was just starting the job a little sooner than they'd originally thought. "If you're sure."

"I am." She returned her attention to him. He didn't miss the sweet smile on her face, nor the longing in her eyes. "We can stop at the Wagon Wheel and pick up something for dinner as well."

Was she simply being kind? He didn't know, but again, he accepted what she offered. "I...uh...thank you."

"We'll see you after six then."

He left the store, a little at odds with himself, realizing he was trusting a woman he'd just met. It was a different feeling for him, but at the same time, it felt right. He hadn't lived this long in a position where one could be killed on any given day without having faith in his instincts. Avery would be all right in Mrs. Morgan's care.

He crossed the street and entered the town square once more, traversing the meandering paths quickly. There were still people there—relaxing, chatting with one another, watching their children play. Once again, they waved at him. He returned the gesture though he didn't stop his stride. Time enough to meet everyone who would be under his protection later, but for now, he wanted to meet his deputies. He was a little apprehensive. Would there be animosity because he'd been appointed to the marshal's position over them, sight unseen, after Marshal Kimball decided to retire from thirty years of service. He'd been assured that none of Serenity's six deputies had wanted to move up and take the job. He hoped nothing had changed.

A few minutes later, he stepped up on the raised sidewalk outside the Marshal's Office on the other side of the town square and let himself in. Instantly, he felt at home. Perhaps the layout was different than his last post, but still, it was all familiar. The Wanted Posters hanging on the wall, a small Ben Franklin stove to heat the place in winter, the cabinet filled with guns and rifles of every sort. He didn't see a coffeepot on the stove, but he smelled coffee, the rich brew filling his nostrils. The jail cells, two of them, were directly in front of him, the doors open as they were both unoccupied, their keys on a heavy metal ring hanging from a hook between them.

He noticed a door to his right, which was wide open, and saw the corner of a table, the arm of one chair, and part of a window, but nothing else, though the smell of coffee seemed to be coming from there. Perhaps it was a small kitchen, though he couldn't be certain.

He turned his attention to the main room, which was organized and very neat, exactly how he thought a Marshal's Office should be—clutter made him anxious. There were four desks, two on each side of an aisle, facing each other, only one of which was occupied by a completely bald-headed man studiously writing in a ledger, the pen scratching the paper.

The deputy looked up from the record book on his desk and gave him a friendly, welcoming smile, the edges of his bushy horseshoe mustache lifting as he did so. "Can I help you?"

He stepped through the small gate that separated the office proper from the entry way. "I'm Devlin Goodrich."

The man stood up immediately, pen still in his hand, his smile widening, making his horseshoe mustache lift even further. He extended his hand over his desk. "Merrill Shotton. A pleasure to meet you."

"You as well."

"Rafael is out walking the town," Merrill continued as he checked the clock on the wall. "He should be back in about ten minutes or so." He gestured to the chair beside the desk. "Please, sit. We weren't expecting you quite this soon, otherwise I would have arranged for everyone to come in and meet you."

Devlin did as he was asked, seating himself in a chair beside Deputy Shotton's desk. "I actually wasn't expecting to have time today, but things worked out differently than I had planned."

"I assume you've already seen Lucy Hart. She give you the key to the house?"

"She did. And arranged for ice and milk to be delivered."

The big man nodded. "That's our Lucy. There's a reason she's the head of the welcoming committee—no detail goes unnoticed, no matter how small." He paused, his eyes narrowing just a bit as Devlin found himself on the receiving end of a very thorough scrutiny. He didn't mind. In fact, he'd be suspicious if the man hadn't studied him. After a moment, as if he'd passed inspection, the man gave a short nod. "What about your horse?"

"Challenger is still at the hotel stables, for now. Mrs. Gonzales said I could keep him there until I was settled."

"You can bring him here. We have a small stable behind the building. Pete Mackinaw's son comes twice a day to feed, water, and clean the stalls."

Devlin took in the information, a little surprised but extremely grateful. Everyone he'd met so far had been friendly and generous. He and Avery could be happy here. At least, that's what he hoped. "Thank you. I'll bring him over later."

"And the house? Everything good?" Merrill asked.

"It's a nice house. Avery and I will be fine."

"That's right. You have a daughter. Lucy mentioned that. So did Marshal Kimball when he told us you were coming. How old is she?"

He couldn't help the smile that twitched his lips. "She's almost five and as stubborn as the day is long."

The big man smiled and nodded again but didn't make a comment regarding Avery. Instead, he asked, "Coffee? I just made a fresh pot."

"Yes, please."

"Black? Or cream and sugar?"

"Black, please."

First impressions meant a lot. They could be the difference between living and dying in this business, and Devlin liked what he saw, as he watched the man stride across the room before he disappeared into the open doorway to his right. He had an innate grace and an awareness of what was around him—a man he'd definitely want in his corner when and if it came down to business.

He returned in moments, a cup of the steaming brew in his hand. He jerked his head toward the doorway he'd just exited. "We have a small kitchen. Just a stove, sink, small ice box, and a table with three chairs." He handed him the coffee. "A back door, too, because you never know when one might need to leave quickly—or sneak in on someone."

"Thank you." He took a sip, appreciating the taste of the rich, dark liquid, his eyes darting toward the kitchen though he could only see the corner of the table. "Good coffee." He put his cup down. "It's just you and Rafael during the day?"

The man nodded as he made himself comfortable in his seat. "Nate Hyler comes in at eight in the evening and stays until eight in the morning, Monday through Saturday. He prefers those hours. I come in at seven then Rafael comes in at eight so there is always someone here." He gestured toward the ceiling. "Nate lives upstairs, by the way. I can go up and get him if you want."

"That's not necessary. Tomorrow will be soon enough."

"Sherm Quincy, Tomas Medrano and Caleb Johnson work mostly Saturday and Sunday, but we're all available if needed, any time, day or night. We all live close by. In fact, I live two houses down from you and Tomas lives on the street behind the Emporium." He took a sip of his coffee then wiped his mouth, not with his sleeve, but with a creamy white handkerchief he pulled from his pocket. Devlin noted the embroidery around the edges and the big letter 'M' at one corner and concluded this man's wife or sweetheart had made it for him before he tucked it away.

"And, of course, we have some citizens we rely on if the occasion warrants, though we've only had to call on them once or twice to my recollection. Esteban Silva over on Montaña del Trueno is an excellent marksman, if you need that sort of thing. His brothers, Teddy and Heath, aren't bad either. There're a few others I would trust with my life. Wyatt MacLean over on Stone Creek Ranch has helped when needed. So has Alfonso Serrano. The Zepedas, too."

He picked up his fancy fountain pen and twirled it between his fingers. "There isn't much that happens during the week. It's rather quiet—" he laughed, the sound warm and welcoming. "Which is just the way we like it. Friday and Saturday nights can get a little hectic, though. That's when all the cowboys from the ranches come into town to blow off a little steam at Connor's or the Silver Spur." He paused, his face taking on a reddish hue. "Or visit Josie's."

"Josie's?"

"That's our…uh…" His mustache twitched as he tried to find a word that would be appropriate. "Parlor house," he finally spit out as his body stiffened, just enough to be noticeable. "Josie's a good woman." He defended her and her business. "She and her ladies do a lot for the community despite their…uh…occupation

—" He narrowed his eyes just a bit though his smile remained in place "—and we have no intention of shutting her down."

"I see." He hid his smile. Parlor houses, more commonly known as brothels, were nothing new. Most towns had one or two, some discreet, some not. "As long as she doesn't break the law, I see no reason to shut her down either."

The man was visibly relieved, and Devlin concluded he'd paid a visit or two to Josie's. Might even have a soft spot for the woman. Nothing wrong with that, if the man wasn't married, but then again, who was he to judge? Live and let live…as long as no laws were broken.

"We haven't had anyone in the jail—" He gestured toward the iron-barred cells with his thumb "—in a while 'cept Fred Somner when he drinks too much and starts fighting with lampposts. We send word to his wife, Maura, when he's here—their house isn't far. We usually let him sleep it off. Other than that, Serenity is just like its name implies. We're a peaceful community. Oh, every now and then, something bad happens, guns will be drawn and so forth, but for the most part, you'll probably be bored here after the excitement of Albuquerque."

Devlin laughed. "That's the hope. I could use some peace and quiet."

The door swung open then, startling him, and Devlin swiveled in his seat to see a young man enter the office with a quick step and a big smile. He carried a pie tin in one hand. Shorter than Deputy Shotton, but stockier, he hung up his hat on the rack, revealing thick black hair, slipped past the small wooden gate and placed the pie on Merrill's desk with a little bit of fanfare and a mischievous grin. When he was done, he turned slightly and extended his hand. "Rafael Zepeda."

Devlin stood from his seat and shook Zepeda's hand, noticing it was warm, probably from the pie.

"You must be Marshal Goodrich."

"I am."

"A pleasure to meet you." Rafael released his hand, then backed up a step and gestured toward the pie. His smile widened as he addressed Merrill. "A thank you gift from Polly."

The big man blushed, the redness creeping up from his throat to encompass his entire face. He licked his lips as he looked at the gift. "Is it her famous strawberry rhubarb pie?"

"It is," Rafael responded with a chuckle. "She just asked that you return the pie tin." His thick, dark eyebrows wiggled. "Whenever you want."

If possible, Merrill's blush deepened, and little beads of sweat broke out on the man's head as the smile on his face grew. "You're in for a real treat, Marshal. Polly Dixon makes the best strawberry rhubarb pie in the whole town." He laughed, pride evident as his broad chest puffed out. "Actually, anything she bakes is enough to make your mouth water, as well it should. She owns the bakery just down the street. Sweet Somethings. Can't miss it."

Rafael's smile widened as he gave him the side-eye. "What's she thanking you for, Merrill?"

The big man whipped out his handkerchief again and mopped the sweat from his head. "None of your business," he said, but there was a teasing tone to his voice as he passed the man on his way to the kitchen. He returned in moments with plates, forks, napkins and a knife then proceeded to cut them each a slice of pie.

"You're right. This is the best strawberry rhubarb pie I've ever had," Devlin admitted a short time later as he scraped up the last bit of crust and shoved it in his mouth, the rich, buttery pastry practically melting on his tongue.

"Saw Tresia Morgan leaving your house earlier." Merrill pushed his plate away and smiled. "Lucy send her over to take care of your daughter?"

"She did." He grimaced. It seemed that everyone knew everyone else's business, but what had he expected? Serenity was a small town, so much smaller than Albuquerque, and he reminded himself that's what he wanted. "What do you know about her?"

"About Tresia?" The man shrugged. "Everything. I've known her since we were in school together. Her folks owned Sullivan's Emporium, until ol' Lyle passed. If they don't have it, then you don't need it," he said, repeating the motto that was on the sign over the store as well as what Paul Jennings had mentioned earlier and laughed. "But if they don't have it and you really want it, Tresia will find a way to get it."

"I've known her about that long, too." Rafael chimed in. "Knew her late husband as well." His smile gentled and Devlin wondered if the man had been in love with her at one time. "She's a good woman. Kind. Smart. Generous to a fault. Big heart." He collected the plates and silverware and disappeared into the kitchen, though he never stopped talking, his voice drifting into the room from beyond the doorway.

"She'd be perfect to take care of your daughter. She has a lot of experience with that." His voice grew louder as he came back into the main room carrying a cup of coffee. "Took care of her mother when she became ill—Tresia was only thirteen at the time—then took care of Brett, too, before he passed. These past two years, she's been taking care of her father. He had a stroke in the middle of the Emporium one afternoon, right in front of her." He took his seat but never stopped talking, not even to take a sip of his coffee. "Lyle passed three months ago. Whole town turned out for his funeral. It was a sad day."

Rafael finally paused long enough to take a drink and leaned back in his chair, as if lost in memory then suddenly wagged his finger as if he thought of a way to diminish the sadness. "The one you have to watch out for is Lucy Hart. That sign she has hanging beside her door ain't just wishful thinkin'."

"What do you mean?" He thought back to when he'd met with Lucy Hart earlier in the day. Standing on her front porch before she'd invited him in and introduced him to her husband, Doctor

Ben Hart, he'd noticed several signs, one of which said 'Doctor,' but couldn't recall what the other two signs had said. "What sign?"

Rafael laughed. "The one that reads 'Matchmaker.' Our Lucy is real serious about that." He puffed out his chest. "In fact, it was Lucy who introduced me to my wife, Ventura. Can't say I'm not happy, either. Best thing that ever happened to me." He glanced at Deputy Shotton, grin in place. "Wasn't it she who gently steered you toward Polly?"

The big man blushed at the mention of Polly's name and once again, beads of sweat popped out on his head. "I wouldn't say that exactly." He turned toward Devlin as he pulled the handkerchief from his pocket and mopped his head. "Lucy simply asked me to pick up pies for the silent auction she was sponsoring..." His voice drifted off as he studied the handkerchief in his hand then shook his head before an expression came over his face, one of disbelief yet at the same time, acceptance. "I'll be damned," he chuckled. "She did."

Rafael laughed and slapped his knee, then turned toward Devlin. "You better watch. You might be next."

Devlin stiffened. He wasn't interested in finding a wife. He'd had Hannah, whom he loved very deeply, and yet, he had *had* a sudden reaction to Mrs. Morgan. Tresia. Was sending her to him to take care of Avery the first step in Lucy's plan? No, that wasn't possible. They'd just met. "I don't think so. I'm not interested."

Merrill laughed. "I wasn't either. And look at me now."

CHAPTER 3

$\mathcal{T}$resia watched the bank of clocks for sale, counting the minutes until she could walk into Arnold's office and announce she was quitting. Anticipation and anxiety made her belly tighten, but she was determined. She tore her gaze away from the slowly moving minute hands on the grandfather clock, as well as the cuckoo clocks on the wall beside it, and glanced at the little girl who was now her responsibility. A smile twitched the corners of her mouth.

Avery had awakened from her nap, still clutching one of the store's dolls. Now she was busy re-arranging the display of soaps Tresia had arranged earlier—and seemed to be doing a much better job at it. The display was so much more attractive now, drawing one's eye and tempting one to pick up a bar and bring it to their nose for a sniff.

She watched Avery take a step back, much as she'd done, cross her arms over her chest despite the doll, and study the display.

She glanced at the clock. One minute to six. It was time. "You stay right here, all right, Avery?"

Avery nodded and went back to moving bars of soap around the little table covered in a forest green tablecloth, which complemented the flowered paper-packaging. Tresia marched toward the door with the little sign which read 'office.' She didn't bother knocking, but simply opened the door. Arnold was in the same position she'd seen him in at lunchtime—leaning back in his chair, both feet up on the desk, crossed at the ankle, blowing smoke rings toward the ceiling. One of his beefy hands lay across his big belly, the other held a half-smoked cigar, the end of which glowed red. Ashes were all over the floor as well as the top of the desk, like he still couldn't be bothered to use the cut crystal ashtray.

She wrinkled her nose at the smell. Oh, there was nothing wrong with a good cigar—her father had smoked them all the time—but combined with the aroma of Arnold's rank body odor and the disgusting cologne he used to cover that odor made her eyes water. She stepped further into the room even though she didn't want to.

"What do you want?" His tone bordered on belligerent, but she didn't take offense. He'd never really spoken to her any other way, not since the moment he'd learned her father had had a stroke and he saw an opportunity to worm his way into Lyle's good graces.

Every muscle in her body tensed. She took a moment to gather her thoughts, choosing to ignore the manner in which he spoke to her. "I quit."

He scoffed at her announcement, his beady eyes drifting over her. "You can't quit. Your father's will states that I have to keep you gainfully employed."

"I most certainly can, Arnold." She smiled, knowing something he didn't. "Daddy's will states that even if you do keep me employed, I don't have to stay if I don't want to. I can quit any time I want. It also mentions that you still need to give me two per cent of the profits, whatever those profits might be, even if I'm not employed here. I listened to the entire will when Mr. Applebaum was explaining it to us and then I read it. Did you?"

She assumed from the way the blood drained from Arnold's face that he hadn't either listened closely to or read her father's Last Will and Testament, simply too ecstatic that he'd gotten everything he'd wanted—the store as well as the apartment above it.

Finally, the man was going to pay for how badly he and his wife had treated her. "We can walk up the street right now and see Mr. Applebaum if you'd like. He's the one who drew up Daddy's will."

His feet came off the desk and he stood up quickly, making the chair crash into the wall behind him. For a moment, she thought he might strike out at her, but it seemed the effort to stand had taken all the wind out of him. "You can't quit," he repeated, his face beginning to redden.

"Of course, I can. I just did." Her gaze roamed over him, noticing a stain on his vest as well as one on his trousers. He blinked then brought his hand up and wiggled his pinky in his ear, as if there might be something wrong with his hearing. The slight action made his cheeks jiggle. It was all she could do not to laugh.

"I will continue to keep the books." The offer wasn't made out of pity. It was made out of self-preservation. If she wanted the store back—and she did—she'd be willing to help him, even though he didn't deserve it. Neither did his wife.

"But...but..." he stuttered, the redness on his face deepening, becoming a little more purple. She'd only seen that color once before, when he'd found out that her father hadn't left all his money to him. Apparently, at the time, he thought he deserved that as well. He was shocked now though. He probably assumed she'd never leave the store, no matter how badly he treated her.

"When?" he asked, an expression of resignation coming over his face.

She glanced at the clock on the wall behind him. "As of two minutes ago."

And with those words, she turned on her heel and left his office, softly closing the door behind her. The feeling of satisfaction made her smile as she heard him fall back into his chair through the panels of the door. She imagined he put his face in his hands, wondering what he was going to do now. He had depended on her love of Sullivan's Emporium—and her late father—to do whatever he wanted her to do, never considering that he might be wrong.

"Come on, Avery, let's go home."

Avery started to put the doll back where she belonged, but Tresia stopped her. "You can keep her."

Avery grinned and clutched the doll even tighter, a look of pure happiness on her face.

Tresia held out her hand and Avery scampered in her direction, slipping her hand into hers. Together, they left the store and headed up the street, then turned a corner.

The Wagon Wheel Restaurant was crowded when they entered, almost all the tables were full, the sounds of customers enjoying their meals, chatting with each other, cutlery clanking against plates, and Oscar calling out orders almost overwhelming. Tantalizing aromas wafted from the kitchen.

She caught Elsie Blake carrying a tray of dirty dishes toward the door that separated the dining room from the kitchen. "Hello, Elsie."

Elsie stopped in mid-stride. "Tresia! So nice to see you!" She looked over the edge of the tray. "And who is this darling little girl?"

"This is Avery Goodrich, the new marshal's daughter. I'll be taking care of her."

The woman's eyes widened, and she put down the heavy tray and placed her hands on her hips. "You quit the store?"

"I did." Oh, how wonderful it felt to say those words. And how utterly devastating at the same time, as it was something she never thought she'd do. For so many years, Sullivan's Emporium had been her life, her solace after her mother, then Brett passed.

Elsie nodded. "Serves Arnold right. He shouldn't have treated you so badly."

"No, he shouldn't have," she agreed. "And now he's going to find out how difficult running Sullivan's Emporium really is. He won't have me to do everything."

"Good for you." She laughed. "And bad for Arnold." She glanced at Avery, her eyes lighting up as a big smile crossed her face. "So, you'll be taking care of little Miss Avery here."

"I will."

"Well, it's about darned time!"

Tresia cringed a bit, knowing how the explanation was going to sound even before she admitted, "Actually, Lucy suggested that I work for Marshal Goodrich."

Her smile widened. "Lucy, huh?"

"It's not a matchmaker thing," she insisted, immediately trying to put Elsie's suspicions to rest as they both knew Lucy's main objective in anything was to have two people meet and fall in love...with her gentle encouragement. And a bit of conniving. She'd done it for so many now that she even had a sign below the Photographer one next to the front door of her home. "I have no intention of falling in love with Devlin Goodrich," she asserted, but wondered if her words fell on deaf ears. It was apparent by the expression on Elsie's face that her explanation was not believed. She quickly changed the subject. "I was wondering if I could pick up three fried chicken dinners to take home."

"Of course. It'll be a minute." She gestured to the crowd. "We're packed tonight. What do you want with them?"

Tresia looked at Avery. "Green beans? Or corn?"

"Corn," she whispered, which was hard to hear over the sound of the Wagon Wheel's patrons.

"And some of those potatoes you make, Elsie—the ones that look like little pillows. Biscuits, too, I think."

"Excellent. Have a seat." Elsie glanced around and pointed to a table beside the big picture window. "There's an empty table right over there. I'll be right back." She picked up the heavy tray and went off to the kitchen.

"Come on, Avery." She ushered the girl to the table Elsie suggested, acknowledging the friendly smiles and greetings from people she'd known most of her life, though some gave her an inquisitive look. By tomorrow afternoon—or maybe even sooner —it would be all over Serenity that she was no longer working at Sullivan's and that she was taking care of the new marshal's daughter. She smiled to herself a little as she took her seat—word spread fast in a small town—like wildfire.

Avery sat across from her and gently rocked the doll in her arms. She didn't speak, but she did croon to the porcelain doll that looked a little bit like her, a sweet, low-pitched hum that signaled her happiness with the gift.

Elsie returned with a pitcher of water and two glasses shortly after but didn't move on. Instead, she stood beside the table, hands on her hips, her gaze going from her to Avery then back again. If the restaurant weren't so busy, she might have dropped into the empty chair for a nice, long chat. "So, tell me about the new marshal."

Tresia shrugged. "He seems like a nice man. We've only just met. Today, in fact." She glanced at Avery, who paid no attention to their conversation at all and lowered her voice. "He's a widower."

Elsie lowered her voice as well and repeated. "A widower?" Sympathy—and something else—flashed in her eyes.

Tresia nodded and eyed her, then darted her gaze toward Avery.

Elsie gave a nod, as if understanding the silent message. "We'll talk later," she said then noticed two more people come into the restaurant. "I'll be back with your order."

It didn't take as long as she thought it would before Elsie was back, their dinners in heavy paperboard boxes in a big paper sack. "Enjoy. I added something extra for the little one."

"Thank you, Elsie." She dug in her drawstring bag and pulled out a few coins then handed them to Elsie. "This should cover it."

Elsie looked at the coins in her palm. "It's too much, Tresia."

"No, it's just enough," she insisted.

A blush settled over Elsie's face even as a wide smile spread her lips. She closed her hand around the coins. "I'll see you at the next Society meeting."

"Yes, you will." She held out her free hand. "Come on, Avery. Let's go home."

Avery scooted out of her seat, slipped her hand in hers and practically pulled her toward the door.

They walked home, cutting through the town square, then over two streets to the marshal's house. She pulled the key he'd given her from her drawstring purse but tried the doorknob first. Most people in Serenity didn't bother locking their doors. The door opened easily, and she stepped inside, bringing Avery with her.

After putting the food on plates, then in the oven to keep warm, except for her own, which she left on the counter, she turned toward Avery. "Would you like to help me fix the threshold?"

She silently nodded with enthusiasm.

"Let's go see what's in the shed. If there isn't a hammer and nails, we'll have to walk back to the store." Even as she said the words, she cringed, just a bit. It would be uncomfortable going back into Sullivan's so soon after she quit. Arnold, being Arnold, and probably incredibly angry with her, might just kick her out—if he hadn't closed up the shop already. It didn't matter if he had. She may have quit, but she hadn't given up her key—after all, she was still going to do the books.

They went outside through the kitchen door and stood on the porch. The shed sat off to the left, although Avery's eye had caught a swing hanging from a limb of a tall sturdy elm tree. She made a beeline for it, placed her doll on the seat, and gave the swing a gentle push.

"We can play on the swing tomorrow. Come help me find a hammer."

Avery quickly retrieved the doll and ran up to the porch, the lace on her petticoat showing as she lifted her knees high. Disappointment showed on her face, but she didn't question the request she'd been given. Apparently, someone had taught her to mind. Had it been the marshal? His late wife?

The shed door creaked as Tresia opened it. "It's dark in here. I should have brought a lamp with me." She opened the door wider, allowing the fading sunlight to filter into the darkness.

Fortunately, the shed did contain a hammer, as well as a myriad of other tools one might need to make repairs to the house. There was even a new box of nails on a shelf. Gathering what she needed, she went back into the house, Avery following behind although she had looked at the swing with something resembling longing.

A short time later, after Tresia had positioned the threshold in place and hammered in three nails, she held out her hand, palm up. "Avery, would you hand me another nail?"

Avery grabbed a nail from the small table beside the door with her fingertips, already warned how sharp the point could be, and handed it to her.

"Thank you." Still, not a word from the girl, though she knew the child had a voice. She'd heard her quite clearly as she crooned to her doll and on a few other occasions as well, but her responses were usually just one-word answers, if she deemed to speak at all. Most of the children she knew only stopped talking long enough to take a breath, and sometimes, not even then. She'd have to ask the marshal if there was a reason—physical or otherwise—Avery didn't speak much. A minute or two later, she tested the threshold, trying to jiggle it out of place but it didn't move. "Well, that's done. We did a good job, don't you think?"

A deeper, gravelly voice, not the one she expected, responded from the parlor behind her. "You did a better job than I did, Mrs. Morgan."

"Daddy!" Avery shouted, excitement in her voice and showing she could speak when she wanted.

Tresia shot up from her position on the floor and whirled around, hammer still clutched in her hand to see Avery safely ensconced in her father's arms. "Oh, Marshal! I didn't think you'd be home this soon." Blood warmed her face. Indeed, she could feel the heat of it rising up from her chest. He'd come into the house from the kitchen door as she'd been backside up, pounding nails into the threshold. How long had he been standing there?

"Dinner's in the oven staying warm. I'll...uh...I'll go take care of that." She dropped the hammer on the table, thankful it wasn't on her own foot...or his...and strode toward the kitchen. He followed with Avery in his arms and moved a chair away from the table with his foot before seating his daughter in the chair.

Tresia quickly grabbed a kitchen towel and removed the plates from the oven, one at a time, and placed them on the table.

The marshal glanced at the plates, then at her as she pulled napkins and silverware from one of the drawers and placed forks, knives, and spoons beside the plates. "You're not eating with us?"

"No, I'll just take mine home."

"Well, that's just plain silly." There was a warm glow in his eyes and a teasing quality in his voice as he turned to his daughter. "Avery, don't you think Mrs. Morgan should have dinner with us?"

"Yes." The word was said loudly and clearly and expectancy lit her face.

She couldn't resist the hope reflected in Avery's eyes or the slight smile on the marshal's face. "All right. If you insist."

"We do."

She quickly plated up her own food and sat at the table though it felt awkward and became even more awkward as the marshal began asking Avery questions.

"Did you do anything fun today?"

Avery simply nodded as she took a small bite out of a crispy chicken leg. There was a smile on her face and a warm light in her eyes.

"Did you meet new people?" Again, he tried, but received the same response, which was nothing other than a nod.

It was obvious that Avery's answers were not satisfactory to him at all. Worry seemed to etch itself into his face. There was sadness in his eyes, too, and Tresia's heart went out to him. She sympathized with the situation as she'd had the same with her father after he'd had his stroke, which had taken his ability to speak.

She wanted to tell him to stop asking Avery questions but was afraid of overstepping. There were some parents who did not appreciate advice coming from anyone in regard to their children. She'd run into that at the store, where some parents let their children do whatever they pleased, ruining her displays or running around and making a nuisance of themselves. She'd asked more than one mother to leave over the years, despite losing a sale.

"Is the chicken good?"

Once again, his daughter just nodded and he gave up—finally —but then he turned his attention to her. "Tell me about yourself, Mrs. Morgan."

She swallowed her mouthful of food then wiped her lips with the napkin. "There isn't much to tell, Marshal—"

He interrupted her. "You should call me Devlin. After all, we'll be seeing a lot of each other."

She gave a short nod even as a little thrill whispered through her. "All right. Devlin. And you should call me Tresia."

He smiled, but it didn't quite reach his eyes. His gaze kept going to his daughter, watching her, waiting for her to speak, which she didn't. "You were saying, Tresia?"

Oh, she liked the way he said her name. It flowed from his lips without effort in his deep, gravelly voice that seemed to send fairies dancing in her belly. She paused, looking for the words, looking for a reason as to why that should be. She'd been married, for goodness sake! She wasn't some young miss mooning over a handsome man. "As I said, there isn't much to tell. I was born here in Serenity. I love this town. It's a good place and it's getting better all the time. The Ladies' Society—"

He interrupted her again. "The Ladies' Society? What is that?"

"It's just a group of ladies Lucy Hart gathered together. We try to do good things for the community. Two years ago, we raised funds to beautify the town square. The benches you see are new, each one donated by someone. There's a little brass plaque that shows who provided the funds for it. And the flowers lining the paths are from Mrs. Dameron. She has the greenest thumb of anyone I know, but we all help with weeding and such."

She watched him as she spoke, liking the fact that she had his undivided attention.

"Tell me more. What else does the Ladies' Society do?"

"Lucy thinks—and we all agree—there should be a lending library. The town hall has two rooms on the second floor that aren't being used. We could put up shelves and fill them with books that would be available to anyone. For free. We just need the books."

"And how will you get those books?"

"We'll have to have another fund raiser, but we haven't decided what yet. It'll have to be something good. We did put together a recipe book and that was popular, but we don't want to do that again."

He didn't eat much, she noticed. He'd only taken two bites out of his chicken leg and pushed the potatoes around on his plate, while Avery ate every bit, including the corn and the cookie Elsie had slipped into the bag. She had a good appetite, which was good to see.

"All right, Miss Avery, I think it's time for bed." Tresia rose from her chair and took the dirty dishes to the counter beside the sink. "You've had a busy day."

"I'll do that," Devlin said as he laid his napkin beside his plate and rose from his seat. "We have a routine, Avery and I, don't we?"

Tresia looked at the girl who still hadn't spoken a word, though she smiled a lot, especially when she looked at her father with such love in her eyes. "Of course."

She watched them leave the kitchen, happy with the knowledge that Devlin Goodrich seemed like an attentive father, much as her own had been.

After she'd finished drying the last plate and put it away, the marshal came downstairs. He stood in the doorway for a moment then glanced at the clock on the wall, his expression one of surprise. "I thought you'd gone home."

She spread the dish towel over the back of a chair to dry. "I was just finishing up."

"Thank you for taking care of Avery and for picking up dinner." He reached into his pocket and withdrew his billfold. "How much do I owe you?"

"Nothing. I was pleased to do it."

"Are you sure?"

"I am."

He put his billfold away and just stood there, his hands now gripping the back of the chair. After a long, tense moment, he said, "You have questions."

"I do." She had to broach the subject carefully, but words failed her. In the end, she could think of no other way to phrase her query except a bit bluntly. "Why doesn't Avery speak very much?"

"You noticed."

"How could I not?" She poured him a cup of coffee and slid it across the table, a silent invitation. She poured one for herself as well and sat, waiting until he did the same. It took a moment before he complied, the legs of the chair squeaking against the wood floor as he moved it, though it was obvious to her that he didn't want to.

"She's a smart child, Marshal. She's aware of everything that's going on around her, but she doesn't chatter on like most almost five-year-olds I know. She's a little shy, I saw that for myself. I also saw that she responds only when spoken to, usually with a nod or a shake of her head. Sometimes, she'll actually use her voice and say yes or no, but not much more, and that seems to be very rare." She took a sip of coffee and waited.

And waited a little more.

He looked at his coffee cup, at the wall, at the tabletop, every-where except at her. For a long time, she didn't think he would answer so she tried again. "I don't mean to pry, Marshal, but if I'm going to be taking care of her, then I think I should know."

He finally looked at her. Pain flashed in his stormy blue eyes. That pain was repeated in the deep lines around his mouth. "You're right. You do need to know." He shook his head as his gaze held hers captive. "She wasn't always so quiet. At one time, she was a regular little chatterbox. Hannah and I could hardly get her to stop talking."

"Hannah? Was she your wife?"

He nodded and once again, that pain flashed in his eyes, telling her, without words, that he still mourned her. Perhaps Avery did as well, but being a child, she might not be able to express herself so she lapsed into silence instead. It was a possi-bility. "Was it the loss of your wife that changed her?"

He stared down at his coffee cup, his body stiff, as if talking about what happened to Hannah hurt him deep in his soul. It probably did. "Yes. And more."

She waited for him to elaborate, but he didn't. He simply sat, staring at his coffee, his jaw clenched. A muscle spasmed in his cheek and his eyes narrowed. Without knowing the man well at all, she did realize he wasn't about to say anything more. Perhaps, in time, he would, but for now, she'd have to let it go. When he was ready, if he was ever ready, he might take her into his confidence, but now wasn't the time. She was here to watch Avery and keep house, nothing more.

"Well then, I should go." Tresia finished her coffee then rose from her seat and brought the cup to the sink. She rinsed it out then turned to face him. He hadn't moved, not an inch. He didn't look at her, either.

Feeling guilty, her entire body flushed, the heat coming from deep inside. "I'll see you tomorrow morning."

He finally looked up at her and the pain reflecting in his eyes made every muscle in her body tense even as her heart went out to him. She shouldn't have asked. She knew the pain of losing someone—the confusion, the unanswered questions, the remorse and yes, sometimes the resentment. From her own experiences, she knew there was no answer to the question of 'why.' She also knew that everyone grieved in their own way, in their own time. In many ways, she was still grieving the loss of Brett, though Brett had passed almost three years ago—sometimes the ache was so intense, it hurt so much, she could hardly stand it. Add to that the recent death of her father, and sometimes, the pain brought her to her knees.

"Good night, Marshal." She left the house, closing the kitchen door softly behind her, determined to bring Avery out of her shell and perhaps, in the process, ease the pain she saw in Marshal Devlin Goodrich's eyes.

CHAPTER 4

*T*he sound of Avery's giggles drifted into Devlin's dreams, making him smile as he awoke. He rolled over in the bed, dragging the light blanket with him. Sunlight warmed his face and he let out a contented sigh.

He opened his eyes slowly, his gaze falling on the lamp on the bedside table. It wasn't familiar. When did Hannah purchase a new one? He reached out from beneath the blanket to trace the engraving on the bedside table. This was new, too, but he liked it. He rolled onto his back, raising his head a bit from the pillow to look at the headboard of the bed he slept in. Made of wood instead of brass, it wasn't familiar either.

Had Hannah redecorated while he'd been chasing Big Bill Cassidy all across the New Mexican countryside?

He smiled. Yes, that was something she would do to let him know she was unhappy with him. She didn't like being left alone when he had to be away performing his marshal duties, although when they first met, she'd been thrilled he was a lawman. That changed over the five years they were married. Redecorating was better than her running to her mother, the esteemed and very demanding Frances Emerson Comstock, every time he had to go away.

He closed his eyes again, listening to the cheerful sound of Avery's giggles, wishing Hannah would come back to bed—

The memories came rushing back to him like a tidal wave— the events of the past, reigniting the pain and loss. Hannah. The woman he'd loved with an intensity that sometimes scared him was gone. And so was his son whom she had struggled so hard to bring into the world.

Fear seized him then, making every muscle in his body scream with the need to move. Panicked as well as disoriented, he whipped the light blanket off and scrambled out of bed, his feet hitting the hardwood floor.

Who was Avery laughing with? Had Frances found them? Had she come to take Avery away from him as she'd threatened too many times to count? He tried to calm himself, reasoning that if it was Frances, Avery would not be giggling. Frances would never have allowed that happy sound.

He pulled on his trousers, grabbed a pistol from the nearby gun belt, and rushed downstairs, his heart beating much too fast for so early in the morning.

He skidded to a stop in the kitchen doorway just as reality came back to him. Relief at the scene before him made his knees almost buckle and he moved the gun behind his back, not wishing to frighten anyone like he'd been frightened.

Tresia stood at the counter beside the sink, her backside swaying gently as she beat something in a bowl. Several thick strands of auburn hair escaped from the loose bun at the back of her head to fall about her shoulders.

He glanced to his right where Avery sat at the table, still in her nightgown, the doll Tresia had given her yesterday—the one she had insisted on sleeping with—clutched tightly in her arms. There was a big smile on her face, which grew wider when she turned toward him.

"Hi, Daddy!"

He found his voice, though he still felt off balance. His heart hadn't found its normal rhythm yet and the abrupt loss of his panic made his body shake. He took a deep breath. "Good morning, sweet pea."

Tresia turned away from the stove, those pretty pansy eyes of hers opened wide even as a blush reddened her cheeks at his attire—or lack thereof. She seemed to recover her surprise rather quickly, faster than he did. He took a step back—or at least tried to but she stopped him.

"Good morning, Marshal. Coffee's ready." She gestured to the coffeepot resting on a trivet on the table as if his near nakedness didn't bother her. Perhaps it didn't. She had been married before, but in truth, it wasn't appropriate. She nodded toward the ice box. "I met Mr. Shaeffer as he was leaving your milk, cream, and butter this morning. I already put them away." She smiled as she waved the whisk toward the bowl in her hand. "Your eggs will be done shortly. I hope you like scrambled."

"Eggs?" He repeated, rather stupidly. Was he losing what little remained of his mind? He didn't recall having eggs in the house. Actually, he hadn't remembered a lot of things when he woke up this morning.

"I stopped at Goldwater's last night on my way home. You have eggs." She nodded, her smile gentle and full of understanding. She then pointed toward the pantry with her chin. "I also picked up bread and a few other things."

A little taken aback, he blinked before he finally found his wits. "Thank you, Mrs. Morgan."

Her smile dimmed a little. "I thought we agreed that you would call me Tresia."

"We did. My apologies. I'm a little—"

"Surprised? Confused? Maybe even a little disoriented?"

He gave her a sheepish smile. She was right. He was that and more, waking up as he had in a strange room with unfamiliar surroundings, the sound of his daughter giggling, a sound he hadn't heard in a while. "All of the above."

She bit her lip, probably in an effort not to laugh. "Did you forget I'd be here?"

"I did."

Avery scooted down from her chair and gently tugged on his hand. "Sit, Daddy."

He glanced down at her little hand then at her face and finally, at his own bare chest. "I should make myself more presentable. Excuse me." He made a hasty exit.

This morning wasn't the first time he had awoken like that—disoriented and not quite knowing where he was or remembering Hannah was no longer with him. He wished it would be the last. He went back upstairs, more slowly this time, in full control of his emotions, the fear that someone had been with Avery—perhaps to take her away—having dissipated. It was one of his biggest worries—that Frances would, once again, try to make his life a living hell. He had vowed he would never be caught off guard again.

He drew a deep breath and went about getting ready for the day. When he came back downstairs, shaven, cleaned up and dressed appropriately, his gun belt riding low on his hips, he was much calmer.

"I'm sorry," he apologized as soon as he took his seat.

Tresia glanced at him as she moved around the table. "For what? You didn't do anything wrong. Clearly you were startled."

If she had seen the gun in his hand, she didn't mention it. Nor did she seem disturbed—now—that he'd entered the kitchen shirtless, though at the time, her eyes had rounded in surprise, and a blush covered her smooth cheeks.

"I was." He gave a short laugh then cleared his throat as his gaze roamed over her. "What are your plans for today?"

"Well, after your trunks arrive and we put your things away, I thought Avery and I would visit Lucy, then do a little more shopping." She poured him a cup of coffee, then one for herself, gesturing toward the bowl of sugar and little pitcher filled with cream. "Would you like anything special for dinner? We can stop by Mr. Crandall's. He's the butcher."

"I can't think of anything. Surprise me."

"And what are you going to do? It's your first official day on the job." She drew his attention back to her, her voice soft and filled with what sounded like compassion. Not only was she forgiving, but sympathetic as well. What Merrill and Rafael told him yesterday was true and he remained glad he'd hired her.

"I'm going to meet the rest of my deputies. I met Merrill Shotton and Rafael Zepeda yesterday and then I thought I'd start getting to know everyone in town."

"Sounds like a good plan. Make sure you stop by Sweet Somethings if you have a sweet tooth. Polly bakes the most extraordinary confections."

He speared a mound of scrambled eggs. "I had a piece of her strawberry rhubarb pie yesterday. It was very tasty." He reached for one of the biscuits; it was still warm. He split it open and smeared it with butter, then took a bite. It was delicious. She could probably give Polly a run for her money in the baking department.

He finished eating and glanced up at the clock ticking merrily on the wall above the sink. "I should go. Thank you for breakfast." He drank the rest of his coffee and rose from his seat. Turning toward Avery, he bent low, holding out his arms. "Come give me a kiss."

Avery scooted off her chair and jumped into his open arms. She squealed when he lifted her high and giggled when he made raspberries on her cheek. Her little arms wrapped around his neck, as if she'd never let go. It filled his heart and made leaving for work a little more difficult, but he had no choice. Well, he did.

He didn't need the money, having inherited a great deal when his mother and father had passed away within days of each other. He could have retired when Hannah died, but that wasn't his way. Despite the danger, he loved what he did.

He gave Avery a quick kiss on the cheek and set her down. "You be good for Miss Tresia now, you hear?"

Avery gave a quick nod, the smile she'd been wearing disappearing. Leaving her in the morning was the hardest part of his day, even harder than facing criminals who could kill him without a by-your-leave. He left after giving Tresia an appreciative smile, grabbed his hat from the rack by the front door, and walked out the door though he didn't go very far. He stopped on the front porch and just stood there for a moment, filling his lungs with the cool morning air, before he walked down the steps and headed to work.

Entering the Sheriff's office by the back door, which was just across the street from his house, he noticed the coffeepot on the stove and the delicious aroma of coffee scenting the air. He heard several voices, his deputies, raised in camaraderie as well. He slowed his pace as he moved through the kitchen and listened for a moment. He smiled. It was clear to him these men shared a closeness, which was to their benefit. It meant that they looked out for each other. Not only did they have each other's backs, it sounded as if they liked each other as well. There was a lot of teasing, especially toward Merrill and his growing affection for Polly.

It had been that way at his last post in Albuquerque. He couldn't ask for more.

He stepped out of the kitchen and into the main room and stopped, quickly noticing that only five men were there, instead of the six he had expected. "Good morning, gentlemen."

The teasing died away in an instant as they all turned to look at him, every one of them instantly alert. Five pairs of eyes sized him up. A tall, blond-haired man laid his hand on his pistol but didn't draw, though Devlin had no doubts he would be quick when he did. Another man, slightly shorter but stocky with hair as orange as a carrot, moved slightly to his left, his eyes narrowing, his body stiff, seemingly ready to defend himself as well as his comrades. He didn't reach for his gun, but his stance clearly said he could…and he wouldn't miss when he did.

Devlin wasn't offended; it was exactly what he wanted to see, which is why he'd come into the building from the kitchen door. Though they'd been in the midst of ribbing Merrill, none of them had forgotten where they were and the danger they lived with on a daily basis.

All in all, he liked what he saw. Confidence radiated from the five deputies, which was so important. Not only that, but trust and loyalty, to each other as well as to the job.

"Good morning, *el jefe*," Rafael greeted him, a big smile on his face as he waved toward him. "Gentlemen, meet our new marshal, Devlin Goodrich."

"Thank you all for coming in. I appreciate it." Devlin sauntered into the room and took a seat at one of the desks, then nodded toward Merrill. "Are we one short?"

"Tomas will be in shortly, I'm sure."

He studied the man, noticing the humorous gleam in his eyes. "Is it normal for him to be late?"

"No, but he probably stopped to help someone." Merrill grinned suddenly. "Maybe he had difficulty tearing himself away from his wife."

The other men laughed.

Devlin hid his smile and directed his attention to the men who were there. "Pull up a seat. We'll talk."

Quickly, they did as he asked, pulling chairs from the other desks, the sound of furniture scraping the wooden floor filling the room. It didn't take long for them to make themselves comfortable, nor for Merrill to bring him a cup of coffee before taking up a position against the wall, arms folded across his chest.

Devlin turned to the blond-haired man who'd dropped his hand to the butt of his pistol when he walked into the room. He appeared to be quite young, maybe twenty, if not younger. He'd have to keep a careful watch on this one. He didn't need some young hothead shooting at everything that moved. "What's your name, son?"

"Sherm Quincy."

"Tell me about yourself."

The man straightened in his seat. "Not much to tell."

"I noticed you were quick to reach for your gun. How long have you been a deputy?"

A blush spread over his features, encompassing his entire face in a reddish pink hue, reaching all the way up to the tips of his ears. Perspiration made his forehead shine. "About six months."

"You ever shoot anyone?"

"No." And then he added, "But I'm a crack shot. I can hit the spade out of a playing card at fifty paces."

"Shooting at cards is a whole lot different than shooting at people."

"I know that." A little bit of belligerence snuck into his tone, which Devlin ignored—for now.

"And you?" He nodded toward the red-haired man.

"Caleb Johnson, sir."

Devlin smiled. "You don't have to call me 'sir'. Devlin will do." His smile grew as he studied the man. "Did you serve?"

Caleb straightened and looked him straight in the eye. "I did, sir. Spent eight years in the Army before coming home to Serenity. How did you know?"

"Just by the way you stood, by the way your body stiffened when I walked into the room, like you were prepared to protect your companions." He laughed. "Or salute me. What rank did you earn?"

"Captain, sir."

"And why did you leave the service?"

"My Pa took ill. I came home to help my family on our farm."

"And how long have you been a deputy?"

"Two years now, sir. I still help out on the farm when I'm needed, but my brother and his wife run it now."

"Do you like your job?"

A proud smile crossed the man's face. "I do. Plan to stay at it for a long time."

"Good to know." He gave a quick nod then focused his attention on the third man sitting before him. Before he could ask a question, the man rose from his chair and reached across the desk, extending his hand, grasping his in a firm grip. "Nate Hyler. Been a deputy for ten years now. I like my job, too." And then he laughed, a big braying sound that was more donkey than human.

Amused by the tall, lanky man's congenial attitude, as well as his unusual laugh, Devlin let out a laugh of his own. "Nice to meet you, Nate."

The door banged open just then and slammed against the opposite wall, startling them all, as a young, dark-haired man half carried, half dragged an older man into the office. Everyone sprang to their feet, except Nate and Merrill, who were already standing. Sherm dropped his hand to the holster around his hips, which Devlin had expected as that seemed to be his defensive way. Others stood at attention, assessing the situation before making a move. Merrill took a step closer to him, as if to protect him, and again, Devlin liked what he saw, despite being surprised himself. His deputies were fast and prepared, more so than he himself was at this moment.

"Sorry I'm late! Found Mr. Somner sleeping on a bench in the town square." The newcomer laughed though he was a little breathless and wrinkled his nose as he dragged the man inside the building. "Smelled him before I saw him. He must have drunk himself silly last night. Maybe someone oughta tell Connor to stop servin' him when he can't walk straight no more."

Merrill stepped forward, as did Nate, and helped the young man deliver Mr. Somner to one of the jail cells, as if this was a frequent occurrence. Perhaps it was. Devlin recalled Merrill saying something about it yesterday.

Mr. Somner didn't resist at all. In fact, he was laughing, complimenting the deputies on how solicitous they were, slurring his words and promising they'd all go to heaven when it was their time for being so nice. They eased the man gently to the cot in the cell. "Go to sleep," Merrill ordered then grabbed a thin blanket from a shelf and spread it out over the man, showing that he'd definitely done this more than once.

"'Night, boys," the man mumbled, then, like a switch had been turned off, he fell asleep. In moments, his delicate little snores filled the small space.

Devlin watched it all with something akin to amusement. All the years he'd spent in Albuquerque, he'd never seen anything quite like it. Yes, there was drunkenness in Albuquerque, but his deputies hadn't quite been so solicitous.

"And now you've met Fred Somner," Merrill chuckled. "As you can see, completely harmless even if he is definitely in his cups." He extended his arm and placed it around the deputy's shoulder. "And this is Tomas Medrano."

Tomas stepped forward and extended his hand. "You must be Marshal Goodrich. A pleasure, sir."

"Nice to meet you, Tomas. Please, pour yourself a cup of coffee and have a seat. I think you've earned it." Devlin smiled in greeting, his gaze sweeping over the young man,

Tomas did as he was asked, disappearing into the kitchen and returning with a cup of the steaming coffee. He pulled up a chair and slumped into it.

"Tell me about yourself."

"Me?"

"Yes. We were all getting to know each other when you came in with Mr. Somner."

Tomas smiled. "What would you like to know?"

"Anything you'd like to tell me." Devlin liked this young man. Not only did his dark eyes miss nothing, but there was a calmness to him, a *serenity* as it were, despite having to drag a very drunk, mostly incoherent man into the office.

"Well, I grew up in Serenity. My folks own *Dos Corazones* Ranch just north of here. I've been a deputy for four years. I'm married to a wonderful woman—Cordelia, and we have two children who are the light of my life." Tomas used his thumb to gesture toward the jail cell. "Welcome to Serenity, Marshal."

Devlin smiled. "Thank you. I'm happy to be here." He studied each of the men before him, clearing his throat after a moment. "I should probably tell you all a little about myself. I run a tight ship, but that doesn't mean I can't or won't be accommodating. Tell me what you need. If it's time off, let me know and we'll make arrangements. If you think we need more help, tell me that, too. If you have a problem with the way I run things, talk to me. I will listen." He took a sip of coffee.

"I will not be changing anything—for the time being, if ever. I see no reason to do so as Deputy Shotton assures me things are going well as they are, so your schedules will remain the same. The main thing, gentlemen, is that the people who live and work in this town are safe. It's our job to protect them and we will do it to the best of our ability. Any questions?"

No one said a word but there were a few head shakes, which pleased him. They looked like good men who knew their jobs though he would keep an eye on Sherm. The young man's penchant for reaching for his gun gave him pause. Though all lawmen wore guns, he was of the opinion it shouldn't have to be used as a first resort. Much can be accomplished by speaking gently but firmly, and an unpleasant situation could turn out well if the right approach were used.

"Good. You're all dismissed then, except for Merrill and Rafael. However, I expect you back for your regular shift." He glanced at Nate, his night-time deputy, who'd stayed after his shift ended. "Get some sleep."

The men shuffled out of the building, talking amongst themselves. If there was any negativity, he didn't hear it and none of his deputies showed that they were upset with his introduction in any way. Devlin finished the coffee in his cup, pleased with what he had accomplished so far.

"Well done, Boss," Merrill said as he grabbed his hat from his desk. He didn't put it on. Instead, he held it in his hands, his fingers caressing the brim.

"You think so?"

"I do. Besides, we all knew who you were before you were appointed. We know about Big Bill Cassidy and Smiley Burdette, two of the most notorious gunslingers ever to roam New Mexico, and how you brought them in when the odds were against you. We may be a small town, but we still get news from across the country. In fact, we have our own newspaper and telegraph office." He fitted his hat to his bald head. "You're a legend among lawmen."

While the praise was earned—sort of—he didn't think he deserved it, especially since it was while he was chasing Big Bill that he'd lost Hannah. No, it wasn't Big Bill's fault that Hannah passed, but he blamed the man just the same—as much as he blamed himself. If he hadn't been searching for the outlaw, he'd have been there when Hannah went into early labor. "I don't know about that, Merrill, I was just doing my job."

As if sensing the subject was a sore one, Merrill changed it. "You ready to start meeting the townspeople?" His hand moved to the gun belt slung low around his hips. He pulled a pistol from the holster, checked that the gun was loaded, and put it back before checking the other.

"You expecting trouble?"

Merrill shook his head and patted the guns at his hips. "Never do, but it doesn't hurt to be ready. Wouldn't be doing my job if I walked out of here unprepared." He turned toward Rafael even as he reached for the door. "We'll be back."

Rafael smiled and gestured to the man sleeping in the cell. "We'll be here."

CHAPTER 5

"*I*s this Marshal Devlin Goodrich's house?" A young man asked when Tresia answered the knock on the door just after noon.

Her gaze swept over him. Big and brawny, he wore a slouch hat, a light jacket and a big smile. "It is."

"Got your trunks." He gestured to the wagon on the dirt road in front of the house then reached into his jacket pocket and removed a folded sheaf of papers. Once he had the papers in hand, he fished around in his pocket a little more and came up with a small stub of pencil. "You gotta sign for 'em." After handing them to her, he signaled to his companion.

Tresia took both and paused as the other young man—just as big and brawny—climbed down from the wagon and grabbed a small trunk from the wagon bed. He lifted it to his shoulder like it weighed nothing, strolled up the walkway and deposited it on the porch. She looked at the trunk, then back at the young man. "Would you mind terribly bringing that upstairs?"

"Uh, we were paid to deliver, ma'am, not bring 'em in."

"Please."

They looked at each other.

"I just made some gingerbread men. You're welcome to them if you'll bring the trunks upstairs."

Again, they looked at each other and the first young man said, "Uh, sure."

"If you'll leave them in the hallway upstairs, I can do the rest."

By the time they were done and had gingerbread men still warm from the oven in their hands, the hallway upstairs contained four small trunks and two big ones. She closed the door behind the delivery men and went upstairs. Now to figure out which trunk belonged to who and put everything away.

She knelt down on the floor and flipped open one of the bigger trunks as Avery watched. It was filled with frilly dresses in all the colors of the rainbow and shoes in Avery's size. She picked up a shoe, recognizing high quality when she saw it, then glanced at the well-worn boots on her charge's feet. Those were high quality, too, but old and well-worn.

She pulled one of the dresses out of the trunk and shook the wrinkles from it as nothing seemed to have been folded—just tossed, like whoever had packed them had been in a hurry. Bright pink, it possessed an inordinate amount of bows, both big and small, and lace—lots of lace. She glanced at Avery, taking in her plain calico dress, sans bows and lace and fancy buttons. It definitely did not match the garments in the trunk.

These dresses looked like the little girl who wore them was more porcelain doll than flesh and blood, a child who did not know the freedom of running around, getting all dirty, a child who was put on display—seen but not heard. She didn't know Devlin well but hardly thought he would insist upon that kind of behavior. In all the interactions she'd seen between Devlin and Avery, she witnessed none of that. Oh, he loved his daughter, that much was evident, but he didn't treat her like she'd break.

Had it been Hannah? Perhaps.

Her gaze rose up to Avery's face and her heart melted a little. There was a smudge of jam on her cheek from lunch and her hair was a curly mess around her head, a soft brown halo of sorts as she had brushed it herself, refusing all help.

"We should put all this away. What do think?"

Avery nodded. Tresia had decided to try to engage the child in conversation. She picked herself up off the floor, closed the lid, then bent low and pushed the trunk toward Avery's bedroom. It was heavier than she thought. She pushed again but only managed to move the thing a few inches. She should be able to do this. She was a strong woman. Hadn't she spent years receiving and unpacking goods at the store?

She glanced at Avery, who simply stood off to the side, clutching her doll, but there was a certain gleam in her blue-gray eyes. "How would you like to give your doll a ride?"

The gleam turned to curiosity.

"Let's put...uh...what did you name her?"

"Cecily."

"Right. Cecily. Why don't you sit Cecily—" she patted the top of the trunk— "right here and we'll push her into your room?"

Avery needed no further urging. Gently, she sat Cecily on top of the trunk then joined Tresia at the back, placing her little hands beside hers.

"Ready?"

Avery nodded, her smile wide.

"Push!"

Avery let out a startling whoop as they pushed and slid the trunk into the other room. She even managed a giggle, which warmed Tresia's heart.

"We did it," Avery said quietly before she grabbed her doll from the top of the trunk and cuddled her in her arms, pride beaming on her little face.

A little shocked, but oh so pleased, Tresia responded in kind. "Yes, we did. Now we can unpack and hang everything up in the armoire." She pointed to the bed she'd made earlier in the morning. "You can sit Cecily on the bed so she can watch."

Avery did just that, placing the doll against the pillows before she started pulling clothing from the trunk.

It didn't take long before the trunk was nearly empty, just a few more items that needed to be folded and placed in a drawer. Tresia pulled out a folded piece of cloth. It wasn't an article of clothing, but something hard. Carefully, she unwrapped it, revealing a silver-framed photograph. The woman in it was beautiful with almost an ethereal quality, an angel among humans. She studied it, noticing the hint of a sweet smile, the wide eyes expressing kindness, the carefully coiffed dark hair and looked at Avery, who had stopped moving and simply stared at the photograph.

"Is this your mother?"

Avery nodded as she took the picture in her hand, holding it with a gentleness that belied her age. Her eyes grew big in her face, yet a slight smile curved her lips. She traced her finger over the glass protecting it.

"She was very beautiful."

Again, Avery nodded and placed the picture on her bedside table. "I miss her," she admitted, surprising Tresia with another full sentence.

She sat on the bed, her heart hurting for this little girl who'd lost her mother at such a young and impressionable age. Though she'd been much older when her own mother passed, she knew that the hurt didn't just suddenly go away. "I lost my mother, too," she said quietly, hoping to draw a few more words from her. "Do you want to talk about it?"

Avery shook her head, looked at the photograph one last time, and snatched up her doll before she ran back into the hallway, prepared it seemed, to push the other big trunk into her father's room.

Tresia watched her go then rose from the bed and joined her in the hallway, reasoning that when she was ready, Avery would talk a little more than what she had.

It didn't take long to empty the other trunks. The marshal didn't have as much clothing as Avery did, and the smaller trunks were filled with incidentals, books, some personal papers and old letters, tied together with a pale yellow ribbon. They looked like love letters, the handwriting on the envelope elegant and definitely feminine. She resisted the urge to look closer. It wasn't any of her business.

There was another photograph, again in an ornate frame, this one with a younger Hannah standing beside Devlin. She held a bouquet of flowers in her hand. He was in a dark suit. She paused and studied the photograph and couldn't help smiling. They looked so happy, so in love. It must have been taken on their wedding day. She placed it on the bedside table so it was the first thing he'd see when he woke up in the morning.

Wiping the sweat from her brow, pleased with the progress she'd made, she glanced at her charge, who sat on the floor on a throw rug and put together a puzzle she'd found in one of the trunks, Cecily keeping close watch by her side.

"How would you like to go see my friend Lucy?"

Avery looked up from her puzzle, her big blue-gray eyes shadowed with—what was that? Anxiety? Fear? Both? She said nothing though. Didn't nod or shake her head as was her usual way to answer a question. She didn't look away either, those eyes of hers seeming to see into Tresia's soul, as if looking for trust, for assurance.

Tresia understood shyness, but this seemed to be something more. Was it too soon to start introducing her to other people? She hadn't appeared to be shy or uneasy around Elsie last night when they stopped at the Wagon Wheel, but then Elsie was so friendly, no one could resist her.

She studied Avery then said, "You've met Lucy before. Yesterday, in fact, when your father picked up the key to the house. Do you remember?"

Avery still didn't respond, oh, but those eyes of hers spoke volumes.

"Lucy's a very nice lady. She's been my friend for a long time. She might even have her niece or one of her nephews at the house. Would you like that?"

Avery blinked and the anxiety Tresia knew she saw seemed to disappear. "Okay," Avery murmured, then rose from the floor, grabbed her doll, and clutched it to her chest.

"We'll bring some of the cookies. What do you think?"

Avery nodded but didn't move until Tresia held out her hand. Avery moved forward, then slipped her little hand in hers.

They left the marshal's house in short order, the remaining gingerbread men they'd made earlier wrapped in a kitchen towel tied with a bow and leisurely walked to Lucy's two-story house, one of the biggest in town, on the street behind the town hall. It had to be the biggest. Doctor Ben, Lucy's husband, had his practice there with his office and examining rooms accessed by a separate entrance. One merely had to follow the arrow painted on the sign proclaiming, 'Doctor.' Lucy, as a photographer, took photographs here, too, in a room just off the formal parlor that she'd decorate for different occasions. There was a dark room, too, where she developed the photographs.

They stepped up to the porch. "Are you ready?" Tresia asked just before she raised her hand to grab the brass door knocker.

Avery gave a quick nod, though it was in no way a confident one. She clutched the doll even closer to her chest, as if looking for comfort. Perhaps, she was.

Tresia used the knocker, let it rap on the brass plate, once, twice, then two more times.

After a moment, the door swung open and Lucy stood before them wearing a full apron with bib to protect the lovely pale green skirt and ivory blouse she wore. There was flour on her cheek, but it didn't dim the unmistakable happiness shining from her mocha-brown eyes as a wide smile of welcome appeared on her face.

"Tresia! Avery! What a lovely surprise!" She opened the door wider. "Come in! Come in! Savannah and I just finished making *Apfelküchle*." She laughed. "I was missing home so I made one of Hilde's traditional German desserts," she said, referring to the woman who'd come out to Montaña del Trueno so many years ago with her *Tia* Evie.

Just the mention of *Apfelküchle* had Tresia's mouth watering. Apple slices, dipped in batter and fried to a golden brown then dipped in sugar and cinnamon was a favorite of hers though she hadn't made them in quite some time. They'd been her mother's favorite as well.

Lucy dropped her gaze and bent low. "Hello, Avery. Do you remember me?"

"Hullo," Avery said.

Lucy straightened then ushered them into the house. "Come to the kitchen."

She led the way, though Tresia didn't need guidance. She'd been in this house many times and felt the comfort she always did as soon as she walked through the door. All the windows were open, the lacy curtains fluttering in the breeze and on the table were the fruits of Lucy and Savannah's labor. Indeed, on Savannah's face was the evidence she had taste-tested more than one apple slice.

Savannah was maybe eight years old now and flew into Tresia's arms and gave her a big hug, despite the sugar granules on her face...and hands...and shirt.

"Hello, Savannah!" Tresia pulled out of the embrace and picked up the end of the girl's pigtail, giving it a slight tug in affection. Out of all Lucy's relatives, her niece, Savannah, the only girl, was her favorite though she held a lot of fondness for little Toughie who had a penchant for running around naked. She was quite fond of *Tia* Evie as well...and everyone else who lived at Montaña del Trueno. "It's been a little while since I've seen you! I think you've grown another inch."

"That's what Mama says!"

"And she'd be right." She turned toward her charge. "Avery, this is my friend, Savannah."

Savannah took her hand like a proper young lady. "*Tia* Lucy has swings in the backyard. Grab an *Apfelküchle*." She pointed to the dessert on the plate. "And let's go play."

Avery looked up at her with big eyes, hesitant, leery.

"Go ahead. You can have one." Tresia encouraged her. "They're good." And to prove it, she delicately pulled an apple slice from the top of the pile and took a big bite. The combination of tart apple and sweet sugar left an explosion of taste…and memory…in her mouth. "Oh, they're perfect." She swallowed and nodded toward Avery. "You try."

Avery still hesitated, her hand hovering over the plate before Savannah nudged her. "Take one. It's all right."

She did finally and took a small bite. A look of pure joy came over her face as she chewed.

"It's good, isn't it?" Tresia asked, her heart full of affection for her.

Avery nodded with enthusiasm and took another bite as Savannah grabbed her other hand and started pulling her toward the door, almost dislodging the doll clutched against Avery's chest. "Come on, you can finish it outside."

Avery allowed herself to be led away—though she really didn't have much of a choice with Savannah. The girls headed for the swings hanging from a wooden frame while Lucy cleared a place at the table, then poured two cups of coffee from the ever-present pot on the stove. Tresia watched the two girls through the window as she took a seat and finished the *Apfelküchle*, then licked her fingertips, getting every speck of sugar. She placed her own dessert on the table. "I brought gingerbread men, but it doesn't look like you need them." She then pulled a folded sheet of paper from her drawstring bag and handed it to Lucy. "I also worked on the layout for the lending library like you asked me. It's just a rough sketch, but I think it's what you're looking for."

"Oh, good! I'll study it later tonight and let you know if it needs any changes," she said as she dropped the folded paper in the pocket of her apron. "I'm sure it's perfect, though." She gestured to the bow-wrapped dish towel. "As for the cookies, they won't go to waste. You know what a sweet tooth Ben has." Lucy pulled out the chair opposite her and slid into it, expectation and curiosity in her expression. "Well?"

Tresia pulled her attention from Avery and stared at her friend. "You lied to me, Lucy Hart. Looked right in my face and straight up lied."

Lucy laughed even as she schooled her features into a look of innocence. "I don't know what you mean."

"Not handsome. No sense of humor. Admit it. You lied." She stirred some sugar into her coffee, the spoon making delicate little tinkling sounds as it touched the side of the fine China cup. "I am not interested in finding someone. I told you that."

"And I told you that I understood. I was not trying to match you with Marshal Goodrich, but I did think you'd fall in love with Avery. And I was right."

Tresia glanced outside at both girls as they swung back and forth, the edges of their clothing fluttering in the breeze, the sound of Savannah's one-sided conversation coming in through the open window. "Yes, you were right. She is a sweet little girl."

"It was love at first sight, wasn't it?"

She had to admit that it was.

"What about the marshal?"

"He seems like a genuinely nice man. He loves his daughter."

"And you like him. You think he's handsome." Lucy raised an eyebrow as she lifted the coffee cup to her lips.

She didn't answer, though the image of Devlin Goodrich standing in the doorway to the kitchen, shirtless, barefoot, popped into her brain. She hadn't seen a man half naked in a very long time, nor one so muscular, his broad shoulders and wide chest tapering down to a slim waist. Though she'd pretended to ignore that earlier, it was proving harder and harder to do.

"What is that look?"

"Nothing," Tresia said and helped herself to another *Apfelküchle* so she wouldn't have to respond.

"Hmm, if it's nothing, then why is your face turning red?"

"What do you know about him?" she asked. If anyone knew anything, it would be Lucy. Not only was she the leader of the Ladies Society and a matchmaker, she *was* the town busybody. Not much happened in Serenity that she didn't know about. She wasn't a gossip though. Whatever anyone said to her, stayed with her. Secrets remained secrets, which was good because so many shared their confidences with her.

"He was an excellent marshal in Albuquerque, or so I've been told. He has a sterling reputation. Above reproach, really. Follows the law to the letter." She quieted for a moment, as if searching her memory. After a moment, she said, "And he's a widower, but you already know that. That's all I really know. You'll have to find out anything else for yourself."

Surprised, Tresia just stared at her. Lucy usually knew *everything*! Her gaze roamed over Lucy's face, looking for a clue that she might know more than she'd shared, but there wasn't anything there. She didn't wink. She didn't smile. She didn't turn away. She simply returned Tresia's stare with one of her own.

It was Tresia who had to turn away. Why did she want to know about the marshal anyway? When she'd told Lucy she wasn't interested in being matched, she'd meant it. She had a plan and it didn't involve getting married again, at least, not until she accomplished her goal. She was being paid to take care of Avery and, by extension, her father. That was all.

She glanced out the window to check on her charge. The girls were no longer on the swings. Instead, they were crouched on the ground, intently inspecting something, but she was too far away to see what it was. Whatever had drawn their attention, it was enough for Avery to release her death grip on her doll.

They talked about the library fundraiser for a while, then about the new dresses Leslie Carmichael, the dressmaker, had in the window at her shop, until Tresia said, "We should go. Dinner is not going to make itself and I still have to stop by the butcher."

Lucy was giving her a straightforward stare, except this time, there was a happy little glow in her friend's eyes.

"Stop thinking what you're thinking, Lucy Hart."

"I'm not thinking anything." She held up her hand as if ready to take a pledge. "I swear. Believe me, I learned my lesson with Tia Evie. I will never place an advertisement for a husband in the newspaper again, though that turned out rather well, but I'm not above a little gentle persuasion. Still, I know that's not what you want and I respect that."

Tresia watched her carefully, especially Lucy's eyes and the corners of her mouth. If she was lying, that's where she'd see it, but there was nothing. No tell-tale give-away. Not even a hint of something not true.

She rose from her seat, took a last sip of her coffee, then headed toward the back door. Lucy did the same, following her out to the porch, closing the kitchen door behind her. For a moment, they just stood there, watching Avery and Savannah, both now laying on their stomachs and studying whatever was crawling on the ground.

"It's time to go, Avery."

Avery popped up from her position and ran toward her. There was dirt on her cheeks and hands. Indeed, her little calico dress was coated, but there was a huge smile on her face.

"We found a caterpillar." Savannah volunteered, her own clothes, hands, and face just as dirty as she joined them on the porch.

"Is that what you were watching so intently?"

Savannah nodded toward Avery. "I don't think she's ever seen one."

"I'm sure you'll see more, but for now, we have to go." She brushed some of the dirt from Avery's dress then gave up...she was only making it worse. "Go get Cecily."

Avery ran back to grab her doll, which was no longer as clean as she had been, her little dress splattered with dirt as well as the remains of dried leaves. There were even leaves in her hair and some of the curls were loosening. It was obvious to anyone with eyes, Cecily was well loved and after only a day.

"Savannah, it was so nice to see you." Tresia tugged once again on one of Savannah's pigtails and laughed. "Stop growing up so fast."

Savannah giggled. "That's what Mama says."

She gave Lucy a hug. "I'll see you at the next meeting."

Lucy squeezed tight. "You will." There was something in her eyes when she let go, something Tresia couldn't miss. Despite the fact that she'd said she didn't want to be matched, Lucy would do as she pleased. She always did. And maybe, just maybe, this one time, it wouldn't be bad if things didn't go as Lucy planned.

CHAPTER 6

*W*ho would ever guess that meeting so many people would be exhausting? And there were a lot of people to meet. Merrill made sure of that.

Devlin stepped up to the back porch and paused before letting himself into the house. His feet were a little sore from walking around the town, not once or twice, but four times in total, as Merrill wanted him to meet as many people as possible, and while he should have been used to it, he admitted to himself he was a little out of practice. Serenity wasn't nearly as big as Albuquerque, but it had been a long time since he himself had walked a town like he had today. That job had been done by his deputies.

His throat was a little sore, too—from talking so much. It seemed like everyone wanted to meet him and shake his hand. He wouldn't be surprised if he had calluses, his hand was pumped so much.

That thought brought a slight smile to his face and he remembered that tomorrow and the following day, Rafael would take him out to the ranches and farms in the area to meet the owners. Not only was it part of his job to know everyone he was responsible for, he actually enjoyed meeting them.

The aroma of something savory assailed his nose and he inhaled deeply. He shouldn't be hungry. Not at all, since the owner of the green grocery, Winston Goldwater and his lovely wife, Gemma, insisted he take an apple. Polly, Merrill's sweetheart at Sweet Somethings, charmed him into trying one of her apple tarts, and a woman named Elsie at the Wagon Wheel twisted his arm to sit and have a piece of pie and a cup of coffee, though she didn't have to try so hard. There were others, too. So many people...and all of them friendly, welcoming him to Serenity, apparently glad he was here.

He let himself into the kitchen and stopped.

Avery sat at the table, the doll Tresia had given her clutched in her arms and looking a little worse-for-wear, a big smile on her face as she rocked and crooned softly to the miniature version of herself.

"Daddy!" The smile on her face grew bigger as she scrambled off the chair and flung herself into his open arms. He picked her up and hugged her, drawing squeals of delight from her, then, with her still in his arms, he walked over to Tresia at the stove, taking a peek into the skillet and various pots. "Smells good."

"I hope you're hungry." She smiled at him as she stirred the gravy. "We're having pork chops smothered in gravy, mashed potatoes and green beans. Avery and I stopped at Mr. Crandall's. He's the butcher. And Goldwater's."

Devlin returned her smile. "I met him today and liked him immediately. He's very funny. Winston Goldwater, too. Nice people."

"Why don't you wash up. Dinner will be on the table shortly."

He lowered Avery to the floor then headed out of the kitchen toward his room. He noticed the trunks in the hallway at the top of the stairs and lifted a lid. Empty, as he knew it would be. The corners of his mouth raised just a bit. Tresia was as good as her word.

Strange how many people he'd spoken to today, who once

they knew Tresia was taking care of Avery, immediately offered their own experiences with her kindness. According to most of the townspeople, she was a paragon among women. The only person who didn't have anything nice to say was Arnold Sullivan. According to him, Tresia Morgan was the worst person in the world, probably because she had quit working for him to take care of his daughter.

He headed toward the bathroom and washed his hands and face, then walked into his bedroom, unfastened his gun belt and placed it on top of the armoire, far enough away from Avery's curiosity though she knew the importance of not touching his guns. It was the first lesson he taught her as soon as she was old enough to understand, even though Hannah hadn't wanted him to. Still, a child's curiosity could get the better of them, but even if Avery pushed a chair to the armoire and climbed atop that chair, she was far too short to reach them. For right now, this was a workable solution. He'd have to invest in a gun safe sooner rather than later.

He turned away from the armoire and stopped, his gaze falling on the photograph of Hannah and him sitting on the bedside table. It had been taken the day they'd married at the county courthouse. He picked it up, the pain in his chest making it hard to draw breath, even after all this time. He traced his finger on the glass over her face, wishing he could touch her again, then put the picture back where it belonged. "Ah, Hannah," he whispered after taking one more glance.

He headed downstairs. The table was now set and a platter of pork chops smothered in a mushroom gravy sat in the center. Avery had positioned her doll on the empty chair beside hers. Apparently, Cecily was joining them for dinner. Whatever made Avery happy at this point made him happy, too.

"Thank you for putting our things away."

"You're welcome." Tresia smiled at him before she turned back to the stove but continued speaking over her shoulder as she scooped green beans from the pot into a bowl and added some butter. "I didn't know where you wanted to store the trunks. There's an attic with access through your bedroom, but I think the bigger trunks are too big to fit through the opening." She faced him once again as she made her way to the table. "There's also storage space under the back porch." She set the bowl of green beans beside his plate. "There might be room in the shed, too. Or you could sell them."

"I'll figure it out tomorrow." He rested his hands on the back of his chair. "Do you need any help?"

"No, thank you. Why don't you start?" She removed dishes of food from the warming box drawer and set them on the table, then sat down.

Devlin turned toward Avery. "How was your day, sweet pea?"

"I saw a caterpillar." Avery announced proudly and smiled at him, her mouth spreading wide like the Cheshire cat.

Flabbergasted she just didn't nod at him, he returned her smile. "You did?"

She did nod at him then, but the smile on her face showed she was happy, happier than she'd been in a long time. It was the best thing he could have asked for and it had all to do with Tresia and the way she cared for his daughter, which seemed to have been instantaneous.

"Where did you see it?" He took one of the pork chops from the platter and placed it on her plate before pulling the plate closer to him. He cut up her meat then dished up some mashed potatoes and green beans for her.

"At Miss Lucy's."

"And what did you do with it?"

"Nothin'. Me and Savannah just watched it crawl." She took a sip of her milk and ate a piece of meat.

One could have knocked him over with a feather. Avery had said more words at one time than he'd heard her say in months.

He glanced at Tresia as she ate, staring at her with wonder that Avery had spoken so much.

"Savannah is Lucy's niece. Avery and I stopped by Lucy's house for a visit today, didn't we?"

"An' we had *Apfelküchle!*" his daughter responded around the food in her mouth though she'd been told that wasn't polite. At this moment, he didn't care about manners. He was simply thrilled she was talking.

"*Apfelküchle?*" he asked, though he wasn't sure he was saying the word correctly. He wasn't sure Avery was saying it correctly either. "What is that?"

She finally shrugged, her mouth full and the conversation apparently over, but it was more than he'd hoped for. Actually, after only two days with Tresia, it was a miracle. He looked at the woman he'd hired to take care of his daughter. She was smiling, her deep pansy-colored eyes bright, apparently pleased with the conversation. Though he'd been told of her reputation for being kind, he couldn't help being impressed by her...and what she'd managed to accomplish with Avery in just a short time.

He returned Tresia's smile. "So what is *Apfelküchle?*"

"It's a traditional German dessert. Sliced apples dipped in batter, then fried to a golden brown and sprinkled with sugar and cinnamon."

"Sounds delicious."

"They are. Lucy insisted we bring some home. We're having them for dessert."

She lapsed into silence as she shaped her mashed potatoes into a well and dumped gravy in the middle. He grew silent, too, and concentrated on his dinner, though he hadn't been hungry when he walked in the door. The food was simple and tasty and as she'd told him, filling. Before he knew it, everything on his plate was gone...even the green beans, which he really wasn't fond of, but somehow the way she made them was delicious.

Avery, he noticed, ate everything on her plate as well, which made him happy. She was much tinier than other children her age, which made him worry. That, and those months of silence after Hannah's passing.

Tresia rose, her plate in her hand. "Avery, would you like to help me clear the dishes so we can have dessert?"

Devlin sat forward in his chair, his hands folded in front of his face, and watched, with something close to amazement, as Avery picked up her plate and brought it to the counter just like Tresia had done. She returned to the table for her silverware then moved closer to him, excitement clearly showing on her little face.

"Are you done, Daddy?"

"I am." He pushed the plate toward her then glanced up to see Tresia watching both of them, her smile warm and gentle as she scraped the scraps into a bucket, and filled the sink with hot water and soap so the dishes could soak. She pulled a plate out of the warming drawer and brought it to the table then brought the coffeepot as well.

Tresia placed two apple slices on his dessert plate then smiled at him, nodding her head toward the treats. "Try it."

Ignoring the dessert fork beside his plate, he tried one, despite how warm they were. "It's delicious! But hot," he said, laughing.

Avery giggled and happily ate her *Apfelküchle*. Devlin watched his daughter, thrilled that she was more like she had been before.

"Finish your milk, sweet pea. It's time to get ready for bed. Why don't you go upstairs and get ready? Pick out a new book for us to read." He smiled gently, his gaze roaming over her little face, so much like Hannah's, his heart skipped a beat. "Don't forget to wash your face and brush your teeth."

"Okay, Daddy." Avery slipped from her chair but didn't leave the room. Instead, she grabbed Cecily by an arm, then went to Tresia, held out her little arms and hugged her. A lump formed in his throat as he watched. How had Tresia managed to do in just about two days what he'd tried to do for months?

"Will you stay for a bit? I'd like to talk to you." He glanced at the coffeepot residing on the stove. "I wouldn't mind more coffee when I come back"

"I will stay and make a fresh pot."

He gave a quick nod, excused himself, and took the stairs to the second floor two at a time.

After he read Avery a story and put her to bed, he went back downstairs. Stopping in the doorway to the kitchen for a moment, he just watched Tresia. She sat at the table, fresh cup of coffee to her left, the last of the *Apfelküchle* on a plate in the middle of the table. The dishes had been done and put away, but the kitchen still smelled of coffee, apples, and cinnamon. She also had a small leatherbound notebook open in front of her, the pencil in her hand moving swiftly over a page. "I met Arnold at Sullivan's Emporium today."

She jumped, startled, dropped the pencil in the book and quickly closed it, then pushed it away, like she'd been caught doing something she shouldn't. Her face took on a pinkish hue as her gaze rose to his. The corners of her mouth tilted upward. "I'm sorry."

"Sorry? Why?"

"Arnold isn't the nicest person—at least to me. I'm sure he isn't happy that I quit. He's probably blaming you."

He laughed. "No, actually, I got the impression he blamed you."

"That's Arnold. He never takes responsibility for anything. He probably never will." She took a sip of coffee, her gaze meeting his over the rim of the mug. "I'm sure he's finding out how hard it is to run the Emporium now that I'm not there."

Her eyes were sparkling with just a hint of what he thought might be mischief. Or maybe it was something else. He didn't know her well enough to know, but he wanted to.

"Who is he to you?"

"My cousin."

He walked past her to the stove, grabbed a mug from the cabinet, then poured himself a cup of coffee. "There's apparently no love lost between the two of you, is there? Why is that?"

She waited until he took his seat before answering. "There's no love lost between his wife, Willetta, and I either. Maybe because they both know what they did to me wasn't right."

His curiosity piqued, he leaned forward in his chair. "What did they do?"

She paused before she spoke, as if choosing the right words. "Sullivan's Emporium was supposed to be mine. I'm not sure how it happened or why, but somehow, Arnold, and probably Willetta, convinced my father to leave it to them instead of me. When Papa died and his will was read, the store and the apartment above it belonged to Arnold." She shook her head, disappointment evident in her eyes. "I was surprised...and devastated. Not only had I lost my father and the store, but I'd lost my home as well."

He could tell how much that hurt her by her expression, the hoarseness of her voice and the fact that her beautiful pansy-colored eyes had lost their sparkle. He sensed the betrayal behind the words—and it was a betrayal of the deepest kind—by both her father and her cousin.

He'd heard from Merrill just how prosperous the Emporium had been when she and Lyle Sullivan ran it, and how, now, Arnold—and Willetta, whom he hadn't met yet—seemed to be pushing customers away with their poor attitudes. That must hurt her, seeing what the store she loved so deeply was becoming.

"I had such plans for the store," she said. "I still do."

"What kind of plans?"

She smiled at him, a smile full of the promise of what could be. "I wanted to make it bigger. Sell more things. Invite the community to participate even more than they do now. Or did."

"What do you mean?"

"Louise Gardner just outside of town has beehives and regularly brought me honey, which I, in turn, sold at the store. And I paid her for each jar of honey sold, taking a small commission for myself. It was the same with Olivia Cudahy. She knits beautiful hats, mittens, and scarves. I sold them for her and took a small commission for doing so. I wanted to expand that practice, but Arnold—or it could be Willetta—I'm not sure which—didn't want to continue."

She stared at her cup. "Olivia was devastated when I told her I couldn't sell her knit goods anymore. So were the customers who came into the store to buy Louise's honey. I suggested they could sell their wares on their own, but they liked doing business with me. I was fair and honest." She seemed to have run out of words but when she looked up at him, the brightness was back in her eyes. "Someday, I might get it back." She gestured toward the notebook and pulled it a bit closer.

"That's what this is for." She opened the book to the page she'd been working on. Even from his position across the table, he could see the swirls and curves of her neat penmanship, even a drawing at the very bottom of the page, though he couldn't see what it was. "Every idea for goods and displaying them goes in here."

"And if you don't get it back?"

Pure determination lit her expression. "I'll get another store and make it my own."

"Is there another place in town that you could buy or rent?"

"No, not right now, but things change every day. There may not be a place for me today, but there might be tomorrow so who knows?" She shrugged, a casual lifting of her shoulders, which moved the lace neckline of her blouse against her throat, but even that movement showed her determination and willingness to go after what she wanted. "I may have to go somewhere else. Santa Fe. Or San Francisco. Or maybe even Chicago."

She meant it. He could tell, which brought two things to

mind. The first was that she was ready to unsettle her life to chase a dream, unlike him who'd left everything he'd known to run away from a nightmare. The second thing surprised him the most. Even though she'd only been in his life for two days, he couldn't imagine her not being there. "So if that is your plan, why did you take this job with me?"

A blush rose to her cheeks. She opened her mouth then closed it and dropped her gaze to her notebook. For a moment, he didn't think she would answer him at all, but then she looked at him. "Two reasons, actually," she said softly as her eyes darted to the ceiling and the bedroom where Avery slept. "Taking care of your daughter, and by extension you, pays a lot more than working for Arnold."

At least she was honest. "What was the other reason?"

Her tone changed and her eyes brightened. "Avery. She's a sweet girl and she…needs me. I think I need her, too."

He couldn't agree more. Avery was starting to come out of her shell, talking more in the past forty-eight hours than she had in a long while, and for that, he was grateful.

"I should go." She went to the sink, rinsed out her coffee cup and put it aside to dry, then came back to the table. She pushed the leatherbound notebook into her drawstring bag.

Funny thing, now that she was ready to leave, he didn't want her to go. He enjoyed her company. Or maybe it was just her presence. She had a very calming, soothing effect on both him and Avery. He rose from his chair as well. "I'll walk you home"

"No. You stay. I'm just across the way, Devlin. I'll be fine. Besides, you can't leave Avery alone even if it's only for a few minutes."

He did walk her out to the back porch and leaned against the railing. A full moon cast its light over everything, though some things remained in shadow. "I'll watch you from here. Good night then, Tresia."

"Good night, Marshal." She smiled as she touched his hand

then skipped down the steps, where she turned to address him. "I'll see you tomorrow."

He watched her walk to the end of the fenced backyard and pass through a gate he hadn't even known was there, her stride sure and, if he weren't mistaken, happy. She disappeared for a moment behind the high bushes bordering his neighbor's yard then reappeared before climbing the steps to Mrs. McMurty's Boarding House. She turned once more and waved, then disappeared through the door.

Devlin waited for her to close the door of the boarding house then went inside, got a fresh cup of coffee, and settled himself at the desk in the small study across from the parlor. He pulled several sheets of paper and a fancy fountain pen—the last thing Hannah had given him—from the drawer and started to write a long overdue letter to his sister. She, at least, needed to know where he and Avery were, but as he began writing, his thoughts, more than once, drifted to the woman who was taking care of his child and some of the things the people in town had told him about her.

Tresia Morgan was everything they said...and more. He did like her—had liked her from the moment they'd met. There was hope in her smile and possibility in her attitude, and as incredible as it may feel, he wondered if there weren't forces he couldn't possibly explain at work here.

He wasn't a man given to flights of fancy, but maybe, just maybe, Hannah was smiling down at him from her place in heaven, approving of their move to Serenity and the hiring of Tresia Morgan. He wouldn't be surprised. For as kind and gentle and sweet as Hannah had been, she also had backbone and determination, which she had passed along to their daughter. Would she approve of Tresia taking care of Avery? Yes, she would have. Before he went back to his letter, he had one last thought that in another time and place, he was certain Hannah and Tresia would have been friends.

CHAPTER 7

"*Think you can bring me in?*"

The voice came from behind him. He didn't need to turn around to know that it belonged to the man he'd been chasing for so long. He didn't need to turn around to know there was a pistol pointed at his back, either. He could feel it though it wasn't touching him. What he didn't know was how Big Bill Cassidy had gotten the jump on him, managed to sneak up on him when every muscle, sinew, and nerve in his body was attuned to everything around him.

"I don't think it, Cassidy, I know it." His hand lowered oh so slowly to the revolver at his hip.

"Uh uh, don't you be movin'!" Cassidy stopped him, his voice filled with derision and—was that a touch of fear?

Maybe it was and if it was, then he might just have a chance to escape this encounter with his life.

"Put your hands up and turn around real slow. Don't be making any sudden moves." Cassidy laughed, though there was no joy in the sound. "My trigger finger's a little itchy."

Devlin did as he was told, raising his hands up and turning slowly to face the man who needed to be brought to justice for the horrible crimes he'd committed. It only took a moment to size up the bandit, notice the bloodshot eyes filled with hate, and the sneer of contempt spreading his lips.

"Drop the holster."

It was the last thing he wanted to do, but it was either that or get shot right where he stood. Cassidy wouldn't hesitate. He hadn't before, and unless he was brought in, he wouldn't again. Some men just liked killing and Cassidy was one of them.

Slowly, so as not to raise suspicion, Devlin reached for the buckle of his holster, even as his mind went over the various scenarios, only one or two of which would leave him not dead, though at this moment, he didn't care if he died. Life without Hannah was too hard.

Still, Avery needed him. Hell, he needed her. And once Cassidy was brought in, he could be with her again.

He unbuckled the holster but didn't let it drop to the ground. Instead, he lowered it until it rested on the dirt then straightened, going over all the possibilities in his head to get out of this alive.

"Who are you?"

"Devlin Goodrich. U.S. Marshal."

Cassidy nodded, the gleam of recognition shining in his dark eyes. "Heard about you. How'd you find me? No one knows about this place."

"Been looking for you for a long time, Cassidy. Caught up with your buddy, Smiley Burdette. He's sitting in my jail cell right now and talking up a blue streak." He tilted his head, knowing he was antagonizing the man who held his life in his hands, hoping, praying that something he said would make this man act irrationally, giving him a chance to act. "He told me where to find you."

He awoke, startled and disoriented, and sat up quickly, the dregs of the nightmare still in his head. It took a moment or two to orient himself. He wasn't in the high mountains of New Mexico—he was in his own bed, in his own home. Moonlight streamed into the bedroom, not the high glare of midday sunlight that had made him squint when he'd finally found Cassidy's hideout.

He let out a sigh. He'd never go back to sleep now. He never could after one of his nightmares. Fortunately, those nightmares were becoming less and less frequent though they still had the power to scare the living daylights out of him.

He rose slowly, grabbed a pair of socks, trousers and a shirt from the bureau and slipped into them, then padded down the hall, boots in hand. He pushed open the door to Avery's room carefully, praying the hinges wouldn't squeak then tiptoed in, leaving his boots in the doorway. He didn't need to light the lantern; he was able to see his daughter quite clearly in the moonlight. She lay sprawled on her bed on her stomach, one arm around Cecily, the other arm under her pillow. The blanket half covered her and one foot hung off the bed.

He smiled. She slept like her mother—hard, deep, and unplagued by the nightmares he himself suffered.

He moved closer to the bed, slowly brought her foot up so it was covered by the blanket, then straightened the covers around her shoulders. She sighed in her sleep, clutched Cecily a little closer, but didn't awaken.

He stood there for a moment, just watching her, listening to her breathe. Pure love filled his heart. It was his duty to keep her —and the world around her—safe, a duty he was proud to perform. Secure in the knowledge that he would never again let someone try to keep her away from him—like Frances had tried to do—he carefully stepped out of the room.

Grabbing his boots, he closed the door, though not all the way. He wanted to be able to hear her if she should call out, then headed downstairs, careful to avoid the riser that creaked. As he passed through the parlor, he noticed that it was only a little after five in the morning. He had another hour or so before Tresia breezed into the house and started breakfast. Her hours, when he hired her, were seven to seven but that seemed to have gone by the wayside. She frequently arrived before that time and stayed well after. She didn't seem to mind. He didn't either. He rather enjoyed sharing a cup of coffee with her after Avery went to bed.

He wandered into the kitchen, slipped into his boots and went about making a pot of coffee then sat at the table and just waited for it to be ready, at odds with himself and the reason he wasn't still sleeping. He couldn't just sit there, though, his fingertips tapping out a rhythm. He had to do something...constructive...instead of simply waiting for the coffee...and Mrs. Tresia Morgan.

He rose from his chair and went into the small study, grabbed the rolled-up tube of new Wanted posters that had been delivered yesterday, and brought them back to the kitchen table. He untied the neat little bow that held them together and spread them out in front of him, placing the sugar bowl at one corner of the papers and the creamer at the other to keep them from rolling back up again. He poured himself a cup of the finally done coffee, then made himself comfortable at the table and studied the posters as he always did, committing the names and faces to memory. If any one of them wandered into his town, he'd make sure they never did again.

The kitchen door opened, startling him, as Tresia entered the house. She stopped for a moment as her gaze landed on him before a big smile spread her lips. "I didn't expect you to be up."

"Avery's still sleeping." He gestured to the coffeepot on a trivet on the table. "I made coffee."

"You look tired. Didn't you sleep?"

"Not very well, if you want to know the truth."

"Have you always had problems sleeping?"

"No, I haven't." Not until Hannah passed and he'd spent the next couple months tracking down Big Bill Cassidy with a determination that made most of his friends doubt his sanity. Hell, he'd doubted his own sanity more than once.

"Maybe a glass of warm milk before bed instead of coffee." She laughed softly as she hooked the strings of her drawstring purse over the spindle of the chair and dropped a bundle of clothes on that same chair. "My father always had a glass of whiskey before he went to sleep, even after his stroke. He always said it helped him. Brett—"

"Your late husband?"

"Yes." A hint of sadness flashed in her eyes but disappeared just as quickly. "He preferred brandy. I do, as well, on occasion, though not very often." She glanced at the papers spread before him and gave him a questioning look. "Are those...Wanted posters?"

"They are."

"Avery shouldn't see those." She glanced at the clock over the sink. "She'll be getting up soon."

"She's seen them before. She knows what I do. She always said she wants to be a lawman like me." He laughed but rolled the posters back into a tube and tied them with the string, then leaned them against the wall behind his chair. "I'll put them away before she gets up."

"Thank you. Even though Avery wants to be a lawman like you, she's far too young to know how bad some people can be. Those lessons will come soon enough."

"Hannah always said the same thing."

"Hannah was right." She turned away to take a cup from the cabinet and poured herself some coffee. She didn't sit down to enjoy it though. She added a bit of cream and sugar, took a sip then got right to work, taking down a bowl from the cabinet and utensils from the drawer and bringing everything to the kitchen table. "I know you haven't even had breakfast yet, but what would you like for dinner?"

He laughed. "Whatever you make will be fine—you're a great cook. I even like your green beans."

Her cheeks blossomed with color as a blush stole over her face. "Thank you!"

He watched her, fascinated with how the deepening redness on her cheeks made her eyes seem darker than the pansies that grew in the town square. A sudden suspicion settled over him—

was she paying for the items she was bringing into his home? She hadn't asked him for money, nor did she seem like she would do so but he didn't want anything to come out of her own paycheck. "Are you paying for everything out of your own pocket?"

She looked at him like he had three heads. "No, of course not. You have a tab with Goldwater's, the butcher, and the ice man." She gathered eggs, vanilla, cinnamon, and milk as she spoke. "You settle up at the end of the month when you get your bill. Did Lucy not tell you that?"

He shook his head. If Lucy had told him that, he'd forgotten. So much had happened on the day he met Lucy and received the key to this house. He'd met Tresia for the first time…and she had proven to be a godsend in more ways than one. Avery was thriving…and he, to some extent, was as well.

"It's the same with your milk delivery." She cracked two eggs, one in each hand, against the side of the bowl and let the contents slide out, never losing her train of thought. "Mr. Shaeffer will leave a bill with the last delivery of the month."

He was relieved but before he could say anything, she spoke again.

"If you'd like, I can take care of it if you leave me the money."

She cracked two more eggs, using the same method, which fascinated him. He didn't recall anyone ever doing that. Not his mother, not his sister, not Hannah, and certainly not his mother-in-law who, he didn't believe, even knew where the kitchen was in her big house.

She added a little milk to the bowl, some cinnamon and finally a dash of vanilla then whisked it all together, creating a frothy concoction.

"What are you making?"

"I thought we'd have French toast this morning."

He nodded in agreement. "That sounds good. I haven't had French toast in a long time." He studied her as she worked. "Do you need some help?"

She glanced at him, surprised, then smiled. "Thank you for the offer, but I have everything under control."

And she did. It was a pleasure to watch her as she cut thick slices of bread and piled them up on a plate then turned away to pull the cast-iron skillet from where it hung on the wall and place it on the stove. Her movements were economical as well as graceful.

"Should I wake Avery?"

Tresia glanced at the clock then shook her head. "Let's give her a few more minutes. It won't take long to cook now that I have everything ready." She took another sip of her coffee and slid into her seat. His gaze swept over her face, noticing, not for the first time, how beautiful she was. His focus stopped on her eyes, which seemed to sparkle with good humor then lowered to her mouth, which was spread into a wide smile. And suddenly, he was tongue-tied. They'd been having such a comfortable conversation...a rather mundane conversation, but comfortable nonetheless, very much like the ones he'd had with Hannah, but now, he didn't know what to say.

He cleared his throat as he searched for another topic of conversation. "Do you know where I can mail a letter?"

"Miss Gemma over at Goldwater's handles the mail. Have you met her yet?"

"I have."

"I can drop it off for you, if you'd like." She nodded toward the pile of clothing on the chair. "Avery and I will be heading over to the church later on this morning to drop those off. Reverend Parker, along with the Ladies' Society, is collecting clothing for a young family who has fallen on tough times."

"I'm sorry to hear that. What happened?"

"Victor Thromball fell from his horse and broke his back. He will mend, but it will take a long time before he's on his feet again. The family is struggling. They have two small children plus the ranch to run so the Ladies Society is helping." She fiddled with her spoon, but her gaze never left him. "Lucy arranged it. Mr. Goldwater is donating some food items like flour, sugar and other essentials. Mr. Crandall offered something from his butcher shop but was told they had plenty of meat, so he's chipping in a few dollars. Elsie—you've met her I'm sure—has promised to bring them dinner a few times, and we've recruited several of their neighbors to help with the cattle."

"I haven't met the Thromballs yet. How can I help?"

"If you could stop by and see them, that would be wonderful, but really, anything will help. We're taking up a collection for them so they can pay their bills. If I'm not mistaken, they have a mortgage on the ranch. I'd hate to see them lose it. Both of them are lovely people. The children, too."

He didn't hesitate. He rose from his seat, and walked into his study, taking the rolled up tube of Wanted posters with him, then returned moments later with a crisp, new twenty-dollar bill. He handed it to her. "I hope this will help some."

Tresia looked at the money. "This is so generous of you, Marshal." She smiled, her eyes wide as she tucked the money in her drawstring purse. "It'll go a long way in helping them. Thank you. The Thromballs will appreciate it."

He smiled in return as he took his seat. "Glad I could help."

Avery wandered into the kitchen then, Cecily clutched tightly in one arm as she rubbed her eyes with her other hand.

"Well, good morning, sweet pea! Did you sleep well?"

Avery nodded, but rather sleepily, as she crawled into his lap and leaned her head against his chest. Such love filled him at that moment, his heart ached. He dropped a kiss to the top of her head as she snuggled a little closer.

"Are you ready for breakfast?"

She nodded against his chest even as Tresia rose and went to the ice box for the pitcher of milk. She poured a glass and set it down on the table in front of the chair Avery usually sat in, then moved to the stove. "We're having French toast," she said as she plopped a spoonful of butter from the crock into the cast-iron skillet.

"Okay." Avery seemed to perk up at that and slid from his lap. She carefully placed Cecily on the chair beside her then took her own seat.

Devlin smiled at his daughter before he moved his focus to Tresia. She moved with an economy of motion—no step was wasted as she dipped the bread into the egg batter and placed it carefully in the skillet. The sizzling sound soon filled the small room, and the tantalizing aroma wafted to him. The first four pieces were done quickly. She transferred them to a plate and placed it onto the table.

Devlin glanced at Avery. "One or two?"

She grinned at him. "Two."

He speared two pieces and cut them up into smaller bite size squares for her. "Syrup?"

She nodded and he drizzled the sweet maple syrup over her French toast. "Enough?"

She nodded again, the curls surrounding her head bouncing as she did.

"What are your plans today?" Tresia asked as she placed more slices of French toast on the table then took a piece for herself. She drizzled syrup over it then took a bite.

"Rafael is taking me out to more ranches and farms in the area." He took a bite of his French toast, allowing the medley of flavors to settle on his tongue. "I've already been to a few over the past couple days, but he wants to introduce me to the rest."

"Have you met the Silvas out on Montaña del Trueno?"

"No, not yet. I think that's today."

"You'll like the Silvas. And you'll love the ranch. It's one of my favorite places. I spent some time there when I was younger. It's Lucy's family's ranch. Her brothers, Teddy, Esteban, and Heath run it along with their wives. Make sure you meet *Tia* Evie."

"*Tia* Evie? Who is that?"

"She's the woman who raised Lucy and turned that ranch into one of the most profitable ones in the area. It's not the biggest but it is, by far, the best, although Hacienda Zepeda is a close second." She gathered the dirty breakfast dishes and placed them in the sink.

Devlin finished his coffee then rose to his feet. "Come give Daddy a kiss."

Avery slipped from her chair and rushed into his arms. As was his habit, he squeezed her tight and planted several kisses on her face, making her giggle. She sobered quickly. "Be safe, Daddy."

"I always am, sweet pea." He let her go, then gave Tresia a brief nod. "I'll see you later." He paused. "And whatever you have planned for dinner will be fine."

Tresia smiled at him, making him feel less anxious about leaving. It was a confident smile—warm and inviting and comforting at the same time—and it made him want to get his day over with so he could come back to spend time with her.

He left the kitchen and went into his study, where he pulled his holster from the gun safe he'd recently purchased and buckled it low around his hips. Taking the Wanted posters with him, he walked to the front door. He took his hat from the hat rack, placed it on his head then headed outside, stopping on the front porch for a moment, which had become a habit. He focused on the beautiful morning, the last dregs of the nightmare that had awoken him gone, but never truly forgotten.

A bounce in his step, he walked across the street and entered the Marshal's Office by the back door. He could hear Merrill and Rafael talking. Merrill, it seemed, was the victim of more teasing about his fondness for Polly.

He stepped into the main room of the office, noticing that the desks were put in order and polished to a high sheen and he wondered who had done that. Was it something Nate did? Or did they have someone come in and clean? He'd have to remember to ask.

"Mornin', Boss." Merrill greeted him with a big smile, his face a little red, probably from the teasing he'd been receiving.

"Mornin', Merrill." He handed his deputy the Wanted posters. "Anything happen overnight I should know about?"

The big man shook his head. "All quiet according to Nate."

"That's what I like to hear."

"Are you ready?" Rafael asked him as he leaned against one of the desks, coffee cup in hand, obviously waiting for him.

"As I'll ever be."

"Good." He finished his coffee. "I'll get the horses ready and meet you outside." He nodded toward Merrill, then left the office through the kitchen door.

Devlin turned toward Merrill as he unrolled the Wanted posters and laid them flat on his desk. The deputy frowned as he studied the top poster and uttered the name written in bold, black letters. "Ned Delany. I don't like the looks of him."

"I didn't either," Devlin admitted, "but it doesn't seem like he would venture this far north. Let's hope he doesn't change his pattern. I don't want him in my town."

"I agree. Serenity is a quiet place. We don't need his kind of trouble." Merrill pulled the top poster from the pile, grabbed nails and a hammer, and quickly tacked the poster to the wall.

"Anything you need before Rafael and I head out?"

"I'm good." Merrill gestured to the posters. "I'll just hang up the rest of these."

"I'll see you later then." Devlin left the office and stood on the raised sidewalk under the awning for a moment, his focus on the town square across the street. Already, the people of the town were going about their business, walking along the paths to get to the other side of the square or sitting on one of the benches and enjoying the early morning sun.

The steady clip-clop of horses' hooves on hard-packed dirt drew his attention, and he walked down the porch steps, meeting Rafael as he led their mounts to the front of the building.

"Where are we heading?" he asked, as he climbed into Challenger's saddle and made himself comfortable.

"I thought we'd head out to Stone Creek so you can meet Wyatt MacLean, then swing over to Crooked River, Alfonso and Damita Serrano's place." He smiled, showing a full complement of white teeth. "Do you play chess?"

"I do. Why?"

"Alfonso. Don't tell him that. He'll break out his chess board before you dismount your horse." He laughed. "He used to come into town on a weekly basis just to play chess with Marshal Kimbel while Damita shopped. He misses that, I'm sure."

"Actually, I don't think I would mind. It's been a long time since I've had someone to challenge me."

Rafael laughed again. "Just remember you said that. We're also going to stop by Montaña del Trueno and finally Hacienda Zepeda."

"Zepeda? Isn't that your last name?"

"It is," he said, his eyes dancing in his face.

"Any relation?"

"My family."

"So why did you go into the law? Why aren't you working your family's ranch?"

"I love the ranch—I do—but the work was never in my blood, and truthfully, you gotta love it to want to do it day in and day out."

He understood. You really had to love what you did, as most people spent their lives doing it. He felt that way about the law, choosing to be a lawman as opposed to becoming a lawyer like his father.

"How does your mother feel about that?" he asked, knowing how his own mother felt about his decision to chase criminals instead of prosecuting them. She never understood, nor did she want to, and it had remained a cause of disagreement between them until the day she passed.

Rafael faced him. "She doesn't understand. She thinks I should be working the ranch like my brothers and sisters. My father, though, he brags to anyone who will listen that his son is a lawman.

"Just so you know, I have two brothers and two sisters...any one of them would be happy to be in a posse if there should be a need, despite what my mother thinks." He lowered the hat on his head to shade his eyes then adjusted the reins in his hands. "Same goes for the Silvas out at Montaña del Trueno, especially Esteban. Sherm thinks he's a crack shot, and he is, but Esteban is better. You'll want him to have your back if the need should arise. MacLean and Serrano, too. I trust those men with my life."

"Good to know." He urged Challenger forward. "Lead the way."

It didn't take very long before they rode through the metal gate at Stone Creek. Cattle lowed in the distance. A few horses were in the corral next to the barn, but the house seemed empty. Abandoned. No life—as if the people who lived here just suddenly...disappeared.

"Is anyone here?" Devlin moved his mount a little closer to Rafael.

"Why do you ask?"

"Doesn't look like it. Feels like the place has been abandoned."

"No," Rafael said. "MacLean's here. He wouldn't just pull up stakes and not tell anyone." He turned his head to focus on the horses in the corral. "And he'd never leave his animals. That's not him. You won't find anyone more responsible than MacLean, even if he didn't want this ranch to begin with. That was Katie, the woman he was supposed to marry."

"Supposed to marry?"

"Didn't quite work out the way MacLean expected. He bought this place like she wanted but it turned out Katie was interested in something else entirely. The day they were supposed to tie the knot, she left him for another man." He looked around. "He's probably out on the property. It's just him and his ranch hands now."

"I'm sorry to hear about that." He knew all too well the pain of losing someone, whether it be because the other person passed or because they'd just left. "Should we wait?"

Rafael dismounted and stepped up to the porch and rang the big bell hanging from a porch post. The horses in the corral responded with whinnies and grunts, moving in unison behind the wooden fence, but nothing else moved. There was nothing but the sound of birdsong and the clucking of chickens in the small coop by the barn.

"Maybe we missed him," Rafael said. "Maybe he went into town or he might be too far out in the field to hear."

"We can come back another day, if you don't think anything is wrong."

Rafael glanced around, his eyes narrowing as he took in everything. "Nothing seems out of place." He pulled a notebook from his pocket, then fished out a small pencil. He scraped the point with the edge of his thumbnail. "We'll leave him a note." He quickly jotted something, ripped the page from the book, and stuck the paper onto a nail near the front door. "Let's go."

Both men mounted up, rode down the driveway, and back to the main road when Devlin asked, "Where are we going now?"

"Crooked River. The Serrano's place," Rafael said as they cantered down the road, a ribbon of brown cutting through green grass. "I'm sorry you didn't get to meet MacLean. He's a good man."

"I'm sure I will soon."

It didn't take long to reach Crooked River Ranch, either. They rode up to a small but cozy house and tied their horses' reins to a post beside a water trough. Devlin was surprised. Somehow, perhaps given the name of the place, he had expected a ranch, but this...this looked more like a farm with wheat to one side of the house and rows of corn extending from the other. There were small rows of other crops as well, ones he couldn't name, but they were all green and healthy looking. A small barn sat on the other side of the drive along with a corral and four big horses—the kind that looked like they could pull a plow all day long. A lone milk cow roamed a grassy area on the other side of the barn. He heard the clucking of chickens as well as the grunting of pigs.

"You ready?" Rafael asked as he stepped up to the porch.

"I am."

He knocked on the door. It swung open almost immediately and a tall, thin man with dark hair and even darker eyes stood in the doorway. A wide smile spread his lips. "Rafael! It's been a while! Who'd you bring with you?"

"Alfonso Serrano, I'd like you to meet Marshal Devlin Goodrich."

"A pleasure. Come inside. Damita just made some sopapillas. You won't find any better in town. Not even Polly at Sweet Somethings makes a better sopapilla." He opened the door wider and stepped aside.

Devlin looked around as he walked in. The house *was* small but nicely appointed with the kitchen and living area open to each other, unlike his home where a doorway separated the two. A huge stone fireplace, cold now, dominated nearly one entire wall of the room with doors on either side, which he assumed were bedrooms. There were photographs on the mantle above the fireplace, men and women staring straight into the camera, as if they were afraid to move. Not one of them smiled, but that was normal, considering how old these photographs were. Alfonso's ancestors? Damita's?

"Damita! We have company!" Alfonso called out.

One of the doors beside the fireplace opened almost immediately and a young woman stepped out. The first thing Devlin noticed was how far along in her pregnancy she seemed to be, her belly rounded and protruding. The second thing he noticed was how lovely she was with her long dark hair, deep brown eyes, and beautiful smile. There was a glow about her, one that reflected happiness and contentment. Her smile widened as she leaned into Rafael for a hug and kiss on the cheek. "Rafael, so nice to see you!"

"You, too, Damita. You're looking well."

Her hand moved to her belly and her eyes lit up. "This one doesn't let me rest," she said, but there was no anger or frustration in her tone. Quite the contrary, she seemed to be happy about it.

"Damita, this is Marshal Devlin Goodrich."

The woman extended her hand and shook his. "A pleasure, Marshal. Please," she gestured toward the table in the kitchen which was covered with a pristine white lace tablecloth. Several candles, unlit, made a small circle in the middle of the table, surrounding a vase filled with fresh flowers. "Make yourselves comfortable. I just finished making sopapillas. They might still be warm."

"I hear you play chess." Devlin addressed Alfonso as he took his seat.

Alfonso visibly brightened. "I do. Every chance I get. Do you play?"

"Why don't you stop by the Marshal's Office the next time you're in town and we'll play a game or two."

"I would like that. How about tomorrow?"

Devlin laughed. He liked this man. "Tomorrow would be fine."

"Here you are, gentlemen," Damita placed a plate of freshly made soft pillows of fried dough sprinkled with sugar in front of them then turned away. She brought small plates and silverware next, then coffee cups emblazoned with pansies, the color of the flowers reminding him of Tresia's eyes.

She poured coffee, then set the coffeepot down on the table, and took a seat.

"So, Marshal, tell us a little about yourself," Damita said, a look of expectancy on her face.

"There isn't much to tell, really. My daughter and I came here from Albuquerque."

"Wait! I've read about you in the newspapers." Alfonso interrupted. "You're the one who brought in Big Bill Cassidy."

Devlin stiffened, the coffee cup halfway to his mouth. He didn't know whether to be proud or disappointed that Alfonso knew of his reputation. Part of the reason for coming to this small town was to forget everything that had happened before. He couldn't do that if everyone kept reminding him of what he'd done. At least, none of the newspaper articles about him at that time mentioned Hannah or Avery, and for that, he remained grateful. He looked Alfonso in the eye and said, "I am."

"His partner, too! What was his name?" Alfonso's eyes closed for a moment as if searching his memory. They flew open a second later as he snapped his fingers. "Burdette. Smiley Burdette. That's it. So glad you brought those men in."

"I am as well," he said, then took a sip of his coffee. He most definitely did not want to talk about this with people he didn't know very well. Hell, he didn't want to talk about it with people he did know well. If everyone forgot about it, he could, too, though he knew that was a lie. He'd never forget what chasing down Cassidy had done to him. Or Hannah. Or Avery.

He forced himself to relax then changed the subject. They spoke of mundane things—the things one speaks about when getting to know one another—and the rest of the visit was pleasant. No one mentioned Big Bill Cassidy again or his partner, Smiley, two of the most loathsome criminals who'd ever roamed New Mexico and occasionally crossed over into Arizona or Texas, especially when evading the law.

"Thanks for the coffee and the sopapillas, Damita, but we need to head out." Rafael finished his coffee, licked some sugar from his fingertips, then rose from his seat. "More people for the Marshal here to meet."

"My pleasure, Rafael." She started gathering the dishes from the table. "It was lovely to meet you, Marshal." She smiled at him as she touched his arm lightly. "I'm glad you're here, especially since Alfonso has someone to play chess with."

"Hey!" Rafael glanced at her, seeming to be offended though he wasn't. "I play chess."

"You do, but no offense, not very well." Alfonso replied good-naturedly as he rose from his seat and walked them to the door.

The deputy said, "That's true. Marshal Kimball was just starting to teach me when he decided to retire."

"Where you headed next?" Alfonso stood in the open doorway as Damita joined him.

"Montaña del Trueno."

Alfonso smiled. "Give *Tia* Evie and Jake our best, and if you should see Teddy, tell him he owes me a rematch."

"I'll remind him." Rafael promised, then glanced at him. "You ready?"

"I am. It was a pleasure meeting you both." He shook hands then followed Rafael outside to their waiting horses.

"Nice people," Devlin said shortly after as they rode beyond the gate.

"That they are. The kind who will give you the shirt off their back. No one, and I mean no one, ever goes hungry with Damita. She'll feed you until you're so stuffed you can't move."

"How long have you known them?"

"Feels like all my life, but it's only been about six years since they bought Crooked River from old man Percy." He paused, his gaze roaming over him.

Devlin stiffened beneath the scrutiny, his hands gripping Challenger's reins tightly. "What?"

"You seemed a little uncomfortable when Alfonso brought up Cassidy. If it had been me, I'd be crowing about it from the time the sun came up until the sun went down and then some."

"I was just doing my job, Rafael. The newspapers made it out more than it was. Let's drop it, all right?"

Rafael tilted his head to the side, his gaze now more intense. After a moment, he said, "Sure thing, *el jefe*. Whatever you say."

He was as good as his word and didn't speak about Cassidy again, but he did talk. A lot. About everything and anything to the point where Devlin wanted to tell him to shut up. He didn't though. He listened and supplied a comment if it was warranted but otherwise kept his own counsel until the big house at Montaña del Trueno came into view. Unlike the house at Stone Creek, and Alfonso's cozy home at Crooked River, this one was huge and very well taken care of. Flowers bloomed from planters on the front porch, which was wide and welcoming and filled with wicker furniture, inviting anyone to take a seat and relax.

Rafael dismounted before him and rushed up to the front door, his weight shifting from one leg to the other, as if impatient. Before the door opened, Devlin glanced around. Tresia had mentioned that Montaña del Trueno was one of the best ranches in the area and from the looks of it he had to agree.

The door opened to reveal a beautiful young woman. She didn't just smile. She beamed, her eyes lighting up with happiness, and she squealed, "Rafael!" before she practically jumped into his arms and hugged him. Devlin hid his smile. It wouldn't be an assumption to say these two knew each other well. "Come in, come in. They're on the patio."

As they passed through the door, the young woman paused, her gaze rising up to his. She held out her hand. "Hello," she said, "I'm Ana. Rafael's cousin by marriage."

"Marshal Goodrich. A pleasure to meet you, Ana."

She gave him a quick nod, grabbed Rafael by the hand and pulled him down a hallway, chattering a mile a minute the whole way. Apparently, she hadn't seen him in a while, and there was all kinds of news to share.

Devlin followed along, listening to everything Ana was telling him about the extended Zepeda-Ruiz-Castillo family, and he bit back a smile as his deputy couldn't get a word in edgewise. They entered the kitchen where the aroma of something sweet filled the air.

"I'll bring out some more coffee," she said as she opened the back door and ushered them through. "Go on."

There were six people on the patio sitting around a table, two older couples and another couple just a little bit older than he was, all of them enjoying a quiet conversation though he couldn't decipher what they were talking about. It didn't matter what the topic was. The love shared between these six people was almost a tangible thing, so much so that he could feel it, deep in his bones.

Conversation on the patio stopped as all eyes turned toward Rafael and him.

"Sorry to interrupt, folks," Rafael said as he drew closer, "but there's someone I'd like you to meet."

The people gathered around the table rose almost as one.

"Marshal Devlin Goodrich, meet my second family."

Introductions were made and he committed the names and faces to memory. The woman named Felicity seemed kind and gentle, but he suspected she had fortitude and backbone, much like his mother had. Another older lady, her steel gray hair braided into a coronet atop her head, gave him the most intense scrutiny he'd ever received before she smiled and introduced herself as Hilde in a thick accent he couldn't quite place.

An older man, introduced as Charley, shook his hand. "If you ever need a consultation about the law, come and see me. I retired from the bench a few years ago, but I still keep up with the legal profession."

"Thank you. I might take you up on that, but I'm hoping I won't have to."

"Antonio Lucero. Welcome." A big man with an impressive horseshoe mustache introduced himself.

"Nice to meet you." Devlin shook his hand and turned to a tall man introduced as Jake Hannigan. Jake appeared easy-going and very likeable, but didn't seem like he missed a thing, and yet, it wasn't obvious—only to someone else who'd spent a lifetime studying people and their habits.

And then there was Everleigh Miller Hannigan—"just call me *Tia* Evie." He liked her immediately. Like Felicity, she seemed kind and gentle, but also like her, she had a quiet strength about her, an air of courage with maybe a touch of stubbornness, but most of all, he sensed her loving, giving nature. No wonder Tresia was fond of this woman.

"We can't stay long. We're heading over to my folks after this," Rafael said, shifting his weight from one leg to another.

"Nonsense. Have a cup of Hilde's coffee and some *Lebkuchen*." Antonio said.

"If you insist," Rafael laughed.

Evie laughed, too, apparently very fond of Rafael. "We do. Sit. Make yourselves comfortable." She gestured to some empty chairs then took her own seat. The others around the table did as well. "Tell us about yourself, Marshal," she said as Ana came outside with the coffeepot and two mugs, which she placed on the table before leaving.

All eyes turned toward him, curiosity in their gazes.

"I was a marshal in Albuquerque before coming here." He accepted the mug of coffee Hilde slid in his direction and continued telling them as much as he wanted them to know, which really wasn't very much.

"I've heard some very good things about you, Marshal," Tia Evie said, her smile wide. "I also heard you hired Tresia Morgan to take care of your daughter."

Lucy Hart was her niece. She would have told her. And if she didn't, then someone else in town probably did. It wasn't a secret, even though he doubted anyone had a secret in Serenity. "Yes, I did."

"You couldn't have made a better choice. Tresia is a lovely woman."

"Yes, she is." He smiled. "Avery adores her."

"Tresia embodies the spirit of kindness, but don't mistake her kindness for weakness. She's a smart, strong, self-reliant woman, given all she's been through."

He'd already seen that much for himself. "Yes, ma'am." He took a sip of coffee then raised his mug to Hilde. "Good coffee."

Hilde beamed then offered him a cookie. "Have a *Lebkuchen*."

"No, thank you."

She passed the plate to Rafael, who didn't hesitate and grabbed several, which he cradled in his hand. "One? I could eat them all."

Devlin laughed, wondering how Rafael could eat so much and still remain thin. "I'll be making regular rounds, like Marshal Kimble did."

"That's good to know," Antonio said. "We haven't had any problems out here. No stolen cattle or horses. Esteban's reputation is well known."

"Yes, I heard."

"*Banditos* would be foolhardy to set foot on Montaña del Trueno." Antonio gestured to those around the table. "None of us would hesitate to protect this place or each other." He turned to Hilde. "And she may not look like it, but my wife here can wield a cast-iron skillet with the best of them."

"Oh stop!" She blushed to the tips of her ears. "I haven't hit anyone in a long time." She laid her hand on his arm. "I'm sure my aim is off now. But I still wouldn't test it if I were you."

"No, ma'am." Antonio laughed.

Devlin laughed as well. There was so much love around this table. It was there in the way these couples looked at each other, teased each other. There was respect, too.

"You ready to meet my family?" Rafael asked, breaking into his thoughts as he finished his coffee and rose from his seat.

He was enjoying the company of these people, but he stood. "Of course."

"Come back any time, Marshal." Tia Evie grasped his hand as she rose and patted it. "And give Tresia my best."

"Will do, ma'am." He picked up his hat from the spindle of the chair and glanced around those sitting at the table. "It was a pleasure meeting all of you."

Devlin followed as Rafael led the way out of the garden toward a gate near the corner of the house. Once outside by their horses, he said, "I like them."

"I knew you would. I've known *Tia* Evie most of my life. She and my mother are very close—closer than most sisters. I spent a lot of time here when I was younger, which is why I call them my second family. My wife, Ventura, loves them as much as I do." He untied his horse's reins from the post. "Someday, I'll tell you how *Tia* Evie and Jake met. You might find it interesting."

"Interesting? Why?"

Rafael laughed. "Jake is a mail-order husband. Lucy arranged it."

Devlin stopped in his tracks, surprised. "A mail-order husband?" He turned though he couldn't see the patio from where he stood then shook his head. "Seems like it worked out all right."

"It did." He mounted up, seemingly anxious to be off, and spurred his horse down the dirt road with Devlin at his side.

It wasn't a long ride to Hacienda Zepeda. Again, Devlin was impressed with the house at the ranch and thought Rafael was lucky to have grown up here. Unlike the two-story home at Montaña del Trueno, this house was a long and rambling one story, made of adobe, and had a courtyard instead of a porch. There were flowerpots everywhere, filled with bright blooms and several wrought iron benches on the flagstone patio surrounding the front door.

They dismounted, tied their horses to a metal ring on a post, and walked up to the big double doors where Rafael opened one.

"Come on in." As soon as the door closed behind him, Rafael shouted, "Hello! Anyone home?"

An older woman, gray-haired and diminutive, bustled from another part of the house and met them in the hallway.

"Rafael!" She squealed with delight, her dark eyes disappearing into the myriad of wrinkles on her face. "It's about time you visited," she scolded him in her heavily accented English, trying to be stern but failing completely, her expression full of love and pride.

Rafael didn't hesitate. He hugged the woman, lifting her off her feet—gently—making her laugh. When he let her down, he kissed her on her wrinkled cheek then turned toward him. "Marshal Devlin Goodrich meet Natalia Chavez y Ruiz, my *bisabuela*."

"*Bisabuela?*" Devlin asked, unfamiliar with the word, as his gaze swept over the woman, noticing her sharp eyes, that, like Jake Hannigan, seemed to miss nothing.

"Great grandmother."

Devlin extended his hand. "A pleasure, ma'am."

She didn't take it. Instead, she spread her arms wide, obviously expecting a hug as well. He obliged, bending low and embracing her tenderly. If there was ever a moment when he felt an instant kinship with someone, this was it. The love in this woman's heart seeped into his troubled soul in that one brief instance. He broke the embrace then took a step back as Rafael's *bisabuela* turned her attention back to her great-grandson.

She reached out to smooth her hand against his face. "What are you doing here, *mijo?*"

"I wanted to introduce the marshal to the family."

"Your brothers and sisters are out in the pasture. It's calving season. As for your *padres*, you just missed them."

"I did? Where'd they go?"

Natalia laughed. "Your *madre* and *padre* went into town to take you for a late lunch." She glanced at the grandfather clock in the hallway. "If you leave now, you might still catch them. They left about twenty minutes ago."

Rafael glanced toward him. "Maybe we still can meet up with them. What do you think?"

Devlin shrugged. "It's up to you."

"Go. Go." Natalia waved her hands in a pushing motion, shushing them both out of the house. "But come back another time. I miss you, *mijo*."

"I miss you, too, *bisabuela*." Rafael stopped in the doorway and faced her. "I promise. I'll bring Ventura by this Saturday for dinner. We might even stay the night."

That made the older woman happy, if her expression was any indication. "I will hold you to that promise." She gestured to Rafael to bend low, planted a kiss on his cheek, then turned toward him, her dark eyes piercing. "You keep my *mijo* safe."

"Yes, ma'am." He touched the brim of his hat. "I will."

He watched the door close, then mounted up. Anticipation filled him. He couldn't wait to get home, where he could share a cup of coffee with Tresia and tell her about everyone he'd met today.

The thought startled him. When had that become important to him?

CHAPTER 8

"*H*ow would you like to come with me to the Emporium, then visit Miss Lucy?"

Avery nodded enthusiastically and pushed her lunch plate away after taking the last bite of her sandwich. She scooted off her chair, as if prepared to go right now, a big smile on her face.

Tresia laughed, loving this child's enthusiasm. She still didn't speak very much, but she was getting better, and a lot of their conversations now were not one-sided. She'd learned in over the three weeks she'd been taking care of Avery that she was smarter than average...and stubborn, like an old mule. That was all right. Sometimes stubbornness was all one had.

"There might be a lot of people there. Miss Lucy seems to always have someone at her house. Will you be all right with that?"

Avery nodded, perhaps hoping to see Savannah again. In one afternoon, the girls had become fast friends, bonding over their love of swinging and the caterpillar they'd found crawling in the grass.

"We'll have to fix your hair." So far, Avery insisted on doing it herself...and it showed. She also insisted on washing her hair herself in the bathtub, though she did allow Tresia to help her rinse the soap from it. Even her father wasn't allowed to brush her hair. "Will you let me do that?"

The words, spoken so casually, made the smile fade from Avery's face. Her lower lip began to tremble as she shook her head.

"We could tie it up in a pretty ribbon to show off your beautiful curls. We could brush Cecily's hair, too, and put in a matching ribbon. Wouldn't you like that?"

Again, Avery stubbornly shook her head and took a step away from the kitchen table, as if at a moment's notice she would dart out of the house, her little legs carrying her far, far away.

Tresia crouched down and calmly reached for Avery's hand, holding it very gently in her own. "Will you tell me why?"

"I promised not to tell," Avery said quietly, clearly miserable, then clamped her mouth closed, as if she'd already said too much.

Those words rushed into Tresia's heart, and suspicion flared. Who had hurt her and extracted a promise that should never have been made? "Promised not to tell who, sweetheart?"

"Daddy."

"I see. But you can tell me, can't you? I wouldn't tell your daddy."

She could see Avery was undecided, but Tresia just continued holding her hand, offering comfort and peace and, perhaps, a little courage. It only took a moment more before Avery's eyes darted toward Cecily sitting on a chair. "Grandmama pulled my hair," she whispered, her words clear and precise though very softly spoken. "An' then she cut it an' hit me with the brush."

Taken aback, Tresia simply stared at her. Yes, Avery's hair was short but curled around her head like a halo—she thought the style suited her. "Why would she do that?"

"She's mean."

"Is she?"

Avery nodded. This was why Avery had been reluctant to

have anyone touch her hair, always saying she'd do it herself. Tresia had thought it was the girl's independent streak, but now, knowing this, she realized Avery was afraid.

She gave her a reassuring squeeze of her hand then released the child. "I promise you I won't be mean or hurt you. Do you believe me?"

Avery nodded.

"Bring me your brush. If you don't like it or if I'm hurting you in any way, you can do it yourself." She stood up, but her gaze never left Avery's. "Can we try?"

Avery nodded again, even though there was a touch of fear in her eyes, then she ran up the stairs to her room. She returned within moments, an ornate silver brush in her hand, but didn't enter the kitchen. She stood in the doorway, shifting her weight from one leg to the other.

Instantly, Tresia's heart flooded with sympathy. "It's all right, sweetheart. I promise I won't hurt you." She pulled a kitchen chair away from the table. "Why don't you hop up here?"

With a great deal of reluctance, Avery entered the kitchen, placed the offending item on the table, and crawled into the chair, lower lip beginning to tremble.

Tresia bent down low so she could look into her eyes. "You can tell me to stop at any time, all right?"

Avery nodded, but her eyes were huge in her face, like she could cry at any moment.

Tresia picked up the brush and very gently, very slowly ran the bristles through Avery's soft, shiny curls. After a moment, she relaxed. Her eyes weren't nearly as wide, nor did she look like she was about to run.

Tresia finished the task quickly, reluctant to push her luck. "That wasn't so bad, was it?"

Avery shook her head, her curls bouncing.

"I think we need a ribbon. A blue one. What do you think?"

"I don't have any ribbons. Grandmama threw 'em away."

Tresia, even though her heart was breaking for this little girl, smiled. "Well, then, we'll just have to get you some. Would you like that?"

Avery smiled and whispered, "Yes."

A short time later, Avery's hand in hers, Tresia stepped into the Emporium as the little bell over the door rang its familiar tinkling sound. Until three weeks ago when she'd quit, that sound, that bell, had been part of her life almost every day. Hearing it now reminded her of how quickly her life could change. Here she was holding a sweet child's hand, walking into this place she had loved for so long, to buy hair ribbons.

The store seemed…empty. Neglected. Shadowed. There were no customers. There was no one on the floor at all—not Arnold, not Willetta. There was dust on the displays and dirt on the floors, as if no one had cleaned since she'd been gone.

A sudden pain flashed in her chest. Seeing Sullivan's Emporium now brought home the truth that Arnold should never have been given the store in the first place. It should have remained in her possession. She would have taken care of it like it deserved. But then, she wouldn't have been introduced to the cute little girl who held her hand and her handsome father. If the truth were told, she loved Avery Goodrich more and more every day. As for Devlin, yes, she was growing quite fond of him as well. He was a good man, reminding her every so often of Brett and her own father.

She clutched Avery's hand a bit tighter and waited. And waited a little longer before moving toward the ribbons on display.

Taking a ribbon from the rack where they hung, she held it up against Avery's face. "I like this one. It matches your eyes. What do you think?"

Avery reached for a purple ribbon. "This one." She held it up and motioned for her to lean down a bit, then held it against Tresia's cheek. A wide smile lit the girl's face.

"What are you doing here?"

The familiar voice startled Tresia, but she didn't have to turn to see who it belonged to. Willetta. Arnold's wife. A harridan who defined the word perfectly. She waited for the beratement that was surely coming as footsteps came closer. She didn't have long to wait.

"I asked what you're doing here," Willetta said as she came closer, her voice rising. "You don't belong here. You quit. Left us without notice. After Arnold and I were so good to you."

The belligerent tone, as well as the lie, struck her immediately, but Tresia straightened and turned to face the woman. She couldn't say, in all honesty, that she missed Willetta Sullivan. Her life was so much better since she didn't have to put up with her cousin-in-law's nasty attitude.

"Is that the way you treat all your customers?" she asked before her gaze roamed the store, landing on several displays that hadn't been touched in days. "No wonder the store is empty."

Willetta's round cheeks turned a bright pink, which matched the dress she wore. The color contrasted sharply with her dull, dishwater blonde hair and pasty white skin. Her equally dull brown eyes narrowed, becoming tiny slits in her plump face. "You're not a customer."

"I am a customer," she insisted, then grabbed a few more ribbons from the display, regardless of color and length, and held them out. "And from the looks of it, I'm the first...and only... customer you've had today." When Willetta did not take the ribbons, Tresia pulled her hand back, calmly walked to the register, and simply waited.

Willetta just stared at her for the longest time then, as if realizing she had no choice, let out a huff of disgust and walked over to the counter.

The sale was made quickly and silently, though the expression on Willetta's face left no doubt she wasn't happy. If looks could kill, Tresia would be dead right where she stood. There was no love lost between them, and at that moment, she knew they would never be anything but civil, if that, with each other though she'd tried at one point to become friends with the woman. Her attempts had been swiftly rebuffed, which had hurt at the time, but no longer mattered.

Willetta placed the ribbons in a small brown bag along with a handwritten receipt, the stub of which remained in the receipt book, and handed it to her, seemingly anxious to have her gone so she could go back to what she was doing…which was probably nothing.

"I'm here to pick up the account books as well."

Willetta stiffened as the bright spots of color adorning her pale cheeks spread to encompass her entire face. "The b…books?" she stammered.

"Yes. I told Arnold when I quit that I would continue to keep the books. He agreed. Seemed relieved actually."

The woman's lips tightened before she let out another huff of disgust. "He didn't mention anything to me."

Tresia stared at Willetta, not willing to give an inch. "Doesn't matter if he discussed it with you or not. I said I will continue to keep the books so if you wouldn't mind…"

Willetta just looked at her, body stiff, mouth pursed in a moue of loathing before she simply…deflated. "I'll get the books." She stepped away from the register, then stopped and turned to face her. "You wait here."

"Of course."

"She's mean." Avery whispered as the woman walked away, tightening her grip on Tresia's hand.

She glanced down at Avery holding the little brown bag with the just purchased ribbons. "She's not mean, sweetheart. She's unhappy. There's a difference."

"Why isn't she happy?"

"I don't know. I do know there are some people in this world who are never happy, either because life isn't treating them like they think it should or because they don't know how to be happy." Her gaze roamed over the little girl's face. "You can't depend on anyone else to make you happy, Avery. You have to start with yourself, and sometimes, it takes a lot of work and searching your heart, but there is always something to be thankful for, and that can make you happy."

Avery looked at her. "Are you thankful?"

"I am. Very much so."

Curiosity sparkled in her bright eyes. "Why?"

"I'm a very lucky person." She bopped the girl on the tip of her nose. "Because I have people in my life that I love....like you."

Avery giggled, which touched her heart. "Like me?"

Tresia laughed in response. Yes, she did love this child, which didn't surprise her. What did surprise her was how quickly she'd fallen in love with her. "Yes, like you."

"And Daddy?"

That answer came swiftly as well. She didn't even have to think about it as she'd grown quite fond of Devlin Goodrich. "Yes, your daddy, too."

How quickly that happiness faded to be replaced with disappointment as Willetta stepped out of the office, the account ledger in her hand. There were scraps of paper hanging out of the book in every which way and Tresia knew, without even opening the ledger, that nothing had been recorded since she'd quit. She'd be lucky if all the receipt stubs were there as well as the total amount from the register at the end of each day. Her gaze fell on the word "Invoice" printed on a piece of paper extending from the ledger and she surmised it hadn't been paid. This was no way to run a business which depended on people acting responsibly as well as ethically and if it kept up, Sullivan's would cease to exist, which made her heart hurt even more.

Reluctantly, Willetta handed over the ledger, stooping low to pick up a piece of paper that fluttered to the floor. She said not a word as she handed the paper to her, but her face was still bright red.

Disappointment rippled through her, but it was her own fault. She should have picked up the ledger last week. Or even the week before. Now, it looked like she had her work cut out for her. "Thank you. I'll have this back to you by tomorrow afternoon."

The woman just nodded, dislike flashing in her eyes.

"Come on, Avery." Tresia tugged on her charge's hand and headed toward the door. The little bell tinkled as she opened it wide.

Avery stopped before passing through and turned to face Willetta still behind the register. "I'm sorry you're sad," she said then skipped outside.

If the words had any effect on Willetta, she didn't show it. In fact, she heaved in her breath, and turned away, but not before Tresia saw her mouth the word 'brat.'

Tresia decided to ignore it as she did with most things Willetta did or said and left.

Once outside, she looked down at Avery. "Are you ready to see Lucy now?"

She nodded. "She's nice." She slipped her hand into Tresia's as they walked up the raised sidewalk. Several men going about their business doffed their hats to both of them as they passed, showing the utmost respect. A few women stopped to talk with them for a bit, while some others simply nodded a greeting.

As they turned the corner, she saw Lucy on her front porch, shaking the hand of Mrs. Filmore, who was surrounded by her eight children, all dressed in their Sunday finery. They must have had their photographs taken.

She waited until Mrs. Filmore and her brood got into the carriage waiting in the street before she moved forward. She waved at them as the carriage pulled away.

"Well, good morning! I wasn't expecting to you see today." Lucy welcomed her with a warm hug.

"I just thought we'd stop by…if you aren't too busy."

"Never too busy for two of my favorite people." She opened the door and ushered them inside, her smile, as always, warm and happy. "I've been taking photographs. Mrs. Filmore was my last appointment so your timing is perfect. My first appointment, believe it or not, was Polly."

"Polly?"

Lucy smiled and closed the door behind them. "Things seem to be getting very serious between Deputy Shotton and her. She wanted him to have a photograph of her."

"Oh, so your plan is working." Tresia laughed.

"It seems so. From what I understand, the man is truly smitten with her. It's a good thing. She deserves to be loved." She bent low and took Avery's hand. "I'm sorry, sweetie, Savannah isn't here today, but we can still have fun. How would you like to have your photograph taken? Have you ever done that before?"

Avery's brow furrowed as she shook her head just seconds before her face lit up. She held up her doll. "Cecily, too?"

"Cecily, too."

"As long as you're here, you might as well have one taken of yourself, Tresia," Lucy said as they walked into the small studio she had set up.

"No, that's all right. Just take some of Avery for her father. I think he'll like that." Tresia let go of Avery's hand, allowing her to explore the room that was filled with expensive photography equipment. She didn't touch anything, but Tresia could tell she was fascinated with the cameras.

"Whatever you say," Lucy said, then took charge of the situation, positioning Avery on the stool in front of a neutral color canvas spread from one corner of the wall to the other.

Tresia took a seat at a little table and opened the Emporium's ledger. A sigh escaped her. She'd been correct when she assumed that nothing had been recorded since she'd quit. A quick glance told her nothing had been paid, either. She gathered all the scraps of paper as well as receipts and invoices into a reasonably coherent pile, then pulled a pencil from her drawstring bag and began cleaning up the mess Arnold and Willetta had made of the previously immaculate ledger.

"So, tell me what's happening with the marshal." Lucy said as she adjusted the height of the tripod that held one of her cameras, put her eye to the viewer and focused on Avery, who sat completely still on the stool and smiled her brightest.

"What do you mean? Nothing is 'happening.' We are becoming friends…I think."

When Lucy didn't respond, Tresia glanced up from the receipt on the table and stared at her. The truth hit her like a sledgehammer. "I can see the wheels turning in your brain, Lucy! You're still thinking the marshal and I would make a great match, even though I've told you, time and again, I'm not interested. He is not part of The Plan."

And yet, even as she said the words, she couldn't lie to herself. The marshal was a genuinely nice man. He had a good heart. He was kind and solicitous. All the qualities she admired. And she did like him. Very much.

Lucy said nothing, her focus on Avery. She adjusted the camera on its tripod a little more, then looked through the viewer again and snapped a photograph. "Ah, that was beautiful, Miss Avery," she said, obviously satisfied with what she saw through the camera lens. "Why don't you cradle Cecily in your arms and sing to her."

Avery did exactly that, her sweet voice filling the small room as she crooned a lullaby to the doll. The sound was so heartwarming and heartbreaking at the same time, that it drew Tresia's attention away from the ledger and piles of paper. Someone sung those words to her so often that she'd memorized them. It must have been Hannah. As far as she knew, Devlin didn't sing. At least, she'd never heard him.

"Why don't you go stand with Avery? I think the two of you would be a beautiful photograph."

When Tresia didn't move, Lucy turned her attention to Avery. "Wouldn't you like a photograph of you and Miss Tresia?"

Avery nodded, so vigorously, she almost lost her balance on the high stool.

Realizing she had no choice, Tresia stuck the pile of receipt stubs and invoices into the ledger and closed the book. She moved toward the set, patting her hair as she did. "Is my hair all right?"

"Pretty," Avery said.

Standing behind Avery, she rested her hands gently on her small shoulders.

"Lovely," Lucy said as she gazed through the camera lens and snapped another photograph. Then another and another. Avery was photogenic, her smile wide. She chattered away, clearly at ease. And she was animated, striking poses and making faces that made Tresia laugh.

"Last one, I think." Lucy stood back, her fingers coming up to tap on her lips. "Avery, why don't you give Miss Tresia a hug?"

Avery climbed up on the stool until she was standing then threw her arms around Tresia. "I love you, Miss Tresia."

Oh, though the words were a surprise, they settled in her heart, and she couldn't help the smile that made the corners of her mouth rise up. "I love you, too, sweetheart."

"Perfect!" Lucy snapped the photograph at that moment then moved away from the camera. "You can pick up the photographs in a few days."

"That's fine. How much do I owe you?"

"Nothing. I enjoyed today."

"I refuse to pay you nothing, Lucy. There has to be some kind of charge, at least for the materials you used and for taking up your time."

Lucy laughed. "I'll send you a bill," she said, though Tresia knew a bill would never come.

She glanced at Avery, who had climbed down from the stool, Cecily clasped tightly in her arms. "Are you ready to see Mr. Crandall at the butcher shop?"

Avery nodded, then approached Lucy. "Thank you, Miss Lucy," she said then tugged on her hand, bringing her closer. As soon as Lucy bent down, she gave her a kiss on the cheek.

To say Tresia was stunned by the action would have been an understatement. Not only had she been surprised by Avery's admission that she loved her, but also how happy and at ease Avery was with Lucy.

She stopped in the process of picking up the ledger from the table. As Tresia watched the transformation of her young charge with something akin to amazement, she was still determined to talk to the marshal about Avery's grandmother. Perhaps, this is what Avery had been missing—people who listened to her when she spoke, people who genuinely seemed to care and let her be herself.

Lucy appeared stunned as well, though she recovered quickly and gave Avery a hug before she looked at Tresia. "Don't forget the Ladies Society meeting next week."

"I won't." She held out her hand for Avery. "Come on, sweetie, let's go figure out what we want for dinner."

"Okay." Avery clasped her hand, then turned and waved. "Bye, Miss Lucy!"

Devlin stepped into the kitchen after putting Avery to bed, fully expecting to have his nightly cup of coffee with Tresia amid pleasant conversation. Avery had chattered nearly non-stop, telling him all about having her photograph taken at Miss Lucy's. His daughter seemed to be coming out of her shell, once more behaving as she did before Hannah had passed and the awful time when she'd gone to stay with Frances while he was burying his grief in chasing outlaws.

But Tresia looked up at him with a serious expression. "Tell me about Avery's grandmother."

"Why?"

"She told me something today that has me...upset."

Devlin moved into the room on feet that seemed to have turned to lead, pulled out his chair and sat down though he didn't like the concerned look on her face. He saw a flash of anger in her pansy-colored eyes. "What happened? What did she say?"

"I won't betray Avery's trust. Suffice it to say she said her grandmother was mean. That upsets me, Devlin." She studied him, unwilling to lower her gaze, clearly expecting an answer. "Was she mean to Avery?"

Devlin sat back in his chair even though he felt his body stiffen with unwelcome memories, recalling the devastation of seeing Avery with her hair cut short as punishment and Frances' cruel and cold attitude that her granddaughter deserved it. That had been the last straw for him, one that started him on the journey to this new place. No one abused his daughter. "Avery isn't wrong. She is mean, but I suppose she had to be. You've heard of *Rancho Gran Cielo* just outside of Albuquerque?"

"I have." Tresia folded her arms across her chest. "It is said to be one of the biggest ranches in New Mexico."

"Frances Emerson Comstock owns it. She's Hannah's mother, Avery's grandmother."

"I see." Her expression didn't change. She was upset.

"Frances has been running it since her husband died a year after Hannah was born. It takes a tough woman to do that, and she is tough."

"I understand being tough, Devlin." She folded her hands around her coffee cup, cradling the mug. "What I don't understand is being mean to a child, a grieving child who had just lost her mother. And why would she cut Avery's hair? Make me understand."

Oh, he did not want to talk about this, did not want to bring up memories that still hurt, but he could see clearly that Tresia wasn't about to give up without an answer. He doubted he could make her understand. He didn't understand that kind of heartlessness himself. "The way it was told to me when I went out to the ranch was that Avery didn't want to sit still so Frances could brush the knots from her hair. Frances lost her patience, which she did a lot...I witnessed that firsthand with Hannah, but instead of taking a moment and walking away, she simply grabbed the nearest pair of scissors and chopped off all of Avery's long hair. I was devastated over what she had done to my little girl. And angry."

"I see."

And he supposed she did see—or at least, understood his anger. It was there in her expression. Hurt for both him and Avery. Anger at Frances who hadn't had a little patience to deal with an emotional child who'd lost her mother. Her own granddaughter. Her grip tightened on her coffee cup. Any more pressure, and the mug might break.

"And Hannah? Was she like her mother?"

"No. In fact, she was the exact opposite, which is why I fell in love with her. Hannah was like...a fresh breeze after a spring rain. Sweet. Kind. Gentle. Generous. You would have liked her. It always amazed me how a woman as controlling, as mean as Avery says Frances is—and she is—could raise someone like Hannah. It defied explanation." He smiled, unable to help himself. "I fell in love with her the moment I laid eyes on her. My deputy and I had been summoned to the ranch to investigate stolen cattle. I saw her coming out of the house, dressed in white silk, the sun shining on her almost as if she were the only one it did shine on. She was laughing with a friend. She saw me, too. It was like the world had stopped spinning."

"Four months later, we snuck off to Socorro and got married. To say Frances was upset would be an understatement. I wasn't good enough for her only daughter. And she let me know it as often as possible. Frances had big plans, which I, apparently, ruined. She wanted Hannah to marry the son of the rancher next to *Rancho Gran Cielo*, even though Hannah didn't want to. It was a political move more than anything else. Frances didn't care that the man repulsed Hannah, didn't care the man had ambitions that didn't include being a faithful husband. He wanted the power and prestige marrying Hannah would have brought him."

"I'm sorry."

He shrugged off her apology. She had nothing to be sorry about. "After Hannah died, I was lost, I guess would be the best way to say it. And angry. I didn't know what to do, especially since it was my fault."

"Your fault? How was it your fault?"

"I wasn't there when Hannah needed me most."

"I don't understand."

His throat constricted, making it difficult to speak, and yet, he had to try. He couldn't have Tresia thinking the worst of him. He'd made mistakes, a lot of them, but he was trying his hardest to make up for everything he'd done wrong—or had been told he'd done wrong. "Hannah was pregnant with our second child. The baby wasn't expected for another three months but Hannah went into labor early, or so I was told. She'd been staying at *Rancho Gran Cielo* because I was desperately trying to find Big Bill Cassidy and bring him in after he killed a rancher and his family. Frances' people found me to tell me what happened. By the time I got there, Hannah was gone and so was our son." He paused, thinking back.

"I missed the funeral by three days." He stared at the coffee in his cup, the pain almost unbearable. "Frances blamed me for everything. I blamed myself for not being there." He looked up and saw the tears in her eyes, which made his guilt worse. "If I had been there, it wouldn't have happened."

She cleared her throat but still, her voice came out hoarse. "How can you be so sure?"

"I promised I would always take care of her. And I didn't. I let the job get in the way."

"It wasn't your fault Hannah went into labor early, Devlin. That happens, probably more than you know."

He shook his head, refusing to allow her to take the blame from him, the guilt that sometimes brought him to his knees. He rose from his seat and began pacing, walking the length of the kitchen, unable to look at her and see the sympathy in her eyes, on her face, on the lips that trembled so slightly as if she held back her tears.

"Frances convinced me that it would be best for Avery to stay with her on the ranch, considering how dangerous my job was— is. I agreed though it broke my heart not being able to see her every day. Big Bill was still on the loose, still evading capture, coming out of his hide-out only to wreak more havoc. I was angry—angry at myself, angry at him. Even angry with Hannah, though I knew that was unreasonable." He stopped, leaning his hands on the sink, looking out into the dark yard illuminated by shafts of moonlight. "I left the Marshal's Office under the control of my deputies and went after Big Bill. It took months to find him and bring him to justice, months of lost time with Avery, months of sleeping on the hard ground, existing on bitter coffee. There were days when I didn't speak to another human being. By the time I found him, I was just as wild, just as desperate, as he was. And in the end, it didn't work. It didn't bring Hannah or our son back."

He turned to face her, only to find her standing there, her expression one of pain, her eyes filled with tears that rolled silently down her cheeks. Whatever anger that had caused her to ask him about Frances seemed to have disappeared, replaced with sympathy and compassion. And it was the last thing he wanted to see.

"I'm sorry, Devlin. I didn't know."

He gave a brief nod, too choked up to speak, and left the room without a word, caught up in the pain that seemed to be never-ending. He heard her gather her things and leave the house, the kitchen door closing softly behind her. He felt overcome with doubt, doubt for telling her about Hannah, doubt about Avery, and worse than doubt, guilt over leaving his daughter with a heartless, cruel woman like Frances.

He stood in the parlor for a long time, staring at nothing, until his vision blurred. All the grief and guilt he had been carrying for so long poured out of him, much as his story had poured out of him to Tresia. She was the first person he'd ever told about what he felt, the pain he carried. His shame. He took some deep breaths, one...two...more, until his breath was slowed and even and calm and he felt as if the weight of dark feelings was slowly lifting. He went upstairs, suddenly exhausted, and laid down on his bed. He was asleep as soon as his head touched his pillow.

CHAPTER 9

A few days later, Tresia noticed the change in Devlin. He seemed different since he'd told her about Hannah. Lighter, if that were possible. Perhaps, he'd forgiven himself...or at least, seemed to have come to terms with the fact he hadn't been there when Hannah needed him.

Tresia hoped she'd never meet Frances Emerson Comstock. If she did, she'd give the woman a piece of her mind. No one had the right to treat a child the way the woman had treated her own granddaughter, especially not a sweet little girl like Avery Goodrich. It didn't matter how tough one had to be. There was always room for kindness, no matter the circumstances, but some people had no kindness in them. She certainly had no right to blame Devlin for what happened to Hannah and his son. Whether Devlin had been there when Hannah went into labor or not, the outcome might have been the same.

Avery was healing, too. The child was coming out of her shell, talking much more, smiling much more, and there were times when the conversation at breakfast or dinner was lively. When that happened, she could see Devlin's satisfied reaction. His daughter was becoming what he called his chatterbox once again.

Tresia picked up the cake platter from the table, her contribution to today's luncheon, and walked into the parlor. She called upstairs. "Are you ready, Avery?"

The chatterbox ran down the stairs, the curls surrounding her head bouncing, the bow of the pink ribbon Tresia had tied in her hair that morning slightly askew. Cecily, wearing a matching ribbon, was in her arms. "Yes, ma'am."

"There're going to be a lot of people there today."

Avery listened, but there was no fear in her eyes, no anxiety showing in her smile. She took Avery's hand and they left the house.

Carriages and buggies were lined up along the street in front of Lucy's house, which wasn't unusual. The bi-monthly meeting of the Serenity Ladies' Society was a raucous affair and those asked to join the 'Ladies' seldom missed a meeting. They did a lot for the people of the town as well as for the ranchers and farmers who lived on the outskirts. Started by Lucy, her aunt, Everleigh Miller Hannigan, and *Señora* Marisol Zepeda just two years ago, the society now had fifteen members. These women, from so many diverse backgrounds, were the heart and soul of the town.

As Avery and she stepped up to the porch, the sound of women and children chatting and laughing sounded from the open windows. She glanced at Avery, hoping the sounds didn't frighten her and undo all the progress they'd made. "Ready?"

Avery nodded and clutched Cecily a little tighter, but that was all.

Tresia reached up and grabbed the brass knocker, gave three quick raps and let herself into the house.

Everleigh Hannigan—*Tia* Evie to anyone who was close to Lucy—opened her arms and embraced her as soon as she stepped through the door. "Tresia, so lovely to see you!"

It was an awkward hug since she was carrying a cake, but they managed. She'd never forgo a hug from this woman, no matter how full her hands were. "You as well."

Tia Evie released her from the hug and took a step back, her gaze sweeping over Avery. "Is this who I think it is?"

"It is." Tresia placed her hand on the girl's shoulder. "This is Avery Goodrich, the marshal's daughter." She squeezed a little in a reassuring way. "Avery, meet Mrs. Hannigan."

Tia Evie bent down and cupped the girl's chin. Avery didn't flinch, nor did she pull away, perhaps recognizing the goodness in the woman, which was evident to everyone, even strangers. "You can call me *Tia* Evie. It's so very nice to meet you."

Avery gave her a perfect curtsy.

Tia Evie rose as a group of children ran past her then she addressed Avery directly. "I heard you've met Savannah, my grandniece."

Avery's eyes widened and a big smile lit her face. "Savannah is here?"

"She is. She's in the backyard with the other children. They're going to play a game of Blind Man's Bluff before lunch is served." She smiled in that reassuring way she had, the one that seemed to put everyone at ease. "Why don't you join them?"

Avery looked up at her, anticipation making her eyes sparkle. "Can I, Miss Tresia?"

Tresia laughed. "Of course."

Avery needed no further urging as she ran after the other children, clutching Cecily tightly in her arms. The kitchen screen door slammed a moment later.

"She seems like a lovely little girl," *Tia* Evie said as Tresia followed her into the dining room.

"She is." Tresia placed the cake on the sideboard, adding to the other desserts and hors d'oeuvres already there.

"And the marshal?" *Tia* Evie smiled at her, knowing all too well Lucy's penchant for matching people. It was she, after all, who put into motion the odd but amusing circumstances that led her to meet the man she'd married, her mail-ordered husband, and it wouldn't surprise her a bit if *Tia* Evie wasn't all in on matching her with the marshal. After all, she'd done it before, helping her nephews to find their perfect wives.

"He's a very nice man," Tresia said.

Tia Evie chuckled. "And handsome. I've met him. He came out to the ranch with Rafael Zepeda to introduce himself."

"Yes, he is." Tresia admitted, but that wasn't the reason she liked him. "He's also kind and loves his daughter. That's what makes him attractive."

"And?"

"And nothing, *Tia* Evie. No romance there. We are becoming friends." She repeated what she'd told Lucy just a few days ago.

Lucy rose from her chair and clapped her hands. "All right, ladies, let's bring this meeting to order."

The fourteen women took their seats at the table, after they'd helped themselves to some of the appetizers on the sideboard and gave Lucy their full attention.

"I have several things on the agenda today so let's get started and then, we can have lunch." She glanced at the sideboard groaning under the weight of all the food. "Which, from the looks of that spread, might take a while."

Everyone laughed.

Tresia pulled a notebook from her drawstring bag and laid it open on the table. She would take notes and transcribe them later, perhaps after Avery went to bed, and she went to her quiet, lonely room at Mrs. McMurty's after sharing a cup of coffee with Devlin.

"The first order of business. I'd like to submit Josie DuBois' name to become a member of the Serenity Ladies' Society."

"Excuse me?" Samantha Graves piped up, her face beginning to color. "Did I hear that right? You want Josie Dubois to join us?"

Lucy gave a regal nod. "I do."

"But she's…she's—" Samantha stammered, her mouth opening and closing as if she were having difficulty finding the words to express herself, which had never been a problem for her before.

"She's what, Sam? A madam?"

"Well, yes," Samantha said, clearly uncomfortable with Josie's chosen profession.

"Does that preclude her from joining us?" Lucy asked, then simply looked at the woman. "The purpose of this group is to do good. For the town. For the ranchers and farmers. For everyone. It doesn't matter what a person does for a living as long as she has a good heart and a giving soul." She straightened, pushing her shoulders back. "Have you ever spoken to her?"

"No, why would I?"

"You should." Lucy smiled. "She's a fascinating woman. Educated. Kind. Intelligent. She takes care of her girls, makes sure they are seen by Doctor Ben, my husband, at least once a month. She's teaching them how to handle money and save so someday they can leave that business and live a different kind of life, if they want." She eyed every woman around the table. "Are any of you aware that she has been secretly donating to whatever cause we come up with? Her donations have always been anonymous, but I caught her slipping an envelope full of cash under my door just the other day for the Thromball family." She laughed. "She was embarrassed that I caught her, as she didn't want anyone to know." She stared at everyone at the table. "All those in favor of having Josie DuBois become a member raise your hand."

Most of the fifteen women raised their hands. Only three dissented.

"Tresia, record the vote."

She dutifully did so, jotting down the names of the women who had voted for allowing Josie DuBois to join the Ladies' Society, as well as those who disagreed.

Lucy looked down at the paper in front of her. "The next item on our agenda is the Lending Library. I've spoken to Mayor Tisdale and he has agreed to let us use those two rooms at the town hall." She tapped the paper on the tabletop. "Tresia has rendered a drawing on what it could look like so now all we need is the funding. Anyone have any ideas on how we can raise money?"

"We could do a bake sale," Polly suggested. "I'll happily donate a few cakes and cookies."

"We could do another cookbook. I know I use mine all the time." Charlotte Applebaum looked across the table at Thelma Pierce. "Thelma's recipe for pumpkin pie is absolutely wonderful."

"Good suggestions, but we need something big, ladies! Something that will bring in a lot of money. We will need lumber to build shelves. We must purchase a desk, and some nice comfy chairs so people can sit and read, but mostly, we need books. Lots and lots of books. I have some I can donate. I'm sure some of you do as well, but that won't be enough."

There was a lively discussion about all the possibilities to raise money, from charity events like a small fair to holding a dessert auction at the church common room. Eventually they decided and voted and agreed to hold a fair later that summer, on July Fourth, with booths and games and races and a dessert auction.

Lucy smiled then glanced down at her notes. "And the last thing on the agenda, ladies. There's a new marshal in town, as you may know. Devlin Goodrich. I'm sure most of you have met him. He has a daughter, Avery, whom Tresia is taking care of."

Tresia's face grew warm as everyone turned to her, chatting and laughing among themselves, giving her big smiles, as they all knew of Lucy's penchant for matchmaking. Some of those around the table had availed themselves of her services...and were quite happy with the outcome.

"Let's make them both feel welcome. And that's it. Meeting adjourned. Let's eat. I've set up little tables outside for the children."

⁓

Later that evening, after the dinner leftovers were put away, the dishes were done, Avery had already had her bath and Devlin was putting her to bed, Tresia took two big coffee mugs from the cabinet and placed them on the table. She couldn't help smiling as she listened to the murmuring of their conversation, interspersed with Avery's laughter coming down the stairs, followed by Devlin's deep rumbling laughter as he responded in kind. Avery hadn't stopped talking about playing with all the children at Lucy's house.

Tresia took the coffeepot from the stove and placed it on the trivet in the middle of the table, looking forward to spending a little time with the marshal for their nightly ritual, which she enjoyed much more than she should.

She removed her apron and hung it on the hook in the pantry then turned to see Devlin standing in the doorway to the kitchen. "Oh, Devlin! I didn't see you there."

"I'm sorry. I didn't mean to startle you."

She studied his face, his eyes most especially. They were warm and filled with...was that concern? "What is it, Devlin? Have I done something wrong?"

"No, not at all." He entered the kitchen but didn't sit. "Avery was telling me how much fun she had at Lucy's house with all the kids as well as the other ladies, especially *Tia* Evie, and I just wanted to thank you."

Startled by his comment, she just stood there, feeling the warmth of the compliment ripple through her. "Thank me? For what?"

"For what you've done for her."

"I really haven't done anything." She poured a cup of coffee for him and slid it across the table then poured one for herself and took her seat.

"Yes, you have. You've worked miracles with her." He pulled out his chair and slid into it. "She's become a regular little chatterbox again. And she laughs all the time now. She isn't the same little girl that walked out of her grandmother's house with me. And that's your doing."

"I just talked to her, asked her questions to get her to answer."

"Well, it's worked and I'm grateful. I accepted the marshal's position here in Serenity because I had hoped it would be good for her. And it has been. You're good for her. I've never seen her take to someone as quickly as she took to you. She feels—" He paused, then shrugged. "—loved I guess would be the best way to say it."

"I'm glad. She's a wonderful little girl. She should feel loved."

His warm gaze swept over her, touching her in a way she hadn't been touched by a look in a long time. There was gratitude in his blue-gray eyes, but that wasn't all, though she couldn't define what it was she saw. Interest? Fondness? Perhaps.

And she shouldn't be looking for those things. She had a plan she was working toward...and it didn't involve falling in love with Marshal Devlin Goodrich. As she looked at his handsome face and soulful eyes, she realized it might be just too late. She was already falling in love with him, little by little, slowly every day. She had to put a stop to the growing feelings she had for him.

She forced herself to look away and concentrated on the coffee in her cup until he spoke, drawing her attention.

"I didn't realize what leaving Avery with Frances would do to her. I thought I was doing the right thing," he confessed and the pain in his voice struck her heart. "After I finally found and brought Big Bill Cassidy in for his crimes, my first and only thought was to see Avery." His eyes darted from his coffee cup to the clock over the sink to the ice box, then finally on her once again. "She was so quiet when I first saw her again, like she was afraid if she spoke she'd get in trouble. She doesn't talk about that time with Frances, except what she said to you about Frances being mean and cutting her hair." He fiddled with the spoon beside his coffee cup. "Do you think she'll forgive me? I was away from her longer than I should have been."

"Have you asked her?"

He stiffened, perhaps startled by her question. "Asked her? No, I haven't. We don't talk about that time at all."

"You should. Tell her how you feel, how sorry you are for having been away from her for so long. Ask her about Frances. She's a smart little girl, and as you've noticed, she doesn't seem to be afraid to talk or laugh or even become angry and frustrated anymore. She loves you, Devlin. She'll forgive you, if you tell her you're sorry. I suspect she has already forgiven you, if she ever blamed you, which I doubt."

He visibly relaxed, his muscles no longer tense, the ridge of worry lines on his forehead disappearing. A slight smile lifted the corners of his mouth. "Thank you. Again."

"You don't have to thank me, Devlin. I haven't really done anything anyone else would have done."

"You listened, Tresia." He paused, as if searching for the words then said, "You didn't judge." His smile widened. "You've been very kind. And understanding."

Tresia laughed. She couldn't help herself. "I have a temper. You just haven't seen it yet."

"I don't believe that."

"You should. Brett always said my temper was a sight to behold." She drank the rest of her coffee. "I try very hard not to show it. I believe in kindness, even to those who don't deserve it. They're the ones who need it the most." She studied him, her gaze roaming over his handsome face. "But I will admit that I would have a very hard time being kind to Avery's grandmother. I also have a hard time being nice to Arnold and Willetta, as neither one of them respond with anything other than meanness. I still try though."

She rose from her seat and brought her coffee cup to the sink to rinse out and took her drawstring purse from the spindle of the chair where she always kept it. "Speaking of them, I should head home. I picked up the books from Sullivan's on my way home from Lucy's and dropped them off in my room at the boarding house. They're a mess, the same as they were the week before when I fixed them." She didn't mention that knowing the books were a mess disappointed her yet thrilled her at the same time. Sullivan's hadn't made a profit since she quit. It was just a matter of time before Arnold might be willing to sell. "I'll see you tomorrow, Devlin. Good night."

"Good night, Tresia. I'm very glad you're here."

"Thank you." She paused at the back door and added, "I am, too."

CHAPTER 10

Tresia stood at the stove, stirring the hearty ham and bean soup she'd made from the leftovers of last night's dinner. She glanced at the clock. Devlin would be home soon—the favorite part of her day. The knowledge brought a smile to her face even as she quickly admonished herself. She had no business thinking that. Marshal Devlin Goodrich was not part of The Plan. Still, she found anticipation skittering through her and looked forward to him coming home, safe and sound.

"All right, Avery, put your picture book away and help me set the table. Your father will be home soon."

Avery did as she was asked, closing her book and placing it on an empty chair beside Cecily, then took the plates Tresia handed her to set the table.

He breezed in through the door a short time later, his smile wide, apparently his favorite part of the day as well—or so she hoped—and her heart skipped a beat. He looked as handsome as ever, his gray-blue eyes radiating happiness, which he deserved. He reached for Avery without a word, lifting her high in the air and making her giggle before settling her in his arms, then kissing her on the cheek. "How's my girl today? Did you do anything fun?"

"We went to the...." She seemed to struggle with the word, licked her lips and tried again. "Emporium."

"You did?"

The girl nodded, her dark curls, which were starting to get long again, bouncing. "And Miss Tresia let me help make soup."

"She did?" He put her down, strode over to the stove, where the steaming soup filled his senses and smiled.

Oh, what that smile did to her!

"It smells good!" He leaned over and dropped a kiss on her mouth—a quick brushing of his lips against hers, like they were married, like he came into the house at the end of each day and greeted her this way.

She felt that one little kiss throughout her entire being. It had been a long time since anyone kissed her and she froze in shock and wonder, the wooden spoon clutched tightly in her hand.

As if one touch of his lips to hers hadn't been enough, he took a step closer, wrapped his arms around her, and dipped his head once more, touching his mouth to hers.

This time, he didn't merely brush his lips against hers. This time, it was a full-on assault of her senses as his mouth moved leisurely over hers, tasting her, teasing her, making the blood rush through her veins. His particular scent of sandalwood filled her, and the warmth of his body seeped into hers. She melted into him, unable to stop herself.

Avery squealed with delight, making Devlin break the kiss and back away, as if realizing he'd done such a thing...without permission, without thought. Blood rose to his face and his mouth opened and closed several times before he uttered, "I'm sorry. I don't know why I did that."

"It's all right." She shrugged like it didn't matter, like her world hadn't just turned upside down and sideways. It did matter. She tensed, trying desperately to tamp down the runaway emotions that his touch ignited. She didn't want this, reminding herself once again that he wasn't part of her plan, and yet, she couldn't deny that she'd thought about him kissing her like that, of being in his arms, wanting so much more than she should.

She dipped the spoon into the pot, stirred a bit and held it up, all so she wouldn't have to think about that kiss, even though her hand shook a bit. Chunks of ham and beans clung to the spoon. "Would you like to try it?"

He took a step closer. He didn't say anything as he took the spoon from her hand and tasted the soup. "Delicious," he said, but she wasn't quite sure if he meant the soup or her. There was a spark of something in his eyes, a look that she'd been seeing more and more often.

Heat curled in her belly as she dragged her gaze from his and washed the spoon, concentrating on stilling the emotions soaring through her.

This is ridiculous! Devlin Goodrich is not part of my Plan! She reminded herself again, though it did little good. She paused, waiting till her head was clear. "It's ready, if you're hungry."

"I am," he said and walked away from her, taking his warmth with him, then sat at the table. Avery made a big production of getting Cecily settled, then climbed on the chair beside him. She took a hunk of bread and pulled the crock of butter closer to her, attempting to butter the bread on her own, once more showing her independent streak.

"Would you like some help?" Devlin asked after a moment.

Avery shook her head. "I can do it myself."

Tresia brought a soup tureen to the table, but her attention was on Avery as she finally managed to butter the bread. It wasn't perfect, but it was good enough and the small success seemed to make her happy. "Good job, Avery," she said as she ladled out bowls of the thick, hearty soup then glanced at Devlin and gave him a quick nod.

He took the hint and heaped praise on his daughter.

Acknowledging a task well done or even the smallest accomplishment went a long way in making a child feel good about themselves. Heck, it could make an adult feel good about themselves, too.

Avery beamed as she took a big bite.

Tresia sat down and gestured toward the bowls on the table. "Eat before it gets cold."

She watched his mouth as he ate, still feeling the touch of his lips on hers, watched him interact with Avery, his eyes so warm and filled with contentment. Yes, that's what it was. Contentment. Too bad she didn't feel the same. That kiss stirred a deep longing in her, something she thought she'd managed to keep at bay, especially when she saw other couples holding hands, their gazes only for each other. Lucy and Ben. Rafael and Ventura. Even Merrill and Polly. And no matter what she told Lucy, she did want love and companionship, someone to share her life with. She also wanted Sullivan's back—or another store like it— and yes, a husband could help her run it. They could do it together, like she and Brett had done along with her father, but she doubted the marshal would ever give up being a marshal. He loved what he did too much. And she couldn't find fault with that.

"How was work?"

"Good. It's quiet here. I like it. The most we've had is Mr. Somner staggering into the office and sleeping off a bender in one of the jail cells. Even at that, he's a pleasant fellow and doesn't cause any disruption, if you can get past his snoring. I'm not looking to change that."

"Mr. Somner drinks a little."

He laughed. "A little?"

She laughed, too. "All right. He drinks a lot. He was an excellent lawyer before his son passed away. He drinks to forget, I think."

There was a long pause of silence before he said, "The memories are always there." Sadness shadowed his eyes for a moment then was gone as quickly as it came. "Polly stopped by to bring Merrill lunch."

"Did she give him the picture of herself that Lucy took?"

"She did. And it's beautiful. It's sitting on his desk now and he doesn't care who sees it." He smiled. "I think there might be wedding bells in their future."

"Good for them. She's a lovely woman, and he's a very nice man. Lucy sure knew what she was doing when she asked Merrill to pick up pies from Polly's bakery."

"Alfonso Serrano came by, too, while Damita shopped. We played a few games of chess. I admit, I'm a bit rusty. He beat me all three games."

"I play."

"You do?"

She nodded. "Even after his stroke, my father and I played almost every night. He may not have been able to speak and he wasn't able to walk very well, but his mind was as sharp as a tack. Some of our games lasted for hours." She smiled. "Brett and I played, too. Marshal Kimball played as well. There should be a chess set here somewhere in one of the armoires or maybe in the bookshelf in the parlor." She nodded toward Avery, who wasn't paying attention to their conversation, but instead mimicked feeding Cecily some of the hearty soup. "You could teach her. She's very smart. I have no doubt she'd be able to pick it up in no time. I was about her age when my father started teaching me." She noticed that his bowl was empty now. "Would you like more soup?"

"I would. Thank you. It's delicious."

She dished it out and watched with satisfaction as he finished his second bowl. She liked this—sitting across the table from him, comfortable in his presence, taking care of him and Avery. If it wasn't for that kiss, she could go back to fooling herself into thinking she was simply fond of this man. It was more than fondness. It was desire, something she hadn't felt in quite some time—something she thought she'd never feel again. Brett had been the love of her life. How could she even think about another man? Of wanting to feel his mouth on hers again, needing to feel his touch?

Stick to The Plan, the tiny voice in her head whispered and she wanted to tell it to shut up.

"What's for dessert?" Devlin asked.

"Avery and I made rice pudding."

A smile crossed his face. "That's one of my favorites. There's a restaurant in Albuquerque that made the best *Arroz con leche*. Do you put raisins in yours?"

"Do you like it with raisins?"

He shook his head, the corners of his mouth moving up.

"Well then, I'm glad I never do." She pulled the pudding from the ice box, then clean spoons and three bowls from the hutch, set everything on the table and dished it out.

He took a bite. A look she didn't quite recognize came over his face.

"What do you think?"

His eyes glowed with pleasure as he ate another spoonful. "It's perfect."

"I'm glad you like it." She glanced at Avery, who had pudding on her chin and cheeks, but she seemed to be enjoying it every bit as much as her father.

Devlin sat back with a sigh. "I'll have seconds if you don't mind."

"I don't mind at all."

The request pleased her more than she cared to admit. She dished out his second bowl and just watched him eat it, that warmth in her heart growing. Oh yes, this was much more than mere fondness. More than desire. This was love, she was certain of it. She had suspected she was falling in love with him, but this…this just proved it.

She quickly tamped down her feelings. She shouldn't be having these kinds of thoughts, but she couldn't seem to stop looking into his eyes, which remained on her. She grew warm under his intense stare until he blinked and focused on his daughter.

"Are you done, sweet pea?" he asked, such tenderness in his voice that it made her miss her own father.

Avery scraped the last of the pudding from her bowl and pushed it away. There wasn't even a grain of rice left. She licked her spoon for good measure.

"Time for your bath and then to bed."

"I don't want to, Daddy. I want to help Miss Tresia with the dishes."

He sat back in his seat, his gaze darting from Avery to her, his eyes dancing with enjoyment. "All right. Just for a few minutes." He pushed his bowl closer to Avery as she slipped from her seat.

Tresia cleared the table and washed the dishes. Avery dried.

"Thank you, Avery. You've been a big help."

"Welcome." Avery took Devlin's hand. "I'm ready, Daddy."

He rose from his seat and took her upstairs for her bath. Tresia smiled, listening to them climbing the stairs, him telling her what a good job she'd done.

A short time later, Tresia dried her hands on a dish towel and spread it over the back of a chair, then went into the parlor and the built-in bookshelf with its many shelves and drawers. She found the ivory chess set and placed it on a small table in the corner of the parlor. She pulled two chairs closer to the table, lit several lamps, set up the pieces then went into the kitchen for the coffeepot and two mugs.

She took a seat in one of the comfortable chairs and just waited, her foot tapping with impatience.

She heard him before she saw him and looked up as he stopped on the last riser of the staircase. He smiled, gesturing to the chess board. "What is all this?"

"White or black?"

He walked over and settled himself in the chair opposite her. "White," he said then made his first move.

She laughed. "That was Brett's opening gambit. Every time."

"Tell me about him. How long were you married?"

"Eight years." She moved a pawn to meet his.

"How did you meet?" He paused with his fingers over a white piece.

"My father hired him to work at the store." She watched him make his second move. "I remember he walked in on his first day, dressed in his very best suit, determined to show Daddy he was a good man and worthy of the job, but he tried too hard. He knocked over several displays, spilled a whole bottle of ink on the ledger, and somehow, I'm not sure how, broke one of the cash registers." She laughed at the memory. "Eventually, he came into his own and I couldn't help myself. I fell in love with him. He was sweet and kind and funny and he made me laugh...until he didn't."

His gaze swept over her, sympathy in his eyes. "What happened?"

"He started not feeling well. He would do things in the store then suddenly have to sit down, exhausted. Climbing the stairs to the apartment became a hardship for him. Someone had to walk behind him to make sure he didn't fall, which he had several times, though we were lucky he hadn't been hurt. I noticed how pale he was becoming and how he struggled to breathe." She paused, remembering what happened, her vision becoming blurry.

"One morning, he just couldn't get out of bed. He complained of being so tired he could barely think. His chest hurt and his lips seemed to be a little bluish. It wasn't influenza. No one else was ill and he didn't have any symptoms. And it wasn't tuberculosis, as he never coughed, not one single time. We knew all the things it wasn't but we couldn't figure out what it was."

She stopped moving her chess pieces and just stared at the board. "We didn't have a doctor in Serenity until Ben Hart graduated medical school, finished his internship, and came back here to open his practice. We did have midwives and a few people who had more common sense than most, but if anyone truly needed a doctor, we had to go to Santa Fe. It's a long trip for someone who is ill, but we took it."

She cleared her throat to remove the sudden hoarseness. "Doctor Walters in Santa Fe said it was his heart. It wasn't beating like it should. He told us that somehow, Brett's heart was damaged and might have been damaged all his life, but he couldn't tell us much more than that. He said to bring Brett home and care for him until..." The chess board became blurry as tears filled her eyes. She swallowed over the lump in her throat. "So that's what I did. I took care of him." She let out a sigh. "He was the same age as I am now, thirty-one, when he just didn't wake up one morning."

He reached across the board and took her hand. She felt the warmth of it all the way to her toes. "I shouldn't have asked. I'm sorry."

"Thank you," she said, because that was what one was supposed to say. "I think I'd best go. We can finish this game tomorrow."

He didn't release her hand, just kept holding it, his gaze warm and radiating sympathy. "Why don't you stay for a while?"

She stared at him, the temptation to stay almost overwhelming, then shook her head and pulled her hand from his.

He gave a quick nod, understanding flashing in his eyes. "I can't let you leave like this."

She rose to her feet, her gaze on him. She sniffed then swiped at her eyes so he'd be in focus then gave a rueful laugh. "He's been gone three years. One would think talking about him wouldn't make me sad after all this time."

"There are no rules for grieving, Tresia." He reached out and rubbed his knuckle against her cheek. She almost leaned into it. Almost. "You don't have to come tomorrow. I'll take Avery into the office with me. She used to like that."

"Thank you, but I'll be here." She moved away from him then quickly went into the kitchen for her drawstring bag and ledger for the store.

"I'll walk you out and make sure you get home safely." His voice came from behind her and she looked up. "Again, Tresia, I'm sorry."

She gave a quick nod, not trusting her voice to speak, and left the house. She could feel his gaze upon her as she went through the garden gate and turned down the street. After climbing the steps to Mrs. McMurty's Boarding House, she turned and waved, then let herself inside.

She wished he'd never asked about Brett. She wished she could have allowed herself to stay with him. She wished...so many things as she closed the door behind her and took the stairs to her room.

CHAPTER 11

"*D*addy kissed Miss Tresia!" Avery blurted out as soon as Lucy released her from a hug. Tresia stood there, speechless.

"He did?"

Avery nodded enthusiastically, then scampered off to join Savannah and her brother, Miguel, who were already in the yard and leaving the statement just hanging in the air.

Heat rushed to Tresia's cheeks as Lucy turned to her, a big grin on her face. "So, the marshal kissed you."

"It was nothing," Tresia insisted, but it wasn't nothing. It was everything and more.

"Doesn't sound like nothing."

Tresia narrowed her eyes as she dropped her drawstring purse and the Emporium's ledger on Lucy's kitchen table and took a seat. "Don't be getting any ideas, Lucy Hart. It was just an innocent kiss. I don't think he even meant it." Oh, it was so hard to lie to her friend. She'd never done so before, but she really couldn't have Serenity's matchmaker believe she'd succeeded again—even if it were true.

Falling in love with Devlin Goodrich just wasn't in The Plan.

At least, that's what she kept telling herself, though, in truth, it was a little too late. Even she had to admit her heart beat a little quicker whenever he looked at her or accidentally touched her. And that kiss! She still felt it…as well as the guilt that kiss had brought. She was betraying everything, her plan, Brett's memory, and yet, she felt a spark of hope that he might feel the same way. It was impossible to be certain. There were times when she caught him watching her, the expression on his face unreadable, but there was a warmth in his smoky blue eyes that spoke volumes.

She just had no idea what she should do about it.

"Tell me everything," Lucy insisted as she poured a cup of coffee for her then set it down in front of her.

Tresia felt her cheeks become a little hotter. At this rate, she'd probably burst into flames. "There's nothing to tell."

Lucy laughed. "If there's nothing to tell, why is your face all red?"

"I'm in love with him, Lucy!" She stifled a groan, wondering how she could have let this happen. "I don't want to be."

"Why not? He's a good man." Lucy sat in the chair opposite her. "You've said so yourself."

"He is a good man, but he's not part of The Plan. You know that."

"Why couldn't he be?" Lucy asked, her voice gentle and full of compassion, perhaps realizing that laughter was not appropriate at this moment.

"I don't know if he feels the same."

"He kissed you."

Tresia fiddled with the spoon, unable to meet Lucy's gaze. "That doesn't necessarily mean anything."

"Are you sure?"

She stopped playing with the spoon and settled it neatly on the saucer. "No, I'm not sure of anything at this moment."

"There's more, isn't there?"

"I've been going through the newspapers and there are a few opportunities. One of them is in Philadelphia. The other is in San Francisco."

Lucy raised a dark eyebrow but didn't say anything. Her eyes were warm and understanding though as she reached across the table and laid her hand on hers.

"Two months ago, I thought I was ready for that challenge, but now, I'm not so sure."

"Why?" Lucy asked.

"I'd have to move. Which would mean leaving Serenity, leaving the possibility of Sullivan's, leaving…them. I don't know if I can now." She bit her bottom lip, not hard enough to draw blood, but hard enough to hurt. "Because I do love him. Love them both and moving…" She paused, unable to find the words to truly convey what she was feeling and then it hit her, like her heart suddenly started beating after being still for so long. "I don't want another store in another place. I want *my* store. I want things how it used to be. I miss Brett. And my father. Sullivan's kept them alive for me, but I feel like…I feel like I'm betraying all their memories as well as my own by even thinking of leaving." Her throat constricted, making it a little difficult to speak. "And by loving him."

"I understand."

She stared at the woman who was her closest friend, the sister she'd never had, and wondered how she could possibly understand. "Do you really?"

"Yes, of course." Lucy squeezed her hand then let go. "Sullivan's was your life, as it was your father's. You spent all of your time there when you weren't in school after your mother passed. It was your solace. Your place of comfort. Working beside your father helped you heal. And then Brett came into your life when your father hired him. All of your happy memories are wrapped up in that place. And then, it all changed, and it must hurt to see what Arnold and Willetta are doing to it." She sighed and even her eyes seemed to glow with unshed tears. "I would feel the same if something happened to Montaña del Trueno, even though I don't live there anymore."

"Why did you do this to me, Lucy?"

"Do what?"

"Offer me the job of taking care of Avery." Tears burned her eyes and she looked out the kitchen window at the little girl she'd fallen for. "If I had never taken this job, Sullivan's would still be thriving."

"No, it wouldn't. Arnold and Willetta are ruining Sullivan's. Neither one of them knows how to treat a customer. Neither one of them knows how to keep the place clean, either, not like you did. I stopped in just the other day and the place is a mess."

"I know. And it breaks my heart." She took a breath. "When I stopped by to pick up the books, Willetta was waiting on Mrs. Ashby and doing it very badly. She was rude to her, one of the sweetest women in the world. It was obvious to me that Willetta is unhappy that she actually has to work. I'm sure she'd rather be sitting in the apartment, stuffing her face with bonbons."

Tresia let out a sigh. "Speaking of Willetta, I need to go. Will you keep an eye on Avery?" She nodded toward the ledger. "I need to return that to the store, though I don't know why. Neither Arnold or Willetta are keeping track of sales or inventory."

There was another reason she wanted to talk to Arnold alone. The numbers weren't adding up. She wasn't sure if they were selling items and simply not recording them. She couldn't tell, not from the receipts stuck so haphazardly into the ledger. She did know they weren't paying their invoices. She'd found several that were marked 'Overdue.'

Arnold and Willetta needed the store. It was their livelihood, but then again, they might not care. They'd gotten what they wanted but had no understanding of how to keep it successfully running. And that broke her heart, too. Not because of the money they were losing, but because it felt like the end of something important.

"Yes, of course, Avery can stay with me. Take all the time you need."

"Thank you." She rose from her seat, grabbed her drawstring purse and the ledger then walked through the kitchen door and out onto the back porch, her gaze sweeping over the three children in the process of digging a hole in the dirt. A big hole.

"Avery!"

She looked up, her face and clothes smudged with dirt but that didn't matter. Beneath the dirt, Avery Goodrich wore a big smile.

"I'll be right back. You're going to stay with Lucy, all right?"

Avery nodded then went back to digging, the sun reflecting off the spoon she used.

Lucy stepped up beside her.

"Are those your good spoons?"

Lucy laughed. "No, not my good ones. I keep those for exactly the purpose they're being used for—digging in the dirt."

"Look at them! All three are filthy!"

"But they're having fun and that's all that matters." Lucy moved closer to the railing and leaned against it, just watching her niece, nephew and Avery.

"All right, I'm going. I'll see you in a little bit."

A few minutes later, Tresia entered the store, not through the front door where the little bell would alert Arnold and Willetta they had a customer, but by the back door, the one that led to the cozy little storage room. She moved through the small room, avoiding pieces of furniture and other items, and pressed her ear against the wooden panel on the other side. All was quiet in the next room. Arnold must be in his office and Willetta—she was probably upstairs, as she'd told Lucy, sprawled out on the sofa, her nose in a book, which wasn't a bad thing, but when one owns a store, one should be in that store.

Leaving the little storeroom, she opened the ledger in the middle, at the ribbon that marked the back half, where the inventory was listed. She dropped her drawstring purse on the counter beside the cash register, fished out a little pencil, and began counting. Five minutes into it, she knew that things had been sold but not recorded. She also noticed that the floor had not been swept or mopped and no one had dusted a darned thing. There was even dust on the counter by the cash register. And the windows hadn't been washed, something that she had done every morning when she opened the store. Anger and frustration surged through her. It wasn't fair. It wasn't right, either.

"What are you doing here?" Arnold came out of his office as she was counting the tea services on display. There were two missing, though no mention was made in either the inventory list or the list of sales.

She glanced at him, beyond disappointed. She hadn't seen him since she'd quit. She'd been getting the books from Willetta, who wasn't happy at all about the arrangement. He looked terrible, haggard, thinner and as if he'd lost weight. "I'm taking inventory."

"Why?"

"Why?" she repeated, stunned he could be so dense. When he convinced her father to leave him the store in his will, Arnold had only seen how profitable it was. He didn't seem to think he had to work to keep it that way. She knew the hard work it took to make Sullivan's the success it was. And apparently, now he knew it, too. When it was almost too late. He hadn't deposited her two percent of the profits in the bank like he was supposed to do, either. And it was probably because there wasn't anything to deposit.

"Look at this place, Arnold! When was the last time you took a broom to the floor? When was the last time either of you dusted the displays?" She held up the ledger. "How difficult is it to record a sale in the book? Or pay the bills? I found four invoices that haven't been paid. That's not how you run a business." She shook her head, still unable to comprehend what he was thinking. Or doing. "And what do you need a new chandelier for anyway?"

He didn't answer, probably because he didn't have a good answer, but then, he didn't have to. She already knew. Willetta had wanted a new chandelier so Willetta had gotten a new chandelier. She'd always been that way, always wanting more than she had. "Give me the store back, Arnold."

"Give it to you? Why would I do that?"

"It's obvious to me, and everyone else, that you don't want it. Not really. Neither you or Willetta know how to take care of it. You just wanted the money it brought in. Or used to bring in." She inhaled deeply and let it out slowly. "You can't make money if you have no customers, and no one wants to come in here. It's dirty and your wife is rude to the customers."

"Get out!" he all but yelled, though, it didn't seem like he meant it. There was something in his voice, something that told her just how tired he was. And perhaps, disappointed things hadn't turned out like he expected.

She didn't care. "I will not."

"You don't own it. I do."

She snapped the ledger closed. "No, I do not, but you are still required to give me two percent of the profits according to Daddy's will, which you haven't deposited in the bank."

He seemed to deflate right in front of her and she gentled her voice. "If you aren't willing to do the work it takes to keep Sullivan's successful, then give it back to me. Or sell it. It's one or the other, Arnold, but either way, the next time I come in here, I want to see it cleaned. I want to see this ledger." She held it up. "In order, inventory and receipts. And I want to see your wife be kind to the customers. It's the only way you'll begin to see profits again." She stalked over to the counter where the only register resided now, dropped the ledger on the glass top, then picked up her drawstring purse and walked past him toward the front door. He didn't say a word. Not one in his own defense nor in Willetta's. He didn't try to explain. She wouldn't have wanted to hear it anyway.

With anger raging through her, she flung open the door, stepped outside, and slammed right into a hard body, the force of which almost knocked her on her behind. A set of strong arms came around her to steady her. "Oh, I'm so sorry," she apologized then looked up at the smiling face of the man who held her. "Devlin."

He let go of her and took a step back, taking his comforting warmth with him. "You rushed out of there like your hair was on fire. Are you all right? Is Avery?"

"Avery is fine. She's with Lucy, but I'm not. I just had an argument with my cousin." She drew in a shuddering breath, wanting more than anything at this moment to feel Devlin's strong arms around her again. "I think Arnold and Willetta are intentionally trying to drive the store into bankruptcy." Sullivan's had been a staple in Serenity for a long time. It made her want to cry to think it was dying.

"What makes you think that?" There was genuine concern in his expression.

"Neither one of them seems to know what they're doing. Inventory is off, either not being recorded correctly or they just don't know how to count. Receipts are off, too." She let out a sigh. "And they're not paying their bills."

"And that hurts you," he acknowledged as he took her hand, placed it in the crook of his arm and started walking up the street.

"Yes, it hurts me. It also makes me angry." They fell into a comfortable stride. "Daddy should never have given the store to them."

"No, probably not, but then..." He didn't pause in his stride, but his gaze swept over her, his eyes warm and filled with both sympathy and something else, something she couldn't define. "I know it's selfish of me, but you wouldn't be with Avery and me right now if the store had been given to you."

She stiffened with his words and almost missed a step. Yes, that was true. And she wouldn't give up her time with them for all the riches in the world, especially now, when she knew she was in love with him. Even if she didn't want to be. Even if she thought being so betrayed Brett's memory in some way.

"I'm very glad you are. With me, I mean. Avery is, too. I wouldn't be able to do my job if you weren't. I know my daughter is safe. I know she is being taken care of. I know she's being loved and that makes me able to leave her every morning without worry."

He meant it. He needed her. Her anger with Arnold and the circumstances seemed to dissipate. Not all the way, but enough so she could think clearly. Maybe it was time to give up her dream and tell him how she felt, even if she didn't know if he felt the same.

He patted her hand and stopped walking. "We're here."

Surprised, Tresia looked up to see they were in front of Lucy's house. How had they gotten here so quickly? She hadn't even noticed.

"I'll see you at home," he said, then reached out to rub his knuckle against her cheek. She leaned into the gentle touch, then, realizing where she was and what she was doing, took a step back, removed her hand from the crook of his arm and moved up the walkway. She stopped in front of the door, knocked then turned around while she waited for Lucy. He stood there at the end of the walkway, watching her, hands on his hips above his gun belt, a slight smile on his face.

Yes, she did love this man and wanted to stay with him and Avery, for as long as he wanted. She loved him, more than she thought possible so why was she so hell-bent on getting Sullivan's back? Maybe, she just couldn't watch it die. There was another option. She could take the time to teach Arnold and Willetta how to run it successfully, if they were willing.

Lucy answered the door, opening it wide. Amusement danced in her mocha brown eyes as her gaze shifted from Tresia to something over her shoulder. Tresia turned, surprised to see Devlin still at the end of the walkway, just beyond the little wrought iron gate. He hadn't moved, hadn't gone on his way. In fact, he leaned against the trunk of the big tree now, his arms folded across his chest, looking like he had all the time in the world.

"It looks like he's waiting for you."

A thrill coursed through her. "I think he is."

Lucy chuckled. "I won't keep you then. We'll catch up tomorrow." She turned slightly and yelled down the hall, "Avery. Time to go."

A moment later, Avery came flying out of the house, running past both of them, her little legs moving fast down the walkway. "Daddy!" she squealed as she jumped into her father's waiting arms, her laughter startling the birds from the trees.

Tresia met them at the end of the walkway, her gaze sweeping over both of them. Just seeing Devlin and Avery made her feel warm all over. And happy. "I thought you were going to see us at home."

"I changed my mind. I'll walk with you." He lifted Avery and settled her on his shoulders then reached out to take her hand. He smiled that charmingly crooked grin and all at once, her heart, which had been beating so normally just a moment ago, began to pound in her chest. "Do you mind?"

"Not at all." She glanced down at his hand holding hers, feeling the warmth of his touch ripple through her, and returned his smile as they started walking down the street.

As Avery chattered on about everything she'd done at Miss Lucy's, Tresia listened, her smile widening, and a feeling of completeness, of overwhelming love, of contentment settled within her. This is what she'd been missing and something she'd never thought she'd have again after Brett passed. The three of them had become a family and her heart swelled with pure joy.

~

Devlin stopped on the last riser of the staircase after putting Avery to bed and frowned. The house felt empty. No chess board was set up on the little table. Only one lantern was left burning in the parlor. And one in the kitchen. He could see the warm glow through the doorway. Had Tresia gone home while he put Avery to bed and read her a story? Surely, she would have waited to say goodnight. "Tresia!"

"I'm out here." He heard her voice and all at once, his mood lightened. She hadn't gone home.

He strode through the kitchen and stepped out the back door to see Tresia sitting in one of the chairs on the porch, coffee cup in her hand, her head tilted back as she stared at the horizon beyond the backyard. The coffeepot sat on a trivet on the little table between her seat and the empty one beside it. His favorite cup was there, too.

"What are you doing out here?"

"It's such a beautiful night, I thought it would be nice to have our coffee outside."

He chuckled as he slid into the empty chair then poured himself a cup of her excellent coffee. He took a sip and leaned back, much the same as she did, his focus first on her then on the stars just beginning to twinkle in the deepening twilight. "This is nice."

"Did Avery give you any trouble going to sleep?"

He laughed. "I think she was asleep before I finished reading one page of the new book. What did you do today to make her so tired?"

"Oh, just the usual."

"The usual?"

Tresia laughed. "We cleaned. We worked on our reading and writing—Miss Palmer will be so pleased when she starts school next year. We went for a long walk, then I took her out to the Jennings' house. Mr. Jennings invited us when he delivered ice this morning. Actually, he extended the invitation from his daughter, Veronica. She's visiting from El Paso. I haven't seen her since she moved there a few years ago so Avery got to play with Veronica's children as well as Mr. Jennings' other grandchildren. It was a good day for her. A busy day." She grew quiet then, as if she ran out of words, but the silence wasn't uncomfortable. Not at all.

It didn't last long though as she turned to him and smiled, which devastated his sense of well-being. She had a beautiful smile, one that lit up her entire face. And invited confidence, too. "I've been working for you for a little bit now, and I realize, I know hardly anything about you. Tell me about yourself."

He took another sip of coffee then placed the cup on the table and folded his hands in his lap, a little uncomfortable talking about himself. "I grew up in Albuquerque. Went to school just like everyone else. Had a lot of friends, many of whom I still keep in touch with." He laughed. "Believe it or not, I'm a great letter writer."

Her brows rose in surprise. "You are?"

"I am. My mother, Primrose—yes, that was her name—was insistent on writing letters and 'Thank you' notes and such. She was a stickler for being proper, which was really hard—for both of us. I wasn't exactly a beacon of propriety. My mother was often exasperated with me and I can't say I blame her." He laughed. "I was a bit of a hellion, as she pointed out every day of my life. Well, almost every day."

"Yes, I can see that about you." She laughed as well. "Do you have any brothers and sisters?"

"I do. I have a younger sister. Xanthia. She lives in Seattle with her husband, Richard, who is, incidentally, a lawyer, which made my mother very happy though she wasn't thrilled Xanthia moved so far away. Richard worked for my father for a few years—that's how he and Xanthia met. He was given a great opportunity in Seattle that he couldn't pass up."

"Are you close? You and Xanthia?"

"We are. We write frequently," he said, then realized he had an unfinished letter to her sitting on his desk. He'd finish it tonight. "She's a good woman. Smart. Friendly. Compassionate. She's very kind, but she also knows how to stand up for herself." He paused after he recited Xanthia's good points and looked at Tresia, realizing he'd listed her good qualities, too. "She's a lot like you."

"Thank you. I'll take that as a compliment."

"You should," he said. "Her husband, Richard, is a good man, too. I don't think my folks would have allowed them to marry, if he wasn't." He took a sip of coffee, his gaze sweeping over her. He loved that he had her complete attention, but Tresia was like that. She didn't listen with half an ear—she listened with both. "I'm the proud uncle to Keara and Richie, their children. At one point, after Hannah passed, Xanthia wanted to take Avery to live with her, but I...I couldn't do it. Seattle is too far away, and I needed to be able to see my daughter."

"I understand." She gave a small nod and he knew that she did. "Have you always wanted to be a lawman?"

"Not always. For a while, I wanted to a cowboy. They always seemed so...free. And then an adventurer, traveling to exotic locations, like Africa, but that all changed as I got older and I realized while those pursuits were honorable, they weren't for me." He laughed, remembering how his father indulged his aspirations without mocking them while his mother did not. "My father, Charles, was a lawyer. I watched him try many cases against hardened outlaws, and he won more often than not. My father was a very smart man. That's why I became interested in bringing in those men before they got to the courtroom, before they had a chance to hurt anyone."

He took a breath, the memories happy ones. "He had a friend, Marshal Fairchild, who visited our little house quite often. I admired him and what he did. It wasn't easy bringing in the lawless, but he was good at it. He took me under his wing, so to speak, teaching me everything I needed to know, and eventually, brought me on as his deputy. Before he retired, he put in a good word for me with the governor and I was appointed marshal." He chuckled, then looked at her. "Mama wasn't happy about that. She wanted me to follow in my father's footsteps and become a lawyer like him. She wasn't thrilled that I put my life in danger."

"I don't blame her. No mother wants to see her child purposely put themselves in peril. It goes against the mother code." She reached out and laid gentle fingers on his arm, and he felt the warmth of her touch through the fabric of his shirt. "I'm sure she is proud of you."

"She was. Eventually."

"Was?"

"She's no longer with us." He let out a long, heartfelt sigh. Losing his folks still hurt, even after all these years. "Both she and my father passed before Avery was born."

"Oh, I'm so sorry. I didn't know." She squeezed his arm then let go.

He thought she would ask how it happened, but she didn't, and that was fine with him. He didn't want to relive the illness that took his mother or the broken heart that took his father. He filled the sudden silence with a question of his own. "What about you?"

"Well, I like strawberries and blackberries, but not blueberries." She laughed. "I like to read and, like you, I'm a great letter writer. I knit and crochet and needlepoint, though I don't like that very much."

"Be serious."

"I am." She laughed again and the sound went straight to his heart and stayed there. "I've lived here all my life, as you know. I had an opportunity to go to college—Vassar—but I didn't take it. I couldn't leave my father. I was all he had after Mama passed. Nor could I leave Serenity. I love this town. I have a lot of friends here."

"Do you miss your mother?"

"I do. Some days more than others, but I was lucky, I suppose. I had—have—some great role models. *Tia* Evie. Bonita Gonzales over at the Serenity hotel. They were both very good friends with my mother. Both took me under their wing, so to speak, after she passed. There are others who hold a special place in my heart."

"Do you regret not going to Vassar?"

"No, not at all. My decision to not go was for the best because if I had left, I would never have met Brett. Besides, why did I need to go to school to learn how to run a business and keep the books? My father had been teaching me since I was old enough to understand." She sighed, though it sounded content to him. "I bet I could teach others better than most though I will admit, some people don't want to learn." She finished her coffee and glanced in his direction.

"Speaking of keeping the books, I should go. I still need to go over the last week's receipts for Sullivan's, though why I try, I don't know. Both Cousin Arnold and Willetta seem to be in the category of those who don't want to learn."

She rose from her chair and brought her coffee cup inside. She returned in moments, the ledger in her arms, drawstring purse dangling from her wrist. "I'll wash that cup in the morning. You can leave your cup in the sink, too." She smiled and walked down the porch steps. "Good night, Devlin."

"Good night, Tresia." He rose from his seat. "And thank you."

She stopped on the bottom step and turned to face him. "For what?"

"For the conversation. For everything you do."

"It's my pleasure, Devlin. Good night."

He watched her walk toward the gate at the back of the yard, disappear behind the tall hedges of his neighbor's yard then reappear as she climbed the steps to Mrs. McMurty's Boarding House. She waved one last time before she let herself in.

He sat in the chair again and took another sip of his coffee, wishing she could have stayed longer. What would it be like if she didn't have to go home?

CHAPTER 12

*D*evlin turned over in bed, dragging the light blanket with him, then flipped his pillow, looking for the cool side. And it didn't work. No matter what he tried, he wasn't able to sleep, though he had no clue as to why.

He lay in the darkness for a long time then smiled. He knew exactly why he couldn't sleep.

Mrs. Tresia Morgan.

He shouldn't have kissed her, but it just felt so right, and he didn't regret it in the least. He wasn't sure if she did or not. She'd seemed flustered, but only for a moment, and when he kissed her again, she responded, her lips conforming to his, the warmth of her mouth like a drug he couldn't get enough of. He would have kept on kissing her if Avery hadn't giggled, reminding him where he was and who he was with.

Avery hadn't seemed to mind that he had kissed Tresia.

He had to admit that he enjoyed seeing her each morning and then again at the end of the day, their ritual of talking over coffee or playing chess. Everything everyone had said about her was true. She was warm and friendly and compassionate and like Hannah, one of the most beautiful women he'd ever known, with her pansy-colored eyes and auburn hair, but she was so much more. It was her innate kindness, her willingness to accept everyone for who they were—her inner beauty—that drew him.

Avery, who'd barely spoken two words when he'd rescued her from Frances, had become, in such a short time with Tresia, the talkative, exuberant little girl he knew and loved. Now, she was hardly ever quiet and that was all right with him. She was joyful again, something she hadn't been in a long time. He was happy, too, as impossible as that seemed. He didn't think he'd ever feel this way again and yet, here he was, grinning in the darkness like an idiot.

Tresia had done that. She'd used whatever magic she possessed—and he was convinced it was magic—to make them both feel almost whole, like they were worthy of happiness.

I'm in love with her.

The words reverberated in his head, not with thunderbolts and lightning, but with a gentleness that swept through him and brought him peace. He turned over, punched his pillow one more time, and closed his eyes, but sleep still didn't come. He should just get up, get a start on his day, but didn't want to leave the warmth of his bed. He rolled onto his back, folded his hands behind his head and let his mind drift and closed his eyes...until a loud, persistent knocking on the front door startled him.

He darted out of bed, pulled on his trousers and boots, shrugged into a shirt and got his gun belt, then rushed downstairs before the noise woke Avery. He buckled on his guns just before he opened the door.

The flash of light from the lantern nearly blinded him as the figure on the porch raised it up. He blinked rapidly until his eyes became accustomed to the light. It only took a moment more before he recognized one of Josie's girls. She was half sobbing and there was blood on her dress.

"Corianna? What's happened?"

"Nate told me to come get you," she blurted out amid a fresh wave of tears. "Josie's been stabbed." She looked down at her hands. "There was so much blood. I don't...."

"Come in." He led her into the kitchen and pulled out a chair for her to sit. "Now tell me what happened."

"A man was trying to get Valentine to go upstairs with him. She didn't want to. She was afraid. He was hurting her. She was crying and begging him to stop but he just kept on hurting her. Josie tried to stop him." She gulped in air. "Lily tried to help, too. The man...he...he...he pulled out a knife and stabbed Josie. Stabbed them both."

"Is that man still there?"

"No. He ran out of the house, almost knocking me down."

"Do you know who he is?"

"I've never seen him before. He wasn't one of our regulars."

"Do you know which direction he went?"

She shook her head, gulped in more air, then swiped at her eyes, smearing the kohl a little.

"Where is Nate now?"

"He's at the house, talking to the other girls. I went to get Doctor Ben before I told Nate what happened."

"You did good, Corianna."

"It wasn't enough." Whatever calmness she managed to achieve disappeared and she dissolved into tears again. "What if...what if Josie..." She wasn't able to finish the sentence.

"Doctor Ben is with her, right?"

She nodded and pulled in a shuddering breath. "Oh, I forgot. His wife, Lucy, is coming to watch your daughter. She had to get dressed. I'm sorry."

A quick knock sounded on the backdoor a few minutes later and Lucy walked into the kitchen. "I'll stay with Corianna and Avery. You go. I'm sure Nate is waiting."

Devlin left the house at a run, stopping briefly to pick up Challenger from the stable behind the Marshal's Office, then rode out to Josie's parlor house at the edge of town.

He walked into chaos. Josie's girls were in various stages of tears, sobbing, barely coherent. Except one, who looked angry enough to spit nails. Lily, the unofficial protector of the group, had Nate backed into a corner, her voice raised in distress as he tried to take notes, writing as quickly as he could in his little notebook.

"The marshal is here!" One of the girls cried out.

Nate turned to look at him, then pointed up the staircase. Without a word, he took the stairs two at a time and stopped in the hallway. Through an open bedroom door he saw Doctor Ben Hart, shirt sleeves rolled up to his elbows.

His gaze drifted to the woman on the bed. Josie wasn't moving. Her bloody gown was bunched at her sides, as if Ben had had to use scissors to cut her clothes away, and blood-soaked cotton pads were strewn on the floor around him.

Bile rose in his throat. It wasn't the sight of so much blood that had him swallowing hard—it was the knowledge of what it meant. He'd seen belly wounds before, from both gunshot and knives. What he saw didn't bode well.

His focus shifted from her belly to her chest. He didn't see it rise, but that could just be his eyes playing tricks on him. Still, he had hope...until his gaze moved to the woman's face. He'd met Josie several times in the course of his official marshal duties and liked her very much.

"How is she?"

Ben Hart turned toward him and shook his head. Devlin didn't know if that meant her wounds were so bad she wouldn't survive...or if she was dead. He didn't ask, but then, he didn't need to as the doctor pulled the stethoscope from his ears, wrapped it around his neck and slowly brought the blanket up to cover her.

Anger flared in him. This shouldn't happen in his town. Hell, this shouldn't happen in any town. Ever.

He went downstairs to find Nate now questioning Valentina,

Lily behind her with her hand resting on the woman's shoulder. It wasn't going well.

"Did he give his name?"

She shook her head as fresh tears consumed her.

"What did he look like, Val?" Nate asked, his voice gentle.

"Mean," Valentina responded, which wasn't helpful at all. Her eye, which was all red, was beginning to swell and close. Her lip had been split and trickled blood. He could see the marks on her arms where he assumed the man had grabbed her.

"Dark hair or light?" Nate persisted, but it was obvious he was becoming frustrated.

"Dark."

"Tall or short?"

She looked at him as she pulled her ripped wrapper closer around her body as if to protect herself, her eye, the one not swollen, shiny with tears and looking glazed from shock. Devlin didn't think she would be able to answer any more questions or even give a decent description.

He approached cautiously. "Let me try," he said, careful to keep his voice calm though he felt anything but calm. He crouched down in front of Valentine but never had the chance to say a word.

"Why are you asking her all these questions? Can't you see she can't answer them." Lily didn't yell, but her voice was strident.

He couldn't say he blamed her. Someone taking advantage of soiled doves wasn't out of the ordinary. It happened though it shouldn't.

"You're not going to do anything, anyway. You don't care if one of us gets hurt."

"That's where you're wrong, Lily." He rose up and looked her straight in the eye. "I'm not like other lawmen. Neither are my deputies. We'll take care of it."

She folded her arms across her chest and glared at him. "I don't believe you."

"Doesn't matter if you believe me or not." He turned his attention to Valentine. "Will you come down to the Marshal's Office with me? I want you to look at some Wanted posters we have. If you don't see the man who did this in one of them, we can talk to Merrill. He's pretty good with a pencil and paper. If you can describe the man to him, he can draw him." He raised her chin with his thumb and forefinger. "Can you do that for me?"

Valentine shook her head but didn't speak and he knew she wouldn't be able to do as he asked. She was too distressed, too distraught, to remember things clearly. He turned his attention to Lily. "You saw him."

Lily nodded as her lips tightened and redness crept into her cheeks. She didn't look like she'd shed any tears. In fact, her eyes were sparked with fury. It was then he saw the wound. She was holding a square of medical cotton, which he assumed Doctor Ben had given her, against her skin between her shoulder and her neck. The square was bloody. She didn't seem as concerned for herself as she was for Valentine.

"Maybe you should sit down, Lily."

"That's what I told her," Nate said from across the room as he spoke to another one of the girls.

Devlin led her and Valentine to a sofa. "Sit." He waited until they did, then said, "Talk to me."

Lily took a breath and told him what happened, the terror and chaos as the man attacked them and how Josie tried to stop him. When she was done she looked up at him and he saw her anger deflate, as if she were too exhausted to feel anything.

Sympathy for her, for them all, rose in him. "Can you describe him?"

"Yes. His face is burned into my memory. I'll never forget it. Dark hair, long, almost to his shoulders, and his eye were almost black…as if the Devil himself had come to life. He was tall. Taller than you. But slim. I think his nose had been broken a time or two. It was a little crooked. And he was angry, so angry, that

Valentine didn't want to go upstairs with him. None of the girls did. Josie tried..." She looked up at him. "You gonna go after him?"

"Yes, ma'am."

"When?"

"As soon as we know who we're looking for."

"Well then, take me down to the Marshal's Office," she demanded, "and let me look at your Wanted posters."

Devlin nodded. "Thank you. I appreciate that."

"Nothing like this has ever happened here before," she said, her voice hoarse. "Josie runs a respectable house, the best one I've known." Her gaze swept the room, stopping on the other girls then came back to him. "She was good to us. Took care of us. Protected us."

He didn't quite know what to say. Any expression of sympathy would be inadequate.

"We always felt safe here."

Doctor Ben came down the stairs, carrying his medical bag and asked, "Where's Lily?"

"Over here, Doc." Devlin waved him over.

Lily watched Doc Ben approach them, her eyes wide and filled with both anger and pain. "Josie?"

"I'm sorry, Lily." He shook his head sadly and set his medical bag down beside her.

Lily's bravado seemed to crumble and tears, the first Devlin had seen from her, filled her eyes.

"Take care of that wound, Doc," Devlin said and looked down at Lily. "We'll need you to come down to the office as soon as you can. I'll send one of my men to escort you," he paused. "I'm sorry. I know Josie was your friend."

She nodded and swallowed hard, as if willing herself not to cry.

Soon after, he and Nate left the house and rode to the Marshal's Office where they compared versions of what happened. "Go get everyone. Tell them what happened and meet me back here."

"Sure thing, Boss," he said, but didn't move as Devlin dismounted and tied Challenger's reins to the post. "Josie was a nice woman."

"Yes, she was," he agreed.

"I've known her a long time."

Devlin recognized the drawn brows and grim expression on Nate's face, seen in the light glowing from the office's big windows. "We'll find him."

Nate gave a short nod, spurred his horse and took off to gather the others. Devlin watched him go, then stepped inside and looked around.

A game of solitaire was laid out on Nate's desk, a cup of coffee, long since gone cold, sitting beside the cards. It had been quiet until that man attacked Josie. It wasn't going to be quiet for much longer.

He paced the office, waiting for his deputies, anxious to gather his posse and go after that man, but there wasn't anything he could do until Lily gave them a description. He walked into the kitchen and made a fresh pot of coffee. They'd need it.

A few minutes later, Merrill came into the office through the kitchen door. "Nate came to get me. Told me a little bit of what's happening." He buckled on his gun belt and tied the strings that hung from the bottom around his thigh.

"Where is he now?"

"Went to Rafael's. Sherm and the others are on their way. Said he would head back to Josie's to escort Lily to the office when he was done so she could look at the Wanted posters." He paused, sadness showing in his eyes and in his expression. "Damn shame what happened. Things like this shouldn't happen in Serenity. Josie was a good woman."

"It shouldn't happen anywhere." He tried to tamp down the anger flowing through him but failed. Horribly. "Do you think you can draw the man if he isn't on any of the posters? Lily said she could give you a description."

"I'll do my best."

They drank coffee and waited as the other deputies drifted in, all in various states of dishevel, having been awakened just as rudely as he had been. Rafael headed for the coffeepot and poured himself a cup. Sherm came in alert, clearly ready. There was none of the usual teasing each other. Not this time. This, they knew, was serious business. They also knew there might be a chance they would not come home. That possibility haunted every lawman.

They didn't need to wait long before Nate came back with Lily. Devlin stepped forward to open the small gate that separated the office proper from the entryway. He took her hand and drew her to a chair beside Merrill's desk. "Are you all right?"

She looked at him like he was the stupidest man on earth. He had to agree with her. It wasn't the most intelligent of questions.

"Do I look all right to you, Marshal?" She snapped, her voice was hoarse and tight. The tension of the night had gotten to her. "I've just lost a very dear friend to some…depraved bastard. I am not all right."

"Forgive me." He patted her shoulder. "Can I bring you a cup of coffee?"

"Do you have anything stronger?"

"Nate, do you still have that bottle of whiskey in your desk drawer?"

Nate flushed then retrieved the bottle, pouring some into a coffee mug. He handed it to Lily then stayed close, the bottle still in his hand. She swallowed the drink in one gulp, which seemed to steady her.

"Are you ready?" Devlin asked as he took her hand and guided her to the Wanted posters on the wall.

She took her time, looking at each poster carefully before moving on to the next and then she froze. Her eyes widened and the blood drained from her face, leaving her pale except for two bright spots of rouge on her cheeks. "That's him! That's the man who killed Josie!"

Devlin glanced at the poster and his heart sank. Ned Delany. "Are you certain?"

Lily took umbrage at the question as she turned to face him. "Of course, I am. I will never forget that face."

He turned to his deputies. "Sherm, I want you and Tomas to start at Josie's house and work your way toward the town square then continue on to the other side of town. Check everything. Look in alleyways and backyards, in wagon beds—anywhere big enough for a man to hide but try to do it calmly and quietly. The last thing we need is to upset the townspeople though I think they should know what's happening. If anyone asks, tell them what's happened then advise them to stay in their homes, doors locked." He took a breath then turned to Rafael.

"We're gonna need Esteban Silva and his brothers and anyone else you can think of. Your brothers will help?"

"They will."

"Good." He pulled the Wanted poster from the wall and looked at Lily. Her face was still white, whiter than the sheets Tresia hung up to dry. She swayed a bit and he wondered how she remained on her feet. She was certainly still in shock. He addressed Nate, who'd come to stand by her again. "Take her over to Doctor Ben's."

"Yes, sir." Nate held out his hand to her.

Lily glanced at the hand Nate offered then raised her gaze and looked at him, her eyes filled with sadness, but at the same time, gratitude. She turned toward Devlin. "As much as I appreciate your concern, Marshal, I don't need Doctor Ben. He has already examined me." She gestured toward the bandage on her shoulder. "I'd rather go back to Josie's, where I'm needed most."

"Whatever you think is best, Lily." Devlin laid a hand on her arm and squeezed lightly. "Thank you for helping us. We're going to find this man before he hurts anyone else." He nodded toward Nate and Caleb. "Take her back to Josie's but keep your eyes open. After you make sure she and the other girls are safe, I want you both to head north to the old mines."

Lastly, Devlin turned toward Merrill. "You're with me. We'll head out to Wyatt's place then Alfonso's." He turned to the rest of the men, who were already checking their pistols, each one knowing that Ned Delany would not be taken easily.

"The sun's coming up." He remarked as he stacked boxes of bullets on the desk and the men loaded up. "You all know who you're looking for. Be careful."

CHAPTER 13

*T*resia entered the marshal's house from the kitchen door, as was her habit, and stopped short, surprised and a little unsure. Devlin wasn't sitting at the kitchen table like she expected. Rather, she found Corianna March, one of Josie DuBois' 'girls,' her blonde ringlets a mess. Lucy sat beside her, rubbing her back in a consoling way. The coffeepot was on a trivet on the table, cups in front of them.

Something had happened. Something bad. Something involving Corianna or Josie or one of the other ladies.

Immediately alert, she came into the room, and looked at both women. "What happened?"

"Oh, Tresia, it was awful," the young woman wailed before Lucy could speak. She used the napkin balled in her hand to swipe at her eyes. It wasn't the first time, considering how damp the cloth appeared.

"What was?" She glanced at Lucy then sat across from Corianna and took the woman's hand, hoping to offer comfort.

"Some man hurt Josie." Corianna hiccupped. "Bad."

Tears sprang to her eyes. She liked Josie. Despite what she did for a living, she was kind-hearted and intelligent. "Tell me."

Corianna related the events as best she could despite the flow of tears. "Lily sent me to get Doc Hart and Nate and then Nate sent me to get the marshal."

"I came over to stay with Corianna and Avery." Lucy still rubbed Corianna's back in a soothing way. "Devlin and his deputies went after the man."

Tresia acknowledged the statement with a slight nod, though her stomach tightened. She forced her anxiety away and looked at Lucy, noticing the dark circles under her eyes. "You're exhausted."

"I am. We both are." She stood and moved closer then lowered her voice. "It took me a while to calm her down. She's doing much better now. Ben stopped by earlier." She shook her head, letting her know, without words, that Josie had died, then returned to her normal voice. "I think I'll go home."

Tresia grasped her hand and squeezed. "Thank you for staying."

"Of course."

"Be careful."

"Always am."

Tresia looked at Corianna after Lucy left the house, fighting to keep her emotions under control. "Devlin will find whoever did this. You can trust me on that. Have you slept?"

The woman shook her head.

"Have you eaten anything?"

"No."

"Let's get you taken care of, then. You need something in your belly."

Quickly, to keep herself busy more than anything else, Tresia rose from her seat and started making oatmeal. She couldn't think of anything else that would stick to the ribs and hopefully help Corianna sleep. She tried to keep up a steady stream of chatter to put the woman at ease.

A short time later, she set the bowl of oatmeal with brown sugar, cinnamon and cream in front of Corianna. "Here. Eat this."

Corianna dipped her spoon into the bowl and took a bite, then another and another. "It's good."

"That's the way my mother always made it. It's Avery's favorite."

Corianna seemed a little better after she finished the oatmeal but she looked exhausted, just as Lucy had. After her emotional night, the best thing for her would be to sleep.

"Let's get you into bed."

She took Corianna's hand and pulled her out of the chair then walked her into the guest room downstairs. She pulled down the covers then helped her undress down to her shift and settled her into bed. Noticing some blood stains on her dress, she said, "I'll wash your dress." She pulled the blankets over her. "You rest now."

"Thank you, Tresia." Corianna smiled at her, despite everything. "You never looked down on me because of what I do."

Like almost everyone else in town, she'd known Corianna for a very long time, but she also knew her circumstances and why she'd chosen to become a soiled dove. There weren't many jobs for women to support themselves and after her father disowned her and threw her out of his house, she had to do something. She'd tried to find decent jobs, but she was too young, or too inexperienced. In desperation, she turned to the only job she could get.

"You've always been kind to me."

Tresia patted her hand. "Call me if you need me."

She gathered Corianna's soiled clothes and closed the door. She stopped short in the parlor. Devlin was in danger, out to get a killer. If something happened to him…she didn't finish the thought. Instead, she forced herself to put one foot in front of the other. She had these stained clothes to wash. Avery would be awake shortly. It wouldn't do for her to see them. She headed into the kitchen to heat some wash water.

~

"Thanks for doing this." Devlin shook hands with Wyatt MacLean.

"Sure thing. I didn't know Josie but that doesn't matter. I don't like the idea of some madman running loose around here."

"That goes for us, too," he gestured toward Merrill as he mounted up. "We'll meet you over at Montaña del Trueno."

Devlin spurred Challenger and rode down the long drive, Merrill right beside him, and headed over to Crooked River, eventually coming to the gate that separated the farm from the main road. Merrill rode up to it and unhooked the rope that held it closed then opened the gate.

The fine hair on the back of Devlin's neck stood up as he passed through the gate. "Something's not right."

"What do you mean?"

"It's too quiet."

Merrill paused and looked around.

Devlin pulled the brim of his hat lower to block the sun and scanned the wide-open space. From here, he couldn't see the house or the barn, but he should have been able to hear something. Instead, he heard nothing—not even birds. "Be careful. Keep your eyes and ears open."

As he and Merrill rode up the meandering dirt drive, he kept looking around, his ears attuned to the absence of sound.

As he and Merrill drew closer to the small structure, his gaze swept over everything in the barnyard. There were horses in the paddock. They seemed skittish, as if they felt his unease. A sense of foreboding settled in his gut. He always trusted his gut. Call it intuition. Call it self-preservation. Call it whatever, but that feeling—and listening to his gut—had saved his life more than once.

Devlin slowly rested his hand on the handle of his pistol. "We're being watched."

"I feel it, too. Like eyes are boring into me." Merrill swept his gaze over the house.

Before he could say anything else, a muffled scream followed by a loud thump startled them both. The front door of Alfonso's home flew open amid a hail of bullets.

They both jumped from their horses and crouched down behind the water trough. Their horses took off.

Devlin crept around to the side of the horse trough, where he could get a better look. Ned Delany was standing in the doorway.

"It's Delany," he said after he crawled back and hunched next to Merrill. Bullets continued to hit the side of the trough, splashing water up. He kept his head low.

It surprised him that the outlaw was such a bad shot, seeming to just continue firing without taking aim, without careful consideration, wasting his ammunition, although if the goal was to keep them pinned down behind the water trough, he was doing a good job.

He glanced at his deputy. "He'll need to reload at some point. It'll be our best chance. Be ready."

Merrill gave a quick nod and pulled back the hammer of his pistol. "Ready as I'll every be."

Devlin removed his hat and moved it above the trough. More bullets slammed into the wood just above his head. There was a click of an empty chamber, once...twice...

"Now!" Devlin stood at the same instant as Merrill, all four pistols trained on the man in the doorway, who was trying desperately to reload his own guns. Several bullets dropped to the ground in his haste.

"Drop the guns, Delany."

The man had the audacity to laugh, but did as he was told,

dropping his pistols to the floor to join the bullets there. "Well, if it ain't Marshal Goodrich." His black eyes darted from him to Merrill, then back. "Heard you brought in old Smiley Burdette."

"I did. Big Bill Cassidy, too." Devlin didn't move. The outlaw was up to something. "Keep your hands where I can see them."

"Well, they was stupid. Lettin' themselves be taken in by the likes of you." He shook his head. "I ain't that stupid. You ain't gonna take me in." He quickly reached behind his back and pulled out a pistol.

Devlin pulled the trigger on both his guns. Merrill's went off as well.

The outlaw dropped where he stood, blood blossoming from the fatal wounds in his chest. He wore a perplexed expression, as if he couldn't believe he'd been shot as his eyes clouded over. He took his last breath and crumpled to the floor.

Devlin turned toward his deputy. "You all right?"

"Son of a bitch hit me." He held up his arm. Blood stained the sleeve.

"Let me see." He ripped the shirt sleeve away and inspected the wound. The bullet had only grazed Merrill's upper arm.

"See? It's nothing. Just a flesh wound." Merrill chuckled though the situation didn't warrant it. "Was it me or was he a bad shot?"

"He was a bad shot. Can't believe out of all the bullets he fired, he only hit you once. Must have gone to the school of more is better for all the good it did him."

"He missed you completely," Merrill said with a laugh.

"Check and see if there is anyone in the barn. It looked to me like he was waiting for someone." He let out a sharp, shrill whistle. In moments, Challenger, along with Merrill's horse, galloped toward him from around the side of the house. Merrill quickly caught their reins and tied them to the porch railing before heading toward the barn, gun drawn.

Devlin jumped up to the porch, stepped over the dead man, and went into the house.

What met his eyes made his blood boil. Both Alfonso and Damita were gagged and tied together on the floor. Bruises marred their faces and from what he could see, Damita's arms. Her eye was swollen shut and nearly purple. Her nightgown was torn, revealing her skin…and more bruises. But they were alive.

They stared up at him in relief.

Quickly, he set about removing the gags.

Alfonso let loose with a string of angry cuss words in Spanish, most of which Devlin had heard before but a few he hadn't. He worked to untie them.

"That *demonio* broke into the house this morning before dawn, guns drawn, threatening to kill us." When he was free, Alfonso gathered his wife close and kissed her on the forehead. Tears made his dark eyes shine and his split lip was swollen. "We were caught unaware. Hell, we were sleeping. He dragged us from bed and tied us up, though we both fought him until he hit me in the head with the butt of his pistol. I went down like a sack of old potatoes." He touched the spot on his head gingerly, winced, then tightened his arms around Damita, his anger palpable. "I hope you killed him."

"Yes, he's dead."

"Who the hell is he?"

"Ned Delany. He killed Josie earlier this morning. He was looking for a place to hide, probably knowing a posse would be coming after him. Your place seemed as likely as any." He didn't say they were lucky to be alive. By the expression on Alfonso's face as he rocked his wife in his arms, he already knew. It might take a bit of time before that reality sunk in. He'd be there when it did. "Can you stand?"

Alfonso nodded and tried but failed. He'd been sitting too long with his hands and legs bound.

He patted Alfonso's shoulder. "Just sit here for a minute."

Devlin looked down at Damita. She'd yet to say anything, but there was a look in her eye he'd seen before when one suffered trauma. "He's dead now, Damita. He won't hurt you anymore."

Her gaze rose to his face as if she'd finally heard his words before every muscle in her body lost their strength. He grabbed her before she fell forward, lifting her effortlessly in his arms, quickly bringing her to the small sofa in front of the fireplace. Alfonso followed, crawling to the couch, softly whispering to her as he gently caressed her face.

"Dear God!" Merrill exclaimed as he entered the house and saw the condition of his friends, people he'd probably known all his life.

Devlin warned him with a quick shake of his head. The deputy closed his mouth but the expression on his face clearly said that if Delany wasn't already dead, he would be. "Did you find anyone else?"

Merrill shook his head, unable, it seemed, to take his gaze from the Serranos. "They need to see Doc Hart."

"Yes. Hitch up their buckboard and we'll bring them into town." He jerked his thumb toward the door and the dead man on the porch. "See if you can find some canvas or burlap to wrap him in."

Merrill scowled, unusual for him. "Let the wolves have him. It's more than he deserves."

. "There's a bounty on him. We can collect the money and give it to Alfonso and Damita."

After a moment, Merrill inclined his head and left the house.

Devlin gathered blankets and pillows to cushion the back of the buckboard to make the ride a little more comfortable. The last thing he wanted to do was hurt the couple even more.

The rumble of wagon wheels over hard packed dirt and the steady clip-clop of horses' hooves drew his attention. He stepped outside as Merrill brought the buckboard to a halt in front of the porch.

His deputy jumped down and grabbed a piece of canvas from the back of the wagon. He threw it over the dead man then dragged him away from the front door by his feet.

Devlin dumped the pillows and blankets into the back of the wagon then sprang into the bed and fashioned a comfortable cocoon for Alfonso and Damita. He looked up to see Merrill standing beside the wagon.

"I'll need you to ride over to Montaña del Trueno. Let everyone know there's no longer a need for a posse."

"Sure thing, Boss." He looked at the blankets in the back of the buckboard. "I'll help you with Alfonso and Damita then head on over." The deputy started toward the porch then stopped and turned toward him. "You gonna be all right?"

Devlin nodded. "Eventually." He stared at the ground, frustrated. "I hate this."

"I know. It ain't easy to kill a man."

His head shot up. "That's where you're wrong, Merrill. Killing him was easy. Much too easy. No, it's Alfonso and Damita I'm worried about, not to mention Josie's girls."

Merrill nodded his understanding then went into the house.

Did his deputy truly understand? He wasn't so sure.

CHAPTER 14

Tresia looked up from the sketch on the table before her when the kitchen door opened. Devlin stood there, his hands hanging loosely at his sides. Pain filled his eyes and was repeated in the grimace on his face. There was blood on his shirt, the brownish stain long since dried.

Despite telling her not to worry, she had been worried, though her anxiety had lessened after Merrill had stopped by to take Corianna back to Josie's house and let her know what happened at the Serrano's. Her worry lessened even further when Nate and Rafael came by the house to give her updates and let her know Devlin was all right.

Still, she was concerned for him. Devlin was a marshal. Hunting down bad men was part of his job, but seeing what had happened to Josie and the Serranos had surely affected him. "Are you all right?"

He didn't answer her question, but one look at his face said he wasn't. "Where's Avery?"

"She's asleep." She put down the pen in her hand as she rose from her chair and took a few steps toward him. She didn't tell him that Avery had been upset that he hadn't been there for breakfast nor that she was even more upset that he hadn't come home for dinner. He didn't need to hear that. Not now, when he seemed to be struggling.

He gave a slight nod, but still didn't move out of the doorway, as if he was frozen in place. She reached out for him, laying her hand on his forearm. He flinched, something he'd never done before. She ignored his reaction, knowing him, sensing what this day had done to him.

"I'm sorry," she whispered, even though the words couldn't possibly help.

He gave her a look she'd never seen before, adding to her concern for him. There was so much pain in that look, etched into the fine lines around his eyes and mouth, that it hurt her, too.

As he seemed unable to move on his own, she took his hand and led him toward the kitchen table to the seat she'd just occupied. She made him sit then got a bottle of brandy from the cabinet, had second thoughts, and chose the whiskey instead. She pulled a glass from the cabinet, her fingers suddenly awkward and stiff and poured some of the liquor, filling the tumbler halfway then set it before him.

He glanced at her then at the whiskey and gave her a slight nod before downing the liquor in one swallow. "Did Merrill stop by and tell you what happened?"

"He did. Nate and Rafael, too."

"I killed a man. I should have remorse for what I did," he said, his voice reflecting the pain on his face and in his eyes. "Delany had to be stopped before he killed again. Merrill says he deserved what he got, that Alfonso and Damita might have been next. I think about Josie, lying dead. She was trying to protect her girls." He looked at her, as if not quite understanding. "How can one human being treat another so cruelly, like their lives don't matter?"

Her heart in her throat, she sat beside him and grasped his

hand, entwining her fingers with his, offering comfort though the sentiment fell far short of what he needed. "Tell me."

And he did, the words seemingly pulled from deep within, his voice much hoarser than usual, telling her so much more than what Merrill, Nate, and Rafael had told her earlier. For a big, brave man, Merrill had had a hard time describing what he'd seen, too. What a close call Alfonso and Damita had. "They're with Doctor Ben right now. I stayed with them for a little while. Ben insisted they stay the night so he could keep an eye on Damita. She didn't lose the baby, but she's been through so much…" He didn't finish the sentence though he didn't have to. She already suspected there was still a chance Damita might lose the child or go into early labor. And knowing that was how Hannah had lost her life, she knew he was reliving that nightmare. Her heart went out to him.

Devlin stared at the tumbler. "I had Lucy come and take pictures of Delany so I can collect the bounty before I turned him over to the undertaker." He glanced at her then and let out a sigh. "I'll be giving the bounty to Alfonso and Damita."

Tresia did the only thing she could do at that moment. She rose from her seat, walked behind him, and wrapped her arms around his neck, offering such little comfort for the things he'd seen. His hands came up and grasped her arms, as if holding on to her for dear life, for sanity.

"I'm sorry," she whispered again, near his ear this time and held him tighter, pouring all her compassion and understanding into him, letting him feel her warmth. "I was worried about you. I was afraid…you wouldn't come home." She probably shouldn't have said it, but she wouldn't take it back.

He grasped her arms a little tighter, though not enough to hurt, only enough to let her know he'd been worried about the same thing. "I'll always come home, Tresia. Always."

She pressed her cheek against his and just held him, knowing his words were a lie. He might say it and he might believe it, but they both knew there were no guarantees.

"I know my job is dangerous. I know there are times when I'm in harm's way. But I wouldn't change what I do. I'd just much rather talk someone down with logic than take them down with guns."

He could have so easily lost his life today and instead of holding him now, someone else—perhaps Merrill or Nate or even Doctor Ben—might have been holding her, telling her that he'd never come home again. The mere thought brought tears to her eyes. For Avery. For herself and the overwhelming feelings of love she had for him. She hadn't meant for it to happen, but truly, she hadn't been able to stop herself from falling in love with him.

She continued to just hold him, offering what little comfort she could. She didn't speak as there was no need for words now. Instead, she hoped her warmth and compassion could soothe his troubled mind.

She felt it the moment his tension eased, though he still held onto her arms and then he moved, grasping one of her hands and bringing it up to his mouth to kiss her soft skin.

"You're all that's good in the world, Tresia. Sweet. Honest. Kind." His voice was hoarse, so much more than usual, as he turned his head slightly, enough so he could touch his lips to hers.

It was the gentlest of kisses, but it was filled with so many emotions, almost too many to name, and then he gently removed her arms from around his neck and stood, turning toward her, even though the chair was between them. He moved it with his foot then took a step closer and drew her into his arms, holding her tight, tighter than she had held him, as if she were his anchor, that if he let go, he would be cast out to sea, adrift on a tide of loneliness and heartache.

She didn't hesitate to rise up on her toes to seek his mouth, molding her lips to his.

He deepened the kiss, which thrilled her. It had been a long time since she'd been touched like this and she felt it deep in her heart, a swift, rising flood of want and need, so much so that her knees grew weak. The need to give this man comfort overpowered her, the urge to wrap her arms around him and take his pain grew as his mouth moved over hers. Blood rushed through her veins, the erratic pounding echoing in her ears. She shouldn't want this, but she did.

He broke the kiss and pulled away a little, his startling blue-gray eyes so much darker, like thunderclouds in the distance. He opened his mouth—perhaps to request forgiveness for kissing her. There was no need for an apology. Or any words at all. In the bright light of day there might be, but not now. She wanted to give him solace from what he'd seen and done, to let him know that everything would be all right. And he needed to take it from her so his healing could begin.

He held her a little tighter, his eyes warm but questioning, before he lifted her in his arms and brought her not upstairs to his room, but to the guest bedroom on the first floor, the room where Corianna had rested before Merrill took her home. He laid her gently on the bed then just stood there for a moment, as if deciding whether or not he should join her.

Tresia took the decision from him. She held out her hand, a silent but unmistakable request.

He took her hand, entwining his fingers with hers for a moment before he released her to unbuckle his gun belt and lay it on a chair in the corner of the room. His vest came next, the shiny star pinned to the leather winking in the moonlight streaming in through the window. Lastly, he toed off his boots then just stood beside the bed, hesitating, his heated gaze, the intensity strong, warming her from the inside out.

She held out her hand once again.

As if finally making his decision, he stretched out on the bed alongside her, his mouth quickly taking possession of hers.

Tresia let out a little sigh, feeling the weight of his body pressed against hers, the touch of his mouth on hers, the pressure building and building, until she was drowning in it, his tongue slipping between her lips to slide against her own.

He broke the kiss then nudged at the lacy collar of her blouse with his lips and teeth, moving the fabric away so he could taste the tender spot beneath her ear, sending a thrill coursing straight to her core, before he deftly unbuttoned the tiny row of buttons, his big, blunt fingers surprisingly dexterous. At this moment, she wouldn't have cared if he simply pulled the fabric apart, scattering all those tiny little buttons to the four winds—as long as he was touching her.

He moved slightly, taking his warmth. "Too many clothes," he murmured against her throat, even as he rose from the bed, bringing her with him. "I need to feel all of you. Every blessed inch."

"Yes."

His mouth came down hard on hers, his lips moving over hers, urging hers to open so he could taste her while his hands made short work of unbuckling the belt around her waist, tossing it on the floor. He drew down her skirt, all while his mouth and lips and tongue played havoc with her senses.

She'd never been undressed by a man before, not even with Brett, which should have shocked her, but curiously, didn't. She would have assumed Devlin would be clumsy as there were a lot of buttons, but he wasn't. He was gentle. Experienced. Fast, yet slow at the same time. As he slid her blouse from her shoulders, his mouth and hands replaced the material, skimming along her skin, awakening feelings she had forced away for much too long. He removed her corset cover then reached behind her, and loosened the ties of her corset. Unhooking the garment, he let it fall to the floor. He pulled her chemise over her head then tossed it on top of her other clothes then slipped the pins from her hair, loosening the tight bun at the back of her head. He thrust his hands into her shining locks, loosening them even more before gently laying the soft strands over her shoulders.

She was naked, except for her stockings, and waited while he removed his shirt and trousers and drawers, the moonlight gleaming on his skin, glinting off the dark hair that covered his chest, revealing his broad shoulders, lean waist and long legs. Her eyes opened wide, trying to see everything in the semi-darkness, as he lowered her to the mattress, his weight and warmth so very welcome.

His breathing deepened, as did hers, as his mouth took possession of hers. She felt a rush of passion deep in her soul. He took his time, exploring her, his hands seemingly everywhere— his fingers skimming along her throat, her earlobe, her shoulders, her collarbone…and lower, followed closely by his lips, until his tongue swept across the taut peak of one of her breasts, making it harder. He pulled it into his mouth and suckled gently.

She felt that gentle tug all the way to her toes, which curled inside her stockings, and let out a small whimper, the feelings simply too exquisite to tamp down.

It had been much too long since she'd been touched like this, but her body hadn't forgotten. Already, there was a tightening deep in her core, a tension that couldn't be denied. And she wouldn't have denied it even if she could.

"Tresia," he whispered as his hand replaced his mouth at her breast and he sought her lips once more, as if he couldn't get enough of her kisses, which was fine with her.

She couldn't get enough of him, loving the way his lips clung to her own, the thrust of his tongue mimicking what he would soon do. She brought her hands up around his neck, pulling him closer, her fingers tangling in the soft curls at his nape.

And then his hand slipped lower, moving away from her breast, slowly caressing her belly, the pads of his fingertips a little rough on her skin. And still, she didn't mind. She wanted this. Wanted him with every fiber of her being.

He broke the pressure of his mouth on hers and left a trail of kisses to her breast then pulled the taut peak into his mouth to suckle gently even as he moved his hand lower still, coming to rest on her mons. He didn't go any lower, and she opened her legs a little wider, granting him access without a word, though there was no silencing her sharp indrawn breath or the fact that she lifted her hips into his hand. She couldn't stop the impatience that skittered through her.

He chuckled lightly, the vibration of which reverberated throughout her entire body, tickling her, adding to the tension building within her. "Patience," he whispered against her breast but she wasn't having any of that.

She was done with patience. She knew what she wanted—to feel him inside her—and she wanted it now so much so that she grabbed his hand and placed it where she wanted it, at the juncture of her thighs.

He obliged by slipping his fingers through the springy curls surrounding that sacred place, parting her folds to find the very core of her. Tresia let out a sigh as his fingers slid against the wetness gathered there, then groaned as he slipped one finger into her, then another, stretching her, filling her.

She was ready. More than ready, her body preparing for the physical explosion she could feel building. And then it happened. Faster than she thought possible as his fingers moved in and out of her in a slow, then fast rhythm, and she couldn't stop the shout of satisfaction that escaped her as her body pulsed around his fingers, her nails digging into his back.

She stiffened, just a bit, a little embarrassed she'd lost control so completely, so quickly, then melted as he moved slightly and settled between her thighs. He pushed into her, inch by incredible inch, stretching her to accommodate his width and girth and then he started moving in her, again slowly as if he didn't want to hurt her, perhaps knowing how big he was and how long it had been for her. And she didn't care how long it had been. She wanted this. Now. Her hips rose up to meet his, searching for the pure joy she knew they could share.

And then all thinking ceased, and she was left to just feel—the heat of him, the heaviness, the exquisite building of bliss waiting to explode again. She could feel it happening as her nails dug into the taut flesh of his backside, urging him faster. His strokes became longer, stronger, as he nearly pulled all the way out of her only to push back in, his whispered words telling her she was beautiful, telling her she felt so good, telling her he needed her as he built momentum so she could touch the stars once more.

The horrors of his day didn't exactly disappear but became more bearable within the heat of Tresia's body. He had thought her comforting before, soothing his soul in ways he'd never imagined, but this—feeling her warmth all around him, hearing her little cries of satisfaction—this is what he needed—and wanted. The comfort was still there, but there was so much more.

He hadn't lied when he told her she was all that's good in the world.

He felt her stiffen as he plunged into her, then heard her cry out, not in pain, but in joy, and finally, finally, he could let himself go. He pushed into her, harder, faster, the muscles in his arms bunching, his heart racing, until he couldn't control himself any longer and spilled his seed into her warm, willing body.

He didn't speak. There were no words. It was so much more than mere satisfaction. So much more than the comfort she offered, the heat of her body pulsating around him. He stayed within her warmth, finding her mouth once more to tangle his tongue with hers.

And though he didn't want to, he slowly withdrew from her, and rolled to his side, bringing her with him, his body relaxed, his mind no longer shadowed, or filled with self-loathing and guilt.

"Devlin?"

He didn't respond, simply held her tighter, her body conforming to his, letting her warmth and understanding seep into him.

"I should go," she whispered, her warm breath ruffling the hair on his chest. "Before Avery wakes up."

He stiffened then forced himself to relax and dropped a kiss on her forehead. "I'd rather you stay. Avery expects to see you in the kitchen when she gets up."

She snuggled a little closer and rested her hand on his cheek. "People will talk."

"They will." He laughed sardonically. "They'll talk anyway. Gossip spreads faster than a prairie fire around here." He turned slightly so he could face her in the semi-darkness. If there were worry lines on her face, he couldn't see them, though he did hear a touch of anxiety in her voice. "But I don't think it'll be about you staying here." He paused as his fingers gently caressed her arm, trying to see into her eyes in the darkness, though he knew he couldn't. "I'm not ready to let you go." He molded his lips to hers before he broke the kiss. "I need you, Tresia."

He did need her. And not just now. She was his light in the darkness. The comfort he so desperately craved but hadn't known he needed. "Stay with me." He claimed her mouth in a kiss and when she wrapped her arms around him, his heart lightened.

CHAPTER 15

*D*elvin awoke to the sound of birdsong and bright sunlight shining in his face. It took all of two minutes to realize he wasn't in his own bed and to remember why.

He'd made love to Tresia Morgan.

Not once or twice, but three times.

Tresia was a wonderful, loving, generous woman. And more.

He smiled as he stretched out his hand, fully expecting her to still be there. He touched an empty pillow. He opened his eyes as he turned his head and stared at the place she should have been. He ran his hand over the empty space. Still warm. She hadn't been gone long.

He rose and dressed quickly, picking up his clothes from the floor where he'd dropped them. Barefoot, he wandered to the kitchen then stopped in the doorway and leaned against the door jamb just to watch her, the smell of freshly brewed coffee drifting to his nose.

She'd twisted her long auburn hair into a tight bun at the back of her head again. He'd rather see it as he did last night, the silky tresses flowing over her shoulders, covering her breasts, the sweet fragrance of honeysuckle subtle yet still staying with him.

His gaze shifted from her hair to the white blouse she wore, which was slightly wrinkled, probably from lying crumpled on the floor. His focus lowered to her backside and hips, which swayed as she bustled about, preparing breakfast. His smile widened. Her hips may be swaying gently now, but last night, they'd been bucking to meet him stroke for stroke. "Good morning."

She jumped, startled, the egg in her hand dropping to the floor, then she turned around quickly to face him. Spots of color adorned her cheeks, but her eyes sparkled, the violet color deeper, richer, more vibrant. "Oh, Devlin!" And quickly on the heels of that, she apologized. "I'm sorry."

"For what?" He gestured to the shattered egg on the floor. "Breaking an egg?"

"No, for…for last night." Her voice was much more strained than usual, as if she fought tears, though why she should, he couldn't begin to fathom.

"Why? Because you offered me comfort? Because I took what you offered?"

She nodded, those eyes of hers growing darker still.

"I'm not sorry, Tresia. You knew what I needed. What we both needed. What I think we both wanted." His voice softened as he approached her, then caressed her cheek with his thumb. "Are you really sorry?"

She leaned into his caress and let out a sigh. "No. I just—" Her mouth opened and closed several times before she inhaled deeply. "I don't normally…there hasn't been anyone since Brett."

"I didn't think there had been." He didn't say that there had been no one since Hannah. Surely, she must know that. He wasn't a man given to visiting bawdy houses unless it was for official purposes. The act of making love was to be revered and shared with someone special. Like she was. He tilted his head to the side. "Are you embarrassed by what we did?"

"A little." The pink glow on her face deepened, and she hesitated before she spoke. "More so by what I did. I'm not a wanton woman, Devlin. I'm afraid my behavior was not appropriate."

He laughed. Actually couldn't help himself, before he cradled her face in both his hands and lowered his head to brush his lips against hers. "Appropriate or not, I don't think you're wanton, Tresia. I think you're passionate and giving and much too generous." And to prove his words, he settled his mouth on hers again, kissing her deeply this time. She didn't resist at all. Indeed, her hands came up to rest against his chest as she leaned into him, the egg on the floor forgotten for the moment.

"Oooh! You're kissing again!" A small voice, one filled with unbridled happiness and just a touch of wonder, interrupted the kiss.

Devlin released her immediately and backed up a step or two, his face now warm. He turned quickly to cover his embarrassment that he'd been caught, once again, kissing Tresia and eyed his daughter standing in the doorway. She looked adorable in her frilly cotton nightgown, her curls twisted up in rags, Cecily in her arms with rags in her hair, too, before he took a few steps in her direction. She didn't seem upset in the least that he had been kissing Tresia. In fact, she was grinning.

"I'm gonna kiss you, too!" He laughed, and lifted Avery up high, smothering her face with little kisses, making her giggle.

"Stop it, Daddy!" she squealed.

"Are you sure?"

She giggled a little more and presented her face to him, upon which he promptly blew raspberries against her chubby cheek then eased her down to the chair. "I think we're having flapjacks this morning." He poured milk into her glass, then grabbed the syrup from the pantry.

Avery's eyes lit up. "I love flapjacks!"

"They'll be ready in a few minutes." Tresia hummed as she worked, happy it seemed. She flipped the flapjacks like an expert after a few moments then placed two on a plate for Avery, four for him, and brought them to the table.

"Thank you." He accepted both plates.

She smiled at him then went back to the stove and spooned more batter into the skillet.

When she finally took her seat, two flapjacks on her plate, he looked across the table at her. There was still a telltale blush on her cheeks, but she seemed to have gotten over her earlier embarrassment. There was nothing wrong with what she had given him when he needed it most and maybe she was beginning to realize that.

She caught him looking at her and smiled and a realization dawned. This is what he wanted to see, every day, for the rest of his life. It seeped into his head, not with a jolt but with a gentle, peaceful flow that filled his heart.

He should ask her to marry him.

The thought didn't startle him despite the fact he'd never thought to marry again. Instead, it made his heart beat a little harder in his chest and happiness, that elusive emotion he never thought he'd experience again, rippled through him. Yes, he would ask her to marry him. He only hoped she would say yes.

He finished his flapjacks, swallowed the last of his coffee, and placed his napkin on the table then hesitated. Duty called though he'd much rather spend the day here with Avery...and his future wife, if she'd have him.

"As much as I don't want to, I have to go to work," he announced as he pushed his plate away and rose from his seat then strolled out of the kitchen.

He returned shortly, buckling his gun belt low around his hips. "What are your plans for today?"

Tresia stopped with her coffee cup halfway to her mouth. "I thought Avery and I would go over to the town hall and look at the rooms Mayor Tisdale said we could have for the lending library, then stop at Goldwater's for some fresh vegetables, and

Mr. Crandall's to get a roast for dinner. Maybe we'll pick up some apple tarts from Sweet Somethings." She lowered her voice even as she lowered her coffee cup. "If you think it's all right, I'd like to see Alfonso and Damita at Doctor Ben's."

"That would be very nice. I'm sure they would appreciate seeing you." He shifted his weight from one leg to the other then broached a subject he'd been hesitant about. "People will have a lot of questions for you today, Tresia. They'll assume—" He didn't finish his sentence, seeing the color on her cheeks spread to encompass her entire face. Even the tips of her ears turned red and he assumed she thought he was referring to them sharing a bed. He quickly eased her mind. "No, Tresia. I'm not talking about that." He smiled, hoping to ease her anxiety though his worries were just beginning. "I'm quite certain word of Ned Delany's death has already spread. People, those you know well and those you don't, including the publisher of the Serenity Times, will assume you know the details of what happened yesterday." His words drifted off, remembering that Avery was still at the table, though she seemed more interested in pretending to feed her doll than what the adults were talking about.

Tresia nodded, though her face remained red. "Yes, of course. I understand."

"I would prefer it if you didn't talk to anyone, especially Mr. Wagner, or any other reporter who comes here, and they will come. Maybe not today or tomorrow, but eventually, they will. Don't speak to them at all if you can help it. They'll try everything to get you to say something you don't want to." He paused, his gaze roaming over her face. He wanted to protect her from invasive questions. She'd never had to deal with that before, but he had.

"I hadn't planned to. I would never betray a confidence, Devlin."

"I know you wouldn't, but some people won't take no for an answer. They'll be persistent."

She stiffened as her gaze rose to his. "You're frightening me, Devlin."

"I'm sorry. I don't mean to." He paused again, and his voice gentled. "Just be careful."

"I will."

He nodded in her direction then held his arms wide toward Avery. "Come give Daddy a kiss."

Avery climbed up on the chair then jumped into his open arms.

"You be a good girl for Miss Tresia."

"Okay, Daddy." She gave him a kiss on the cheek. "Be safe."

"Always am." He gave her another kiss, this time on her forehead, then lowered her back to her chair. He turned toward Tresia still at the kitchen table, then strolled in her direction, a swagger in his step. "I'll see you tonight," he said, then dropped a quick kiss on her utterly kissable mouth.

He left the house with a touch of uncertainty, not happy about leaving Tresia and Avery alone. He stopped on the front porch as had become his habit and noticed there seemed to be more people walking up and down the streets. More carriages, too. He recognized some but not all. His lips pressed together in annoyance. It had begun and it hadn't even been twenty-four hours since he'd killed Ned Delany. He concentrated on keeping his temper under control, then headed over to his office, ready though not quite willing to take on whatever the day brought.

Two minutes after entering the Marshal's Office through the back door, he wished he'd stayed in bed …preferably with Tresia. A chorus of raised voices met his ears. Citizens of the town peppered Merrill and Rafael with questions. It was going to be a long day.

≈

"Are you ready?" Tresia slipped her drawstring purse over her wrist then added the shopping basket to her arm as well.

Avery nodded as she tied the laces of one of her shoes in a perfect bow, an accomplishment she'd just learned. She was pretty proud of herself and Tresia praised her. "Good job, sweetheart."

Avery beamed, picked up Cecily then clasped Tresia's hand as they left the house and walked over to the town hall.

As soon as they stepped inside and she saw all the people gathered around Mayor Tisdale, demanding answers about what happened to Josie, the Serranos, and Ned Delany, and she realized Devlin had been correct when he said people would want to know everything. The mayor caught her eye then motioned for her to join him. She shook her head, held Avery's hand a little tighter, and rushed up to the second floor, where the rooms for the lending library would be.

She pulled a small notebook, the one containing the drawings from her last visit to the rooms, from her drawstring purse, and started sketching. "I think we can fit four rows of shelves in here," she murmured as she drew.

"I think so as well."

The voice was not one she'd expected to hear and she jumped, as skittish as a newborn foal, then turned quickly to see the mayor now standing in the doorway, one hand on the door jamb, the other on his chest, like he suffered from indigestion after eating a heavy meal. "Oh, Mayor Tisdale! You startled me."

"I'm sorry for that, Mrs. Morgan. I didn't mean to." He shrugged as if scaring her didn't matter and remained in the doorway. "I've been getting questions all morning," he said without even a greeting. "What do you know?"

"About what?"

"Come now, Mrs. Morgan." He gestured to Avery. "You take care of the marshal's daughter. Surely, he must have talked to you about what happened yesterday. Taken you into his confidence, as it were."

Tresia tucked her notebook away. "You'll have to ask the marshal any questions you might have." She held out her hand to Avery. "Come on, sweetheart. We need to go."

Avery slipped her hand in hers as they moved toward the doorway, but the mayor didn't move. His big body blocked the way. "You must know something."

"I don't, Mayor. Devlin and I do not discuss his job." She moved a bit closer to him, standing up to him. He'd never been a bully, had always been friendly toward her, but then again, he'd never had such mayhem in his town before.

He smirked, a light coming into his eyes, as if he suspected she did more than just care for the marshal's daughter. "Devlin, is it?"

Her face heated. "Yes. Devlin. That is his name. Now, if you'll excuse us, please."

He stared at her for the longest time, then finally moved his big belly out of her way. She and Avery practically ran out of the town hall.

It was the same at Polly's bakery and Goldwater's, where everyone she met, the shop owners as well as their customers, asked her questions, too, wanting to know something, everything, forcing her to change her plans. Considering what she'd already been subjected to by people she knew and liked, she wouldn't visit Alfonso and Damita but simply go home after picking up the roast.

But there was no escaping the rumors and gossip. It spread through the town like wildfire, unrestrained, blazing uncontrolled, as stories about what happened at Josie's and Crooked River were repeated, usually incorrectly. Everyone knew of Josie's passing. Some rejoiced, thinking she'd repaid her perceived sins with her life and that her house would close while others were saddened by that thought. There was plenty to be said about Devlin and Merrill killing Ned Delany, too, most of that untrue as well.

Simply walking through the town square on the way to the butcher shop, people stopped her, even those she didn't know well, wanting to know what happened. They assumed, like the mayor, that Marshal Goodrich took her into his confidence, considering she was taking care of his daughter, as if one thing had anything to do with the other. Of course, there were innuendos as well, putting the marshal and her together, as if they knew or suspected she hadn't left the marshal's bed all night, which was most likely just her own conscience talking. With the hours she kept, no one could know she didn't sleep in her boarding house bed.

She ignored everything as best she could, repeating over and over again that they should ask the marshal for details of what happened. No one seemed happy with that answer and continued to press her for details she refused to divulge.

"Heard the marshal killed Ned Delany," Mr. Crandall said as he wrapped the roast she'd just purchased in butcher paper and handed it over the glass counter to her, though he didn't let go. "Heard about Josie, too. And the Serranos. Do you know what happened?"

"No, I don't." Frustrated, losing her patience, not to mention becoming angry, she reached for the package, but Mr. Crandall didn't let go, as if he were holding the roast hostage so he could get some answers from her. "You'll have to ask at the Marshal's Office," she repeated for the twentieth time at least. "My roast, please."

He finally let go. She dropped it into the shopping basket. "Come on, Avery. Let's go home."

They left the butcher shop, but didn't get very far before she heard her name shouted from behind her.

"Mrs. Morgan!"

Tresia stopped in the middle of the raised sidewalk, making

others try to avoid her and Avery, whose hand she held. She turned quickly to see Mr. Wagner, the owner and publisher of the Serenity Times, running toward her. A groan escaped her. He was the last person she wanted to see.

A bit breathless, his face red and perspiring, he caught up with her. "Thank...you...for stopping," he puffed, then quickly whipped out a small notebook from his pocket. "What can you tell me about Marshal Goodrich's shootout with Ned Delany?"

A little taken aback by the abrupt question, it took her a moment to gather her wits and tamp down her frustration, which was growing by the second. "I think you should ask the marshal about that."

The man grinned. "I did. He wouldn't talk to me. He kept saying he had no comment."

She smiled at that. Yes, that did seem like something Devlin would say. "If he won't talk to you, what makes you think I will? What makes you think I know anything at all?"

He glanced down at Avery and smirked. "Everyone knows you're taking care of his daughter." His gaze rose to hers. "Everyone knows you're...close." There was an unspoken message in his eyes, as if he were intimating that she wasn't just taking care of Avery, but that she was taking care of the marshal, too, and not in the way that was respectable.

Blood rushed to her face and her entire body flushed. "Mr. Wagner—"

"Just give me one statement, Mrs. Morgan," he insisted. "This is big news. Ned Delany, wanted for murder and so much more, dead, killed by our very own Marshal Goodrich. He'll be even more famous than he is now!"

She took umbrage at his statement. It was obvious he didn't know Devlin at all. Devlin didn't want to be famous. He'd never wanted that. Fame and fortune could go to someone else. He just wanted to do his job and be good at it, having a respectable reputation was all he needed. She knew that and admired him for it. "I have nothing to say, Mr. Wagner."

There was something else as well, something that occurred to her as Mr. Wagner stared at her, waiting for her to make a statement, which she wouldn't. It had been different when her friends and casual acquaintances had asked about what happened, but Mr. Wagner was a newspaper man, a reporter. Devlin had specifically warned her about him. A story in a small-town newspaper might not mean much, but when other newspapers picked it up, which they sometimes did, who knows how far and wide the story could go?

"I have nothing to say except that you should talk to Marshal Goodrich." Her hand tightened around Avery's and she made to move away from the man, but he was persistent. He stepped in front of her again. She didn't know Vann Wagner well. They didn't travel in the same social circles though he had come into the store several times to purchase items for his house or his office. She had always considered him a nice man, but that was changing—fast. "Mr. Wagner, if you'll please just step aside, I'd like to take Miss Avery home."

"Just one statement, Mrs. Morgan."

"Please leave us alone, Mr. Wagner."

And yet, he wouldn't. He did step aside, but as soon as she started walking, he followed, shouting questions, making a nuisance of himself as well as frightening Avery. She picked Avery up then tried to maneuver around the people on the sidewalk, some of whom were stopping and staring.

Her heart pounded a little harder as she quickened her pace, nearly running with Avery in her arms, the groceries in her basket almost toppling to the ground. Perspiration made her chest clammy beneath her chemise and sweat trickled between her breasts. Breathing became a little more difficult between running and the sudden onset of panic. And she was panicking.

"Why is that man following us?" Avery hugged her more tightly, her voice echoing her fear. "Is he a bad man?"

"No, sweetheart, he's not a bad man," Tresia said, trying desperately to keep the panic and fear from her own voice. She didn't want to upset Avery any more than she already was. She glanced at her as she quickened her pace a little more. Avery's eyes were huge in her face and watery, like she could cry at any moment. She just hoped that this incident didn't revert her back to the quiet child she'd been. She rather liked the chatterbox. "He's just persistent."

"Tresia!"

She heard her name called again and glanced around, fear making her mouth dry. There, walking out of the Wagon Wheel, was Lucy, accompanied by her brothers, Teddy and Esteban. Just the sight of them made her knees weak and the knot in her stomach started to unravel, just a bit. Still, she held Avery a little tighter.

She rushed toward them, finally feeling safe, though still rattled by Mr. Wagner's behavior. "Lucy!" She huffed, trying to draw air into her lungs. "Thank God!"

Lucy took one look at her and frowned even as she extended a hand to help steady her. "What's wrong? You're shaking like a leaf."

Her throat constricted as she tried to tamp down fear-born tears. When she could finally speak, she said, "He wouldn't leave me alone."

"Who?" Teddy and Esteban asked at the same time, both, it seemed, ready to defend her.

"Vann Wagner. He wants me to give a statement about Devlin and what happened with Ned Delany." She gulped in air as her panic decreased just being with friends she trusted. "He actually chased us down when I refused to answer any of his questions."

"Not to worry, Tresia." Teddy pressed her arm, glanced at his brother then further down the sidewalk, where the person in question suddenly stopped and turned around quickly, possibly realizing that Tresia wasn't alone and vulnerable anymore. "We'll take care of it," he said then looked at his sister. "Lucy, why don't you take her home?"

"I think that's a fine idea." She took Avery from her arms and held the girl close to her heart. "Come on. I'll make you a nice cup of coffee."

"Thank you."

"And I'll stay with you until Devlin comes home."

Gratitude made the tears she tried so hard to keep at bay flood her eyes, especially now that her panic was dissipating and her heartbeat was returning to normal. Her knees weren't as weak anymore, either, but she didn't trust herself to walk any distance alone. "I love you, Lucy Hart. You're a good friend."

Lucy smiled. "The *best* friend." She hooked her hand into the crook of Tresia's arm and walked her home, leaving Teddy and Esteban to take care of Mr. Wagner.

CHAPTER 16

*D*evlin slammed into the house, his anxiety as well as his temper high. Killing Ned Delany had been necessary, considering the man had wanted both him and Merrill dead. Alfonso and Damita probably wouldn't have survived the encounter, either.

He knew doing so would attract all kinds of attention, but he'd expected that attention to be on him and his deputy, not Tresia and his daughter. He'd barely kept his anger under control after Teddy and Esteban Silva came to the Marshal's Office and told him what had happened with the newspaper man.

"Tresia!"

"In here." Her voice came from the kitchen and he stopped in the doorway to just look at her, relief running rampant throughout his body. She stood at the table, peeling potatoes. She didn't look worse for wear, but her face was pale, highlighting the shadows under her beautiful, pansy-colored eyes.

"Are you all right?" He crossed the room and took her in his arms, regardless of the peeler still in her hand, and held her close, wanting to protect her from everything. "Is Avery?"

"We're fine. A little shaken, but we're all right." She spoke into his chest, clinging to him like he was the only thing holding her to this earth. She was still trembling. He could feel it as he held her in his arms and that just made his anger flare hotter. Vann Wagner had a lot to answer for.

"Avery was scared—so was I—but I was able to calm her down. She's napping now."

"Oh, thank God!" He inhaled the sweet honeysuckle scent of her hair and just held her tighter then dropped a kiss on the top of her head. "Teddy and Esteban stopped by the office and told me what happened….after he and Esteban had a little conversation with Vann Wagner. I talked to him, too. He won't be bothering you anymore." He finally pulled away from her a little so he could see her face then looked deeply into her eyes. "I made sure he understood that he is to stay away from you and Avery. If he sees you walking down the sidewalk, he is to cross to the other side of the road."

She smiled a little at that. "You didn't hit him, did you?"

"No, but I wanted to. Chasing you down, scaring both you and Avery. In fact, you can expect an apology from him."

"Thank you." She moved away from him and went back to peeling potatoes. "You warned me there would be questions. I didn't realize how bad they would be. Or how invasive to my privacy. And yours." She looked at him, her eyes wide and shining with what he assumed were tears she tried to repress. "People know."

"Know what?"

A flush colored her cheeks. "About us. About what we did."

He reached out to cup her cheek. "They don't know, Tresia. They only think they do, but it doesn't matter. I don't care if everyone knows how I feel about you."

She stiffened as her gaze rose to his, the peeler and potato still in her hands.

"I love you, Tresia. I didn't think—"

"I love you, too," she blurted out before he could finish.

He smiled and his heartbeat picked up its pace to pound in his chest, so much different than the anger that had made his heart thunder just moments before. "You love me."

She nodded, her gaze roaming over his face, touching him without touching him. "Yes, I do. Very much."

"Marry me?" he asked, surprising himself, but now that he'd said the words, he couldn't—wouldn't—take them back. It's what he wanted, and had from the moment he met her, only he hadn't realized it until a short time ago.

"What?" Tresia whispered, her eyes widening. Apparently, he had surprised her as well. It felt right though, and the more he thought about it, the better it sounded.

"Marry me." This time it wasn't a question, but a demand. "We're good together, you and me. You've brought joy back into my life, hope back into my heart. And Avery adores you, almost as much as I do." He took a step closer and pulled her into his arms again, his gaze sweeping over her face to settle on her eyes, which were still wide with surprise...and now, shining with the love she so clearly had for him. How had he missed that before? He was supposed to be observant. It didn't matter. "Will you do me the honor of marrying me and making me the happiest man on earth?"

"Yes, Devlin, I'll marry you."

Pure bliss flooded him as she uttered the words he wanted to hear. He tightened his arms around her, but still he had to ask again, not sure he'd heard correctly, but hoping he had. "You will?"

She nodded then reached up to smooth her fingers against his cheek, rubbing against the stubble growing there though he'd shaved just this morning. "Yes."

"Thank you, Tresia. You've made me very happy." He dipped his head and captured her lips with his. When he broke the kiss, he simply smiled, so happy his heart filled with love for her. "We can go to the Justice of the Peace...unless you want a big church wedding."

She shook her head, her eyes once more tearing up. "I don't need a big church wedding, Devlin. I just need you." And to prove her words, she rose up on her tiptoes and touched her lips to his.

~

A few days later, Lucy came over, bringing her niece, Savannah, with her. The girls were in the yard, playing on the swing, their laughter coming in through the open window. Tresia poured coffee and set a plate of molasses cookies on the kitchen table in front of Lucy, when she asked, "Will you stand up for me?"

Lucy's eyes widened. "Does that mean what I think it means? Devlin asked you to marry him?"

"He did."

Lucy jumped up from her chair, excitement making her squeal, and pulled Tresia in for a hug. "Oh, Tresia, I'm so happy for you! I knew—"

Tresia broke the embrace. "Yes, you knew." She eyed her friend. "I should have known, too, when you asked me to take care of Avery. Even though I wasn't looking for someone." She let out a sigh, still reeling from the fact that Devlin had asked her to marry him. "In fact, I was dead set against ever getting married again and here I am, waiting for the Justice of the Peace. None of it was part of my Plan."

Lucy took her seat, then added sugar and cream to her coffee. "Yes, your plan," she said with a smile, as if there had always been doubt in her mind.

"Oh, I still want Sullivan's back, but now, I worry. Do I have to give up on my dream of owning the store to become a wife and mother? What will happen to Sullivan's then? Arnold and Willetta are running it into the ground."

"Have you talked to Devlin about it?" Lucy dunked the cookie in her coffee then took a bite.

"No, I haven't. It's all still new." Tresia lowered her voice and fiddled with her napkin. "I think he was as surprised as I was when he asked me to marry him."

Lucy chuckled. "What makes you think that?"

Tresia related the circumstances of Devlin's proposal, making Lucy laugh. "I do believe you're right. I'm sure he'll support you with whatever you want to do, just like Ben supports me. Talk to him."

"You're right. I will. I just need to find the right time...and the right words." She smiled, anticipation bubbling inside her. "We have to tell Avery, too. We haven't yet."

"What do you think is going to happen? Avery will say no?" Lucy laughed. "Or that she'll blab it to the entire town before you're ready?" She shook her head. "Tell her. I think she'll be very happy."

"I hope you're right. I'm not looking to replace her mother."

"And I don't think she'll see it that way. She's young. She adores you. Does she talk about—what was her name?"

"Hannah. Not very much. I know she misses her. I know Devlin still misses her, too. From everything I've heard, Hannah was a good woman. Sweet. Kind. A gentle soul and a good mother."

"I don't think you have anything to worry about. As I said, Avery loves you. And so does Devlin. Whatever happens, you'll make it work."

By dinner that night, the opportunity to tell Avery presented itself sooner than she thought it would, and it was Devlin who brought it up after dinner. He pulled his daughter into his lap as they both ate the rice pudding she'd made earlier.

"It's good, huh?"

Avery nodded before she shoveled another spoonful into her mouth.

"I want to talk to you about something very important."

"Okay, Daddy."

Tresia's heart beat a little faster, watching the two of them. There was no denying Avery was his daughter. They shared the same dark hair, though Avery's was curly and Devlin's was slicked back. Even their eye color was the same. They shared the same mannerisms as well as facial expressions, but it was more than a physical resemblance. There was love. That special kind of love between a father and daughter, the same as she had shared with her own father, which made her miss him more. She blinked to remove the moisture from her eyes as she watched them across the table.

"Miss Tresia and I are going to get married."

"Okay."

She didn't know what she thought would happen, but she didn't expect Avery's response to be a simple 'okay.'

"So that's all right with you?"

The girl nodded and went back to eating her rice pudding, scraping the bowl with her spoon to get every last bit, seemingly unconcerned.

Devlin looked at her across the table and raised an eyebrow, obviously surprised Avery hadn't reacted with anything other than complete agreement. He dropped a kiss on the top of Avery's head. "Are you all done?"

She nodded then placed her spoon in the empty bowl.

"All right, then, it's time for bed. Why don't you go brush your teeth, wash your face and get ready? I'll be up in a minute."

"Okay, Daddy." Avery slid off his lap and brought both his bowl and hers to the sink, then scampered over to her. She reached up and gave her a kiss on the cheek. "Good night, Mama."

Tresia was stunned. Yes, she knew Avery loved her—had actually told her that before—but she'd never ever called her 'mama.' The love she had for Avery made her heart swell and tears spring to her eyes. "Good night, sweetheart," she managed over the lump in her throat before Avery dashed for the door to get ready for bed.

Another thought occurred to her, one that brought anxiety to mix with the wonder of Avery's words. She glanced at Devlin, still overwhelmed. "Do you mind that she called me that?"

There was a gentle smile on his face but his eyes, so much like his daughter's, held a touch of sadness. He shook his head, as if unable to speak, then rose from his chair and walked over to her, gave her a quick kiss on the lips, then left the kitchen. A moment later, she heard him whistling as he went upstairs.

Still stunned, Tresia did the dishes, then set up the chessboard in the parlor while he was upstairs putting Avery to bed. She poured two small glasses of brandy, then made herself comfortable at the table to wait for him.

She looked up as he came down the stairs. There was a bounce in his step and the gentle smile he'd worn earlier had grown. She waited until he took the chair across from her before she said, "I won't ever let her forget Hannah." She meant what she said.

"I know you won't," he said then reached for her hand over the chessboard, giving it a squeeze before letting go and taking a sip of brandy.

Again, that touch of sadness glowed from his eyes, but it was fleeting. If he wanted to talk about it, she'd be more than willing to listen, but for right now, there was another subject she'd been worried about discussing.

"I wanted to ask you something."

Devlin looked up from the white pawn he was preparing to move and gave her his full attention. "What?"

"It's about Sullivan's," she began but didn't quite know how to continue. She looked across the table at him, searching his face. He hadn't lost his smile. It was still gentle and filled with so many possibilities.

"What about Sullivan's?" he prompted her after a few moments of silence.

"You know I want it back, right?"

"I do."

She took a deep breath. "So what will happen if I can somehow manage to get it? We'll be married. I'll have you and Avery to take care of. I—"

"You're worried that you couldn't have both—a happy marriage and a successful business," he supplied the thought she had trouble with. "But I can't see a reason why you couldn't, Tresia. As long as Avery is happy and healthy." He smiled at her over the chessboard. "And you have time for me." He laughed. "Doesn't Elsie at the Wagon Wheel have children?"

"She does. Her mother watches her girls while Elsie and Oscar are at the restaurant."

"They seem happy. The children are well taken care of." He sat back in his chair but never took his gaze from her. "Doesn't Gemma over at Goldwater's have children?"

"Yes."

"And Mrs. Gonzales at the hotel?"

She nodded. "But their children are a bit older and actually help out. Avery is so young."

"Didn't your father take you to the store with him when you were young?"

"He did."

"And you loved going there with him, spending your time helping, learning everything he could teach you."

Fond memories filled her head, bringing a lump to her throat. "Yes."

"I'm sure Avery wouldn't mind being with you at the store. In fact, I think she'd love it." He sat up and moved his pawn then looked at her. "I can help, too, here at home so you wouldn't have to worry. I would hate for you to give up your dreams because we're getting married. You should be able to do the things you want to do."

Tresia just stared at him, a little surprised though she shouldn't have been. Devlin Goodrich was a good man in so many ways—understanding, kind, thoughtful, and right now, he was making a lot of sense. In fact, he was going out of his way to show her that she could manage all of it, if she so chose. She could have a successful marriage as well as a successful store. Other women had done it and were still doing it.

"You could also hire one or two people to help, but aren't you getting a bit ahead of yourself? Has Arnold or Willetta said anything to you when you pick up the books? Are they willing to give up Sullivan's?"

"No, they haven't said anything, but they haven't done what needs to be done either." She let out a sigh, disappointment rifling through her. "The last time I went in there, no one had dusted or swept the floor. And the books are a mess even though I clean them up every time I take them. They're not paying their bills, either, probably because they're driving their customers away and they're not making any money."

"Let's just wait and see what happens. Who knows? There could be a different opportunity. Another building up for sale that you could purchase and make your own." His gaze held hers steadily, a different kind of light dancing in his eyes now. "I don't want to play chess," he finally admitted.

"You don't?"

He shook his head. "Why don't we go upstairs and celebrate our upcoming marriage."

Tresia didn't need a second invitation. She rose from her seat, reached out her hand to grasp his and led him upstairs to his bedroom on the second floor.

CHAPTER 17

*H*e liked this part of his job—walking the streets of Serenity, exchanging greetings with the people of the town, making sure everything was as it should be, except now it seemed to be a little different. The decision to come here remained a good one though. He'd met and fell in love with Tresia Morgan here. They would be married as soon as the Justice of the Peace came to Serenity, which was just a week from now. Finding Tresia, loving her, was more than he could have hoped for. After losing Hannah, he hadn't thought himself capable of loving anyone ever again. She made him realize that he could.

Avery was doing well, too, a regular little chatterbox once again. She was happy—he saw it every day in her smile and loved listening to her laugh. She loved Tresia almost as much as he did.

They would be a family, and the world seemed a little brighter, a little better.

The reporters were still here, swarming into town from all over, some as far away as San Francisco, like locusts, all of them looking to talk to him about Ned Delany and the circumstances of his death, looking to write the story that would make them—and him—famous.

A week after the outlaw had been buried in the cemetery at the edge of town, the reporters were still coming. Mrs. Gonzalez at the hotel told him just yesterday that all her rooms were filled. Elsie at the Wagon Wheel said she was busier than ever. He heard the same from several other shopkeepers.

Killing Ned Delany, it seemed, had been good for business, though it wasn't for his frame of mind.

Devlin didn't want any part of it. He had more to lose than Merrill or anyone else. He wondered how long it would be before Frances saw his name and showed up on his doorstep.

"Marshal Goodrich?"

He turned toward a man sitting on a bench along one of the pathways in the town square. Another person he didn't recognize. There were so many of them. "Yes?"

"May I have a moment of your time?"

He eyed the man, suspicion making him stiffen. "Who are you?"

"Sebastian Jones with The Albuquerque Journal."

It was just as he feared. Another reporter, but at least this one seemed to know the boundaries. He was polite. Respectful. He hadn't camped out in front of his house, waiting for a moment with him, like the two he'd run off this morning. He was grateful, though, that none dared to approach Tresia or Avery again.

"I have nothing to say, Mr. Jones. Please just leave me alone."

The man smiled, white teeth gleaming. "I can't do that, Marshal. Like you, I have a job to do, and my job, at this moment, is to get an interview with you."

Mr. Jones was persistent; he'd give him that. And he remained respectful. "I'm afraid you've wasted your time. I have nothing to say to you." He started walking away, but the newspaperman wouldn't give up.

He rose from the bench and followed, almost on his heels, making the hair on the back of Devlin's neck stand straight up. *So this is what outlaws feel when I'm pursuing them. Hunted. No peace. No rest.* If it weren't so sad, he'd laugh, though he wasn't in a laughing mood.

"Just one quote, Marshal."

Devlin stopped in the middle of the street in front of the Marshal's Office, pulled in his breath and let it out slowly. "All right. You may have one quote."

Mr. Jones pulled a notebook and pencil from his pocket, then flipped the book open to a blank page.

"Are you ready to take this down?" he asked and the reporter nodded eagerly. Devlin smiled. "Here's your quote: No comment."

He walked away then stepped up on the raised sidewalk and let himself into the Marshal's Office. He closed the door—firmly—behind him. If there had been a lock on the door, he would have used it, but the Marshal's Office was never closed.

He glanced out the window, his gaze on the reporter who was now on the raised sidewalk outside the office, pacing back and forth. It wouldn't be long, he was certain, before Mr. Jones tried the doorknob and let himself in.

"You all right, Boss?" Merrill asked, startling him.

Devlin turned slowly and forced himself to move away from the window. "No, I'm not all right. I'm pissed. I can't even walk across the town square without someone accosting me."

"Killing Ned Delany is big news. They all want a story about it."

"At what cost, Merrill?" He slowly unclenched his hands and forced himself to calm down, though it was harder than he thought. "Vann Wagner scared the shit out of my little girl, not to mention Tresia. Neither one of them can leave the house now without being followed, though I will admit no one has approached them since Teddy, Esteban, and I put the fear of God into Wagner, but still, Avery is only five years old, for cryin' out loud! She doesn't understand."

"Why don't you sneak out the back door and go home." Merrill suggested. "They haven't figured out there's another entrance to this place, although they did realize that Nate lives upstairs. Heard someone banging on his door early this morning. Nate wasn't too happy. I can handle the reporters." He paused, then added, "I hope you don't mind, but I've talked to a few of them."

"You're not telling me anything I don't already know. I read the interview you gave to Wagner for the Serenity Times. It was a good interview. Wagner asked some particularly good questions, and he didn't embellish the answers—or straight out lie. You can talk to anyone you want to, Merrill. Just keep my name out of it as much as you possibly can."

His grin was back. "I'll do my best."

Devlin let it go. No matter how careful Merrill would be, his name would be mentioned and there was nothing he could do about it. He settled his hat on the desk and pulled his chair away, then sat down. There was paperwork on his desk, reports needing to be finalized and filed away, but none of it seemed to matter, and frankly, he just didn't feel like doing it today. After a moment, aware that Merrill was looking at him, he glanced at the man. "What?"

"I heard you asked Tresia to marry you."

"I did. How'd you hear about it?"

"Small town, Dev. Everyone knows." He moved away from his desk and came to stand beside him. "My congratulations. She's a wonderful woman."

"Thank you. I agree. She is. Avery adores her."

"Can't see how she couldn't." He moved away and took a seat at his own desk, then leaned back in his chair.

Devlin didn't take his gaze from the man. Of all the people he knew now, out of all his acquaintances and friends, it was Merrill he was closest to. There wasn't a man he trusted more to have at his back. "Speaking of getting married, would you stand up for me? I'll need a witness."

Merrill's smile was sincere. "I'd be honored. When?"

"The Justice of the Peace will be here next Friday. I've already wired him. We'll meet at the courthouse at two in the afternoon."

The man nodded. "As I said, I'd be honored." He went back to the papers on his desk, but his smile remained in place. After a moment, a merry tune whistled from between his lips.

Devlin smiled as he picked up a piece of paper and read the report Rafael had submitted regarding the theft of several pairs of shoes from Mrs. Loving's front porch. The perpetrator, a black and white spaniel with the name of Lucky, had been caught, and released to its owner and all the stolen shoes had been returned.

On any other day, the crime would have made him laugh, but not today. The threat of Frances coming to town hung over him like a heavy mantle. It was only a matter of time before she showed up at his door. He would have to deal with her at some point, but he wasn't looking forward to it.

"My earlier offer still stands, Dev." Merrill interrupted his thoughts, making him jump. "Why don't you slip out the back door and head on home. Spend the day with Tresia and Avery. Do something fun. Maybe rent a carriage from the livery and go on a picnic. There's a nice spot not far from MacLean's ranch that Polly and I found. It's quiet and peaceful and there's a stream-fed lake you can swim in. Rafael and I can handle things here."

"You know what?" He rose from his seat, then picked up his hat, and jammed it on his head. "I think I will. I'll see you tomorrow."

"Sure thing, Boss."

He let himself out of the Marshal's Office through the back door as Merrill suggested. No reporters roamed about and he moved swiftly to the livery the next street over. He conducted his business with Mr. Yancy quickly then climbed into the open carriage, shook the reins to get the horse moving and drove home.

He entered the house quietly, the aroma of fresh baked bread filling his senses and strode to the kitchen. Tresia stood at the sink, rinsing something then placed a bowl on a towel on the counter, though her gaze never left what was outside the window. He watched her for the longest time.

"Oh, Devlin!" she exclaimed when she finally turned around and saw him, her eyes wide, her smile even wider. "I didn't expect you to be home so soon. Is everything all right?"

"Yes, everything is fine," he lied. "Where's Avery?"

"She's out back on the swing." She spread out a dish towel over the back of a chair, her gaze on him.

"How would you like to go on a picnic? Merrill was telling me about a place not far from Stone Creek Ranch that has a lake."

She took a few steps closer to him then reached out her hand and smoothed it along his cheek. "I would love that. Avery would, too."

"I rented a carriage from the livery. Mr. Yancy says hello, by the way."

"Oh, he's a sweet man. Just give me a few minutes to fill a picnic basket. I'll make some sandwiches out of that leftover ham from last night." She set to work quickly.

Devlin enjoyed watching her for a few moments then opened the kitchen door and stepped outside onto the back porch. Avery was on the swing toward the back of the yard, her little legs pumping hard, her curls dancing in the breeze of her own creation. Cecily leaned against the tree trunk, all but forgotten for the moment. The tension he'd been carrying around with him eased just a bit.

He stepped off the porch and walked the length of yard, stopping in front of her.

"Daddy!" Avery squealed with delight then jumped off the

swing at its highest point. He hadn't expected that and opened his arms, heart in his throat, to catch her in mid-flight.

"Avery!" he shouted, ready to issue the reprimand hovering on his tongue but then he looked at her—all grins and happy giggles, her eyes wide and filled with the utmost confidence that he would catch her. The reprimand died in his throat, replaced with a wry chuckle. She was a daredevil and so much like him he couldn't be upset. Still, he had to say something, for her own protection as well as his peace of mind. "You shouldn't do that."

"But you caught me."

"That I did, but I might not always be there."

She nodded with enthusiasm and conviction. "Yes, you will."

His heart, now beating again as it should, swelled. Yes, he would. Always. He'd never let her down. Ever. He set her down, then took her little hand in his. "How would you like to go on a picnic? Miss Tresia is making sandwiches."

"Okay, Daddy." She pulled him toward the house, excited, apparently, to go. He was just as eager for the opportunity to find a little peace and quiet with his favorite girls.

It wasn't long before they reached the lake in the little spot Merrill had told him about. He climbed out of the carriage, then reached up to help Tresia and his daughter. "Stay close, Avery."

She glanced at him, her eyes questioning. "Can I put my feet in the water?"

"Yes, but don't go too far in without me or Miss Tresia. Up to your ankles only."

Avery gave a nod and headed toward the water, where she promptly sat near the water's edge and pulled off her shoes and stockings. In moments, she was in the water up to her ankles.

"That's as far as you go, Avery," he reminded her. "Promise?"

"Promise," she called back over her shoulder.

He took his gaze off her for a moment to grab an old quilt, then spread it out on the grass beneath the wide limbs of a cottonwood tree. He settled himself, stretching out his long legs, his focus once more on Avery.

Tresia sat beside him and started removing what she'd packed from the basket. "This is nice."

"Yes, it is. A beautiful day. And exactly what I needed." And it was what he needed, far away from the prying questions from reporters, not to mention every single townsperson he ran into. So many wanted him to relive the killing of Ned Delany and he just didn't want to. Yes, Delany was a bad man, but he hadn't enjoyed ending his depraved and cruel life. He would have much rather have him pay for his crimes in prison, convicted by a jury of his peers.

"Is everything all right, Devlin?"

"It is now." He reached for her hand and just held it, the comfort exuding from her by such a simple touch easing his troubled mind.

"But it wasn't before." She looked at him, her gaze steady and inquisitive, her smile tremulous but reassuring, letting him know he could tell her anything. "Why did you come home so early? Did something happen?"

He took his eyes off Avery for a moment and glanced in Tresia's direction before focusing on his daughter again. "I'm tired, Tresia," he finally admitted. "And if you don't mind, I'd rather not talk about it. I just want to sit here in the peace and quiet and spend time with you and Avery."

She squeezed his hand, confirming her understanding. "All right. We can do that." Her gaze settled on him and he knew that even though she agreed not to talk about it now, she would want to later. And maybe later, he would be ready to share his concerns. She was, after all, a good listener, offering sound advice but only when asked. And she was going to be his wife. She deserved to know the fear that lived in his heart, but for now, he simply wanted to enjoy spending time with Avery and her.

Something definitely wasn't right. Tresia studied Devlin's profile, or as much as she could see in the moonlight coming into his bedroom. She was worried about him. He didn't seem like himself.

Ever since their picnic—even during their picnic—Devlin had remained quiet, much too quiet. Not even Avery could pull him out of the darkness that seemed to have taken control of him. Something was weighing heavily on his mind. He even made love differently, still gentle and thoughtful, bringing her to the heights of passion, but with an almost desperation in his actions.

And she wasn't having it.

They were to be married. She was to be a helpmate to him, a companion, someone he could confide in. That's what marriage was supposed to be.

"What's wrong, Devlin?

"Nothing."

"It's not nothing, Devlin." She rose up on her elbow and looked down at his face, his features more visible. "Something is bothering you. It's like…you're just waiting for something to happen."

He let out his breath in a long sigh. "I am."

"Can't you tell me?" She traced her fingers along his cheek and chin, feeling the rough stubble of the beard he'd shave off in the morning. "Perhaps sharing your concerns might lessen the burden."

"You're a good woman, Tresia," he whispered as he entwined his fingers with hers. It took another few moments before he seemed to come to a decision. "It's these reporters coming into town, wanting interviews, asking too many questions. I met one from Albuquerque today and then I made the mistake of reading the piece Wagner put in the Serenity Times. He mentioned my name several times, mentioned the town. He didn't mention Avery, thank God, but I feel like it's only a matter of time before Frances shows up."

Her heart went out to him. She loved this man with every fiber of her being and what worried him, worried her. What frightened him, frightened her as well. "I see. And you're concerned."

She could tell he was loathe to admit it but admit it he did. "Yes."

"Why?"

He remained silent for the longest time. When he finally did speak, his voice was raw and conveyed exactly what concerned him. "Because, knowing Frances as I do, she'll come here and try to take Avery and it's a fight I don't want to deal with. I don't want her around Avery. She will cause trouble."

"She can't take her. You're her father."

He stiffened then released her hand. "But she can try," he sighed then admitted, "Frances has a lot of influence. And a lot of power. I'm more than certain she has several judges in her pocket, not to mention her family lawyer who may or may not have broken the law for her. There's even a senator or two. They're all willing to do her bidding, either because they're not good men or under threat of blackmail. She seems to have a hold over these men. I'm not sure why or how." He paused, as if to gather his thoughts.

"When Hannah and I got married against her wishes, she did everything she could possibly do to break us apart and make our marriage go away." He reached for her, pulling her closer, perhaps searching for the calmness he said she brought to him. "She didn't like me very much. Still doesn't like me to this day. She threatened to have our marriage annulled. Said she knew people who could do that for her. I believed her."

He laughed wryly, but the sound struck Tresia as odd. She

didn't say anything—just wanting him to talk, until he didn't feel like the bottom was about to drop out of his world.

"Frances told that to Hannah, too. I think that was the first time Hannah stood up to her and told her no, threatened that if she didn't stop her interference, Hannah would never see her again. Frances loved her daughter—as much as Frances knows how to love—so she stopped with the intimidation. And then Avery was born and things were better in one way but seemed to get worse in another. The dislike she had for me turned into downright hate. Frances wanted Hannah and Avery to move back to the ranch and stay with her, using the dangers of my job to frighten Hannah, telling Hannah she didn't know how to raise a child, telling her that I had been with other women, which I would never do. Frances did everything she could to get Hannah to hate me, too."

"But it didn't work, did it?"

"No, the more Frances pushed, the more Hannah dug in her heels. She was stubborn that way. She still went out to the ranch to visit but left any time her mother started berating me and our marriage. As I said, she will cause trouble." He drew in his breath. "Avery is happy now. I don't want to see that change."

"What can we do?"

"Nothing until she shows up." There was such defeat in his voice.

"I think you should talk to Mr. Applebaum. He's a good lawyer. He might be able to help. Maybe there's a way to keep her away from Avery."

"I doubt Mr. Applebaum has much influence over someone like Frances," he scoffed, not willing to believe it.

"It's worth a try, isn't it?" she asked, hoping he would see her suggestion as an answer to the problem that was Frances Emerson Comstock. "Doing something is better than worrying about it. That won't get you anywhere except a sour stomach and a racing mind."

His body relaxed as if he considered her suggestion. "You're so good for me, Tresia."

"Yes, I am." She smiled at him even though she wasn't sure he could see it. "We're good for each other."

"Yes, we are. I agree. It's worth a try. I'll see him in the morning, but for now—" He didn't finish the sentence. Instead, he rolled toward her and took possession of her mouth, his lips moving over hers. Tresia felt that kiss all the way to her toes and her belly quivered.

"Again?" she murmured when he broke the kiss and smoothed his fingers against her face.

He didn't answer, just kissed her. And this time, his kiss was a little less desperate and she gave him all that he needed from her.

Early the next morning, Devlin, taking Tresia's advice, climbed the outside stairs to Philip Applebaum's office above his home. He let himself in, determined to find a way to protect himself—and Avery—from Frances. There was a small desk as soon as one walked into the office, but it was unoccupied.

A door to the left of the desk was wide open. He strode toward it and peeked in to see an older man, elbows on the desk, his hands pressed against his cheeks to prop up his head as he studied an open law book.

He cleared his throat. "I'm sorry for the interruption, Mr. Applebaum, but do you have a moment for me?"

The man looked up and smiled. "Of course, Marshal! Come in. Come in." He gestured to a deep leather chair in front of his desk. "Please. Sit." He slipped a bookmark into the book and closed it, giving Devlin his full attention. "What can I do for you?"

"Tresia Morgan suggested I talk to you."

Mr. Applebaum nodded, his pale green eyes lighting up. "Nice woman, that Tresia. Smart, too. She's probably right." Obviously, he knew Tresia and liked her, but then, to his knowledge, Devlin hadn't met anyone who didn't.

"I need some advice." He rubbed his suddenly damp palms on his trousers. "In fact, I think I need to hire you as my counsel."

"Do you need counsel, Marshal? Is this related to the killing of Ned Delany?"

"Yes, I think I do, but not for that. As you may know, it was a righteous kill. No, this is for something different and for my own protection." He drew in his breath. This was harder than he thought it would be. "I don't know what you know about me, but I have a daughter."

The man smiled, which transformed his face and made him seem younger. "Yes, I'm aware. And she's as cute as a bug's ear. I've seen her around town with Tresia."

"I also have a mother-in-law. She's a woman of great influence and power. She's wants Avery."

"I see." The smile disappeared as quickly as it came. "And who is this woman?"

"Frances Emerson Comstock."

"*Rancho Gran Cielo*'s Frances Comstock?" He let out a low whistle. He'd obviously heard of her and by the expression on his face, what he'd heard about her wasn't good. He turned his chair toward a bookshelf behind him and selected a leatherbound journal. Flipping it open to a blank page, he placed in on the desk, pulled a fountain pen from its holder, and asked, "Why does she want your daughter?"

Anxiety made him clench his teeth and he forced himself to relax, though it didn't help much. He wasn't certain, at this moment, that he should have come here and tell a complete stranger his worst fears, but Tresia was right. He needed help with the possibility that Frances could take Avery. He couldn't let that happen. In fact, he was willing to do anything to keep that from happening. "She holds me responsible for the passing of my late wife and son."

A muscle twitched in Mr. Applebaum's jaw before he took a deep breath and asked, "Are you?"

"No, I am not. Hannah died in childbirth. Frances can't—or won't—accept that. Like I said, she blames me."

He jotted some notes in the journal then looked up. "Can she say you're not a good father?"

"She can say it but it wouldn't be true. I love my daughter, Mr. Applebaum. I would do anything for her."

"Yes, I can see that you do. You wouldn't be here otherwise." Kindness crept into the man's eyes. "Can you get statements from people who know you and know your daughter? Know how you are with her?"

He didn't have to think about it. "Yes. There are a number of people who would be more than willing to write letters of recommendation for me."

Mr. Applebaum dropped the fountain pen on top of the journal then leaned back in his chair and steepled his fingers in front of his round face. "What about your job as marshal? It's dangerous. She could use that against you."

He'd thought about that. Actually, Frances had used that argument when she kept Avery so he could chase down Big Bill Cassidy. She could certainly use it against him in a court of law, but if it meant losing Avery, he'd willingly give it up the profession he loved. "I'll quit."

"You'd do that?"

"Yes, I would."

Mr. Applebaum shook his head. "Before you do something so drastic, let me talk to a few people—some judges I know—and read up on the law regarding this matter." He rose from his seat then came around the desk to pat him on the shoulder. "In the meantime, try not to worry. I won't let anyone take your daughter from you."

Relieved, but not completely—Mr. Applebaum didn't know the depths to which Frances would go to get what she wanted—Devlin rose to his feet as well and held out his hand. "Thank you. I appreciate anything you can do for me."

esia removed a pecan pie from the oven, slid a knife into the center to make sure it was done, then set it on the windowsill to cool. Her gaze settled on Avery on the swing, her little legs pumping hard, Cecily, the doll, on her lap. Her giggles drifted in through the window, causing Tresia to smile. Oh, how she loved this little girl! Loved her father, too, though that had come as quite a surprise.

And she was going to marry him. It would be a small wedding, just Devlin and her in front of the Justice of the Peace. Lucy and Merrill would witness their vows. Avery, too.

She took a step away from the window, then set about washing the dishes and cleaning up the kitchen. Her hands were deep in the hot water when a knock sounded on the front door.

"Coming!" she called out, dried her hands, and then hurried through the parlor. She didn't open the door, not with the reporters about. Instead, she looked through the etched glass at the woman standing on the front porch. Porcelain skinned and dark haired, dressed in the latest fashion, she was beautiful...in a hard, cold kind of way. In that one instance, Tresia knew this woman was used to giving orders and expecting them to be carried out without question. A woman of authority, whether real or perceived.

Beyond the woman was a carriage in front of the gate—a big, fancy carriage, not something she'd normally see in Serenity. Even the richest man in town did not drive a carriage like that. A man sat in the driver's seat, his arms folded across his chest, his head moving back and forth as if afraid he might miss something.

She let out her breath, unaware she'd been holding it. She knew, without a doubt, who stood on the front porch. Frances Emerson Comstock.

Tresia backed up, choosing not to open the door, but the decision was taken out of her hands as the door flew open and Frances took a step over the threshold, barging into the house without invitation or permission, her piercing deep brown eyes narrowing as she studied her from head to toe. The corners of the woman's mouth turned upward, but it would never be mistaken for a smile. Tresia backed up another step, startled by her audacity.

"I saw you looking outside. Who are you?" Frances' voice was almost as brittle as her smile on top of being haughty.

Taken aback by the bluntness and pure arrogance of the question, Tresia started to answer, but Frances waved her off. "It doesn't matter who you are. You're just some whore he's taken to his bed after what he did to my daughter."

Tresia bristled beneath the words. She was no whore and to be accused of such struck her to the core. And Devlin hadn't done anything to this woman's daughter except love her. "I beg your pardon."

The woman laughed and brushed past her like she didn't even exist then walked over to the settee beneath the window. She made a production out of pulling a handkerchief from her reticule and swiped at the sofa cushions several times before sitting down, indicating in silence that Tresia wasn't a good housekeeper.

Tresia could do nothing except stare at her, stunned beyond comprehension. Devlin had told her what Frances was like, but she'd never seen anything like how this woman acted. All of her acquaintances, even the public she dealt with at Sullivan's, were kind and polite, with the notable exception of Arnold and Willetta. They could both take lessons from Frances in pure contempt. "What do you want?"

If Frances was surprised, she didn't let on. "So you know who I am."

Tresia straightened. "I do. Devlin told me about you."

"Devlin, is it?" She flashed that smile, which wasn't a smile at all, as she tugged the pristine white gloves from her hands. "Hmmm, I suspected as much." She glanced around the neat parlor, apparently noticing the carved wooden horses on the floor. Her nose scrunched with distaste before she turned her attention to her. "Where is my granddaughter? I want to see her." Her dark eyes narrowed. "Now."

"No." The word slipped from Tresia's mouth before she could stop it.

If possible, Frances' eyes narrowed even more, becoming dark slits, and her mouth dropped open before she closed it with a snap of her teeth. She acted like she'd never been told no before. Perhaps she hadn't and from all appearances, she didn't like it one bit.

"Excuse me?" Frances rose from her seat in one fluid motion and took two steps toward her. Tresia noticed how her hand clenched and unclenched, as if preparing to hit her for her defiance. After what Avery told her, it wouldn't have been the first time Frances resorted to violence. She could see why Avery had been so quiet, so afraid to do or say something wrong, when they'd first met. Frances was intimidating, bordering on frightening. Devlin hadn't lied when he said the woman was a force to be reckoned with.

"I said no." Her heart thundered in her chest. Where she got the gumption to defy this woman, she didn't know but defy her she would. For Avery. For Devlin. For herself. "Not without Devlin here."

She took another step in Tresia's direction. There was barely a foot between them now, so close, Tresia could see the fine lines surrounding her eyes. "You have no right to keep her from me. I am her grandmother. Her blood. You—" she scoffed "—you're nothing. No one."

"I may not be anyone to you, but I am to that little girl. This is wrong as your behavior and your demands leave something to be desired." Surprised by her own bravado, she straightened as she looked Frances in the eye and continued, "I will not be intimidated or spoken down to, not by you or anyone."

A spark of—was that appreciation?—lit the woman's eyes and the brittle smile returned to her mouth, though it was still not quite a smile. She turned and headed back to the settee, seating herself again. Every muscle in Tresia's body tensed, waiting to see what Frances would do in the face of her boldness.

"Well, then, where is my no-good bastard of a son-in-law?"

"He's working."

Frances raised an eyebrow. "Why don't you go get him?" she asked, too sweetly to be anything other than a ploy.

"No, I don't think I will." She glanced out the window at the carriage and the man sitting in the driver's seat. "Why don't you send your driver for him. I'm sure he's in the Marshal's Office. I'm also sure you know exactly where that is and why you came here instead of going there. If you think, for one moment, I'm going to leave you alone with Avery, you are sadly mistaken so either go get Devlin yourself, send your man for him, or wait."

"I'll wait." Frances settled herself more deeply into the settee and folded her hands neatly on her lap, beaten for the moment, but probably not for long. Indeed, she was probably thinking of ways to get exactly what she wanted, which was Avery.

Tresia gave a slight nod. "Fine. I'll make some coffee." She left the room, smiling to herself a little. Just because Frances was rude and nasty didn't mean she had to be. She'd show her how to be a gracious hostess...even if it killed her.

She started the coffee on to boil then glanced out the window, not trusting the woman who sat in the parlor one inch. If there was a man in front of the house, there very well may be another in the back, one willing to take Avery while she was distracted. Avery was fine though. She'd gotten off the swing and was now happily digging another hole in the ground. No one lurked in the shadows. She just hoped that Avery would stay outside for the time being. No reason for her to see her grandmother and become upset.

She gripped the edge of the sink, her heart once more settling into a steady rhythm and not the chaotic pounding seeing Frances Emerson Comstock had caused, then she moved away and put the coffee service on a tray. Several times, while she waited for the coffee to be done, she peeked through the doorway to make sure her guest was still there. She was. In fact, she hadn't moved at all though she looked like she could jump out of her skin at any moment.

"Hey, Dev, I saw a carriage, pretty fancy one, too, in front of your house. You got company?" Rafael said as he entered the office, his usual smile in place.

Devlin glanced up from the paperwork on his desk to get the bounty on Ned Delany paid. "Fancy carriage? In front of my house?"

Rafael nodded as he came closer. "Got a big burly cowboy sitting up front, just watching the road, like he's looking for trouble."

He rose from his desk, his stomach clenching.

Frances.

She was here.

His heartbeat picked up its pace as adrenaline rushed through him. He grabbed his hat, slammed it on his head, then stalked through the kitchen.

"What's going on?" Rafael called after him, then followed on his heels. "Do you need help?"

He glanced at his deputy, his jaw clenched, his hand on the doorknob. "I might need you to keep me out of my own jail."

Rafael stiffened. "What?"

Devlin opened the door and walked through, his pace quickening. Rafael followed him as he made a beeline past the small stable and into the street, coming up behind the carriage, speaking over his shoulder as he did so. "That man...that's Seth Humbolt."

"Is he an outlaw?" Rafael huffed, forcing himself to keep up with Devlin's near run.

"No, but damned close to it," Devlin answered though he didn't have time for all these questions. "I want you to keep an eye on him. Make sure he doesn't move. Hold him at gunpoint if you have to."

"What's going on, Dev? Who is at your house?"

"Frances Emerson Comstock. My mother-in-law."

"Shit."

As they approached the carriage, Rafael drew his pistol and aimed it at the man. "I wouldn't move if I were you."

"What the hell!" The man turned to look at him, a surprised gasp escaping him, then stiffening when he saw the gun as well as the person holding it on him. His eyes narrowed as they moved off the pistol and onto Devlin. "Goodrich. Bet you didn't think you'd see me again."

"Humbolt," Devlin returned the greeting, knowing the man's calm voice belied his violent nature. "Give me your guns. Slowly." He gave a nod of his head toward Rafael but never took his eyes off the man. "My deputy won't miss."

Frances' henchman did as ordered and unbuckled his gun belt. He didn't seem happy about it, though. Not only had he been caught unaware and forced to give up his guns, but there would be hell to pay when Frances found out what happened. She was not a forgiving woman, as they both knew too well.

"The knife, too."

Humbolt started to reach for his foot a little too quickly. "Carefully." Devlin warned, knowing the man's penchant for taking risks. Humbolt sighed as he slowly pulled up the leg of his trousers and reached for the knife he kept in his boot. He reluctantly handed it over. "You'll pay for this," he said.

Devlin handed everything to Rafael. "Don't take your eyes off him. And if he tries anything, shoot him."

"My pleasure."

He left Humbolt under Rafael's watchful eyes and strode up the walkway, trying to keep his temper under control. His heart was pounding much too quickly, feeling as if it were thundering against his rib cage, and his mouth was dry to the point he couldn't even swallow. He entered the house, not at a run, but cautiously, as one never knew if Frances had another one of her henchmen with her or if she herself held a gun pointed at the doorway. She wouldn't miss him at this distance, and he just didn't feel like dying today. He had too much to live for.

He stopped short in the parlor, stunned yet suspicious of the tableau before him. Tresia and Frances sat at the little table where the chessboard was usually set, a coffee service between them. It was all very civilized, except it wasn't. The tension in the room was so suffocating, he could feel it stealing his breath.

Tresia jumped from her seat and moved toward the kitchen doorway, nodding toward the back door, letting him know that Avery was outside in the yard. His gaze swept over her, noticing the paleness of her face, the darkness of her eyes, the stiffness of her body. He could only imagine what Frances had said to her.

Despite whatever words had been said, Tresia's first thought had been for Avery's safety, for which he was grateful.

He turned his attention to his mother-in-law. She hadn't changed at all, except maybe to become more arrogant, more forceful…and older, like she had aged ten years in the space of a few months. She was still as beautiful as she'd always been. "Frances."

Frances smiled, but there was nothing warm or welcoming in it, and the hatred in her dark eyes was a tangible thing. "Are you surprised, Devlin? Did you think I wouldn't find out where you took my granddaughter?" She remained seated, though her muscles were tense, as if she would jump up at any moment and attack him with her bare hands. Or pull that gun he was worried about. It was just a small derringer she carried in her pocket, but she wouldn't hesitate to shoot him right where he stood.

"I want to see her," she demanded, but he wasn't having it. He opened his mouth to deny her but never got the words out.

"Why don't you ask Avery?" Tresia asked from the doorway, a little hesitantly, her voice shaking just a bit, her face still much too pale.

"Excuse me?" Frances turned on her, her eyes narrowing to slits, and the hatred he'd felt when he walked into the room doubled. "Who asked you to be part of this conversation?"

He saw Tresia stiffen and blink several times, yet she held her ground. "I'm the one who has been taking care of her. She should have a choice on whether or not she wants to see you."

"That's ridiculous! She's a child. She needs to be told what to do." Francis laughed, a hard, cold, brittle sound that had nothing to do with humor and everything to do with thinking she was better than anyone else. She turned toward him. "Tell your paramour her opinion is neither required nor sought. In fact, tell her that her duties—" she emphasized the word "—are no longer needed."

"You remember what I did to Dr. Chambers, yes?" Frances

stared at him, one perfectly shaped eyebrow raising upward, her hands still primly folded on her lap.

Yes, he remembered exactly what she'd done to the poor doctor who had the bad fortune to allow Hannah to die during childbirth. Frances had ruined his reputation, took everything from him. His patients, as well as his wife, left him, all because Frances was angry and vindictive. The last time Devlin had seen the good doctor, he'd been thrown out of a saloon, his clothes disheveled and stained, and too drunk to stand. A shell of the proud man he'd once been, before Frances began her campaign to discredit, demoralize, and just plain ruin him.

"If you don't fire her, I will do the same to you. And her. You know I can. I have the money. I have the power. Actually, it would be my pleasure to ruin you both as I did him." She smiled smugly, her thin lips stretching over her teeth in a grin that was more brute than beauty. "And then, I'll take Avery. No judge or jury will allow her to stay with you after I'm done. She belongs with me anyway."

He glanced toward the doorway to the kitchen, expecting to see Tresia still standing there, but she was gone and again, there was nothing he could do about it at the moment. He couldn't chase after her, not with Frances sitting in his house, just waiting for the opportunity to snatch Avery and take her away. Perhaps Tresia had just gone to sit outside with Avery to make sure she didn't come in the house.

"Good. She's gone." Frances laughed softly, but there was no humor in the sound. "She seems to be a little smarter than you."

His jaw clenched as he turned to face the woman who'd been the bane of his existence since he'd met her. "How dare you!" He roared, heedless of the consequences. If he wasn't a man of law and order, he would happily strangle Frances and just be done with it, but as much as he wanted to, he couldn't.

"It's just as well, Devlin," Frances fairly purred, thinking—and looking—like she'd gotten her way. Again. "Now, Avery can come home with me."

"The hell she will!" He ground out between his teeth, his hands clenching into fists at his sides. "I made that mistake once. I will not make it again. And Tresia is a good woman. A kind woman. She doesn't deserve your rancor or your rudeness. She has done nothing to you and you will not talk to her that way."

"Bah! She is nothing but someone you took to your bed!" Frances exploded, spots of color adorning her white cheeks, her voice no longer modulated and cold, but fiery and harsh. It was the first time he'd ever seen Frances lose control and it pleased him no end. "Though how you could after Hannah, I don't know. Don't you have any remorse for what you did to my daughter?"

"I did nothing to Hannah except love her." Anger burned in him though he tried to tamp it down. "And I will no longer allow you to make me feel guilty for doing so. I loved her, Frances. I love her still. That will never change." He paused as he looked at her, really looked at her, his gaze roaming over her face. Her dark eyes glittered, red patches adorned her pale face, and her lips were stretched thin over her mouth, but beyond all that, he saw something else. For the first time, he realized that Frances didn't know how to love, and he pitied her. "I'm sure you don't understand."

That seemed to take some of her anger, but not enough. "I want to see my granddaughter."

"No. Until you can show me that you have patience with Avery and not cut her hair to punish her or hit her with a brush because she wouldn't sit still or berate her for imagined slights or for being a child, you will not see her. On this, I will not budge." His voice lowered as he gained full control of himself, no longer afraid of what Frances might do. "Once you can show me these things, then I will let Avery decide whether or not she wants to see you."

She opened her mouth to say something, but he held up his

hand, stopping her. "Go ahead, Frances. Fight me on this. Try to ruin me as you did Dr. Chambers and so many countless others. I promise you though, you will lose. I am no longer a man full of grief and guilt. The law is on my side. Tresia helped me to see losing Hannah was not my fault, no matter how much you blamed me." He smiled, knowing that was true. "She and I are getting married."

Frances sucked in her breath, her eyes narrowing to slits in her face. "You're going to marry her?"

"Yes. I love her."

For the first time he could ever remember, Frances seemed to shrink before his eyes. He'd never seen that before and it shocked him, but the moment was fleeting as she drew herself up and stared at him.

"You win," she conceded. "For now. My lawyer will be in touch."

It wasn't the threat she thought it was, not anymore. "I look forward to it." He walked to the front door and opened it then turned to look at her.

Lips pursed, jaw clenched, Frances flounced from the room in the most unladylike way, which made his smile grow. He followed her outside but didn't go any farther than the porch steps. "Goodbye, Frances," he said to her departing back then signaled to Rafael, who still stood with his gun trained on Humbolt, to let them go.

He watched the carriage pull away, then walked back into the house. Tresia stood in the doorway to the kitchen, her eyes bright, her mouth turned down into a frown, her face as pale as he'd ever seen it. And she was shaking. He could see it from where he stood and his heart hurt for her.

"Is she gone?"

"For now, but I'm certain this isn't over." He took the few steps toward her and gathered her in his arms, relieved for the moment. "Are you all right?"

She placed her hand on the side of his face. "I am. Oh, I'm still angry the way she barged in here, thinking she could get her way, but I'm all right."

"How much did you hear?"

"I heard you tell her that you loved me and that we're getting married." She smiled, though it wasn't up to her usual standard. "Are you certain that was wise?"

"Wise or not, she'd find out anyway, but at least she'll know what she's up against. I'm not the man I was. I am no longer afraid of what she might do. I think she knows I'll fight her until my last breath."

She nodded as if agreeing to his statement. He had no doubts that she would fight for Avery as well. She tightened her arms around him, snuggling closer. "Can she really ruin you?"

"She can try, but she's not going to win—" he lifted her chin with his finger and gazed into her eyes, so beautiful, so filled with uncertainty, then rubbed his thumb against her cheek. "—not with you by my side. We'll fight her together."

Again, she nodded, the doubt vanishing. "Yes, we'll fight her together."

He laughed, unable to help himself. How had he ever gotten so lucky to have this smart, beautiful—fierce—woman come into his life? "Where's Avery?"

"I took her to Lucy's. I didn't want to run the risk that she would come into the house and see her grandmother. I doubt it would do her any good. She's made such great strides since the first time I met her, I didn't want to undo all that progress." She pulled out of his arms and leaned against the door jamb. He noticed that she was no longer shaking and color returned to her face. "What do we do now?"

"We wait, I guess, to see what Frances will do next."

∾

Tresia let herself into the boarding house later that evening, secure in the knowledge that Devlin loved her and couldn't wait for them to be married though she knew this was far from over. Frances wasn't one to give up so easily and she steeled herself to fight for what she wanted—what she needed—a family with Devlin and Avery. Let Frances try to do her worst. Let her try to ruin Devlin. The woman had no idea what she was up against. She and Devlin were stronger together.

"Tresia!"

She stopped, her foot on the riser of the staircase going up to her room but didn't turn around. She didn't need to. She recognized the voice. Arnold. Why was he here?

"I need to talk to you."

He was the last person she wanted to talk to right now after Frances had tried to turn her world upside down. She closed her eyes for a moment, looking for strength and kindness, though both seemed to be in short supply, then she turned to see him lumber across the parlor's carpeted floor.

"What is it, Arnold?"

He removed the bowler from his head and worried the brim with his blunt fingers. "I don't want the store anymore."

It was the last thing she expected to hear, and it took her a moment to fully grasp what he'd said. He didn't want Sullivan's anymore? Her emotions soared though she tried to keep herself under control, lest she only heard what she waited so long to hear. "Excuse me? Did you just say you don't want the store anymore?"

"I did." He pulled a handkerchief from his pocket and ran it over his face. "Willetta hates it, hates living here in Serenity. She even hates me now. She's moving back to Santa Fe." He swallowed hard. "She said she'll go without me." His eyes glowed with what she thought were unshed tears. "I can't lose her."

Willetta may not be the nicest person in the world, but Arnold obviously loved her, so much so that he was willing to give up

Sullivan's to keep her. She understood what someone was willing to do, all in the name of love.

He reached into his jacket pocket and withdrew a thick packet of papers, neatly folded. "I had Mr. Applebaum draw up the papers reverting the store back to you."

Tresia unfolded the papers and scanned them quickly. It seemed everything was in order. She rifled through the stack and found the deed to the store.

He gave her a tremulous smile, his face reddening even more. "I'm so sorry, Tresia. I never should have convinced Uncle Lyle to give me Sullivan's. It was wrong of me. I only did it to keep Willetta." He looked...relieved. "We'll be out of the apartment in an hour or so. You can move back in if you want."

"Thank you for this, Arnold." She waved the packet of papers. "Good luck to you."

He planted his hat on his head and walked toward the door, then paused with his hand on the doorknob. Turning to face her once more, he said, "Again, I'm sorry for everything. Neither Willetta nor I realized how hard it was to run the business, especially after you left. You are the embodiment of Sullivan's while Willetta and I were not. And everyone knows it." He touched the brim of his hat in a two-fingered salute of respect, then opened the door and left.

Tresia stared at the closed door, waiting for him to come back inside and proclaim that it was all a joke. She wasn't getting the store back. She blinked to remove the moisture from her eyes and counted to ten as she watched the door, then counted to ten again.

He didn't come back.

She inhaled deeply, swiped at her eyes, and went upstairs to her room. Overwhelmed with the turn of events, she sat on the bed and simply smiled. Her life had—in a few short hours—changed dramatically, and she couldn't be happier. She thought about packing her things and moving into the apartment tonight, but given how badly Arnold and Willetta kept the store, she was afraid of what the upstairs looked like. She couldn't stay there until it was cleaned.

Still, she hugged herself, her excitement growing. She couldn't wait to share all this wonderful news with Devlin and Avery.

"Arnold gave me the store back," Tresia announced, barely able to hold back her excitement as she passed through the back-yard gate and saw Devlin sitting on the porch, a portable writing desk on his lap. Avery sat beside him, tenderly, gently, brushing the knots from Cecily's hair. Tresia understood how Avery was still affected by her grandmother's cruelty as that beautiful little girl carefully, patiently, separated every tangle of her doll's hair.

Devlin put aside the desk and rose to his feet. "He did what?"

"Gave me the store back," she replied, perhaps a bit too smugly for her own way of thinking but she couldn't help herself. "He met me at Mrs. McMurty's after I left here yesterday. He said Willetta hated working at Sullivan's and that she was going back to Santa Fe, with or without him. He said they'd made a mistake taking it from me to begin with and that he was sorry." She pulled the paperwork from her drawstring purse and handed it to him as she stepped onto the porch.

Devlin unfolded the documents and quickly read them over. "Congratulations!" He wrapped his arms around her and lifted her up off the ground to whirl her around. "This is what you wanted." He placed her gently on her feet then tilted his head to the side and looked at her. "We are still getting married, right? Justice Peabody will be here the day after next."

She wrapped her arms around his neck and pulled him closer, her forehead touching his. "Yes, we are. My dress is almost ready, so you're not getting out of your proposal that easily."

"I wouldn't dream of it." He laughed then lowered his head to capture her lips with his.

"You're kissing again!" Avery exclaimed, but there was a big smile on her face, as she looked up from the doll in her lap. "It's okay. You can kiss 'cause we're gettin' married." She went back to brushing Cecily's hair, completely ignoring them once more.

"So, what are you going to do with Sullivan's now?" He kept her in his arms, holding her tight where she felt loved and wanted.

"Clean! Though I'm a little frightened with what I'll find when I get to the apartment. The store is bad enough. I can only imagine what it looks like upstairs." She kissed him, reveling in the taste and feel of his lips beneath hers. "After breakfast, of course. Avery, do you want to help me?"

"Okay." Avery gently placed Cecily on one of the chairs and scampered inside the house, apparently anxious to help make breakfast.

"I really am happy for you, Tresia."

"I am, too." She gave him one more kiss then followed behind Avery.

A little while later, breakfast dishes done, Devlin off on his rounds protecting the community, Tresia changed into the extra clothes she'd brought with her and called out through the open kitchen door. "Avery! Come on inside."

"Okay, Mama!" She jumped off the swing as it was just starting to rise and landed gracefully on her feet, then picked up Cecily, who she rested against the tree trunk, and ran toward the porch. She stopped on the bottom step, her face registering confusion. "Why do you look like that?"

"Like what?"

"You got a thing on your head." She pointed to her own head as she climbed the steps and entered the kitchen.

Tresia followed, smoothing her hand over the bandana she'd

tied around her head. "This? It's so my hair doesn't get dirty and stays out of my face."

Avery grinned. "And you're wearing pants. I never seen a lady wearing pants."

She glanced down at the trousers she'd put on and laughed. "I am, aren't I?"

"How come?"

"We're going to clean today and I don't want to ruin any of my good clothes."

Avery looked around the kitchen and frowned. "It's already clean."

"Not this house. My house. At least where I used to live. You know my store?"

Avery nodded.

"There's an apartment over it and it's mine again. The store, too."

A curious expression came over her features. "Are you gonna live there after you marry Daddy?"

She'd always known Avery was smart, but not this smart. "No, my girl. I'll live here with you and your daddy. I'm thinking of renting it out."

"What does renting mean?"

"Someone will live there and pay me money to do so, but before I can do that, I'll have to clean it. Make sure it's presentable."

"Okay." She tilted her head to the side. "Do I have to clean, too?"

"Only if you want to help me, but you don't have to. I have a lot of books and things in my old room. You could draw if you want." She bent down and gently took Avery's chin between her finger and thumb. "I think I might have some watercolors, too, but I'm not sure if the paint is still good."

They left the house, carrying all the things they needed to

clean, and cut across the town square, then walked around to the rear of Sullivan's Emporium. Climbing the steps to the balcony which ran the length of the building, Tresia shifted the items in her arms and fished through her drawstring purse. She pulled out the key and unlocked the door. After she opened it, she stopped short, unprepared for the mess Arnold and Willetta had left her.

She should have known it would look like this, judging by the condition the store had sunk into. It didn't look like either one of them had swept or mopped...or even done the dishes, as the sink was overflowing with used, dirty plates and glasses, some with dried food still on them. They hadn't taken out the trash, either, which overflowed the bin.

Most of all, she wasn't prepared for the smell, a combination of sweat, and Arnold's cologne, and rotting food. It brought tears to her eyes, but she wasn't sure if it was just the smell or the sheer disappointment of seeing what Arnold and Willetta had done to the home she'd lived in all her life. She thought it might be a bit of both. She inhaled through her mouth to prevent retching.

Avery held her nose closed with her fingers. "Pew! It stinks in here!"

"I know." Tresia rushed into the apartment and started flinging back the curtains and opening the windows in the small, but well-appointed kitchen, allowing fresh air to circulate. She did the same in the parlor, and the bedrooms, too, until all the windows were open and the stench didn't seem so bad. She came back into the kitchen and noticed Avery hadn't moved from the doorway.

"You don't want to come in?"

She shook her head. "Uh uh."

She couldn't say she blamed her. If she didn't have to do this, she wouldn't. "All right. You can sit right there." She pointed through the open door to a chair on the balcony. "I'll bring you a book."

She left the room, wanting so much to hold her own nose, and found a book in the bookshelf, one with pictures of birds for Avery to look through. "Will you be all right out here?"

Avery nodded and opened the book.

"I'll be right inside if you need me." She left the door to the balcony open, both so she could hear Avery and continue airing out the apartment, then just stood there, in the middle of the kitchen, her hands on her hips. "I don't even know where to begin."

Hours later, Tresia dropped onto the sofa, whipped off the kerchief tied around her head, and let out a heart-felt sigh. "I'm done! I don't think I could wash another window or another dish! Look at my fingers! They're all pruny." She held up her fingers to Avery, proving that they truly were wrinkled like a prune.

Truthfully, she was exhausted, but the apartment reflected her hard work. Avery's, too, as she had decided to help her after all.

Avery flopped down on the sofa beside her. "Me, too!"

"And I'm hungry." She reached out to tickle the girl's tummy.

Avery giggled and tried to pull away, then moved closer for more. "Me, too!"

"What do you say we go home, change out of these dirty clothes and wash up, then take your Daddy out to dinner at the hotel? We could pick him up at his office. Would you like that?"

Avery nodded and ripped the matching kerchief she insisted on wearing off her head. "We can surprise Daddy!"

"Yes, we can. And I can tell him what a big help you were today."

Avery jumped up from the sofa, her excitement seeming to overwhelm her. "Do you think Daddy will let me have some ice cream?"

Tresia rose as well and took Avery's hand. "Absolutely, my sweet girl. It's our reward for all the hard work we did today."

CHAPTER 19

Tresia stared at her reflection in the mirror, watching as Lucy swept her long auburn hair away from one side of her face to pin it back with an ornate gold comb, then did the same to the other side.

"Perfect!" Lucy said as she took a step back to admire her handiwork.

Yes, it was perfect. The whole day was perfect. The sun was shining, the birds were singing, a light breeze ruffled the lacy curtains hanging from the window, and in a few short moments, she would marry Marshal Devlin Goodrich and begin her new life with the man she loved.

Last night, Mr. Peabody, the Justice of the Peace, had arrived in town in time to go over last-minute details and now waited downstairs in Lucy's parlor, which she had graciously offered instead of the courthouse.

"Stand up. Let me look at you."

Tresia rose from the dressing table after one last glance in the mirror and turned to face her friend.

"Oh, you look lovely. Leslie Carmichael did a beautiful job on your dress."

Tresia looked down at the ivory gown embroidered with tiny white and gold flowers. "She did, didn't she?" She turned toward Avery, who sat on the bed, Cecily clutched in her arms. She, too, had a new dress, compliments of Miss Leslie, the seamstress, who had created a matching dress for the doll. They both looked adorable. "What do you think, Avery?"

"You look beautiful, Mama!" Avery scrambled off the bed and held out a small red box she pulled from the pocket of her dress. "Daddy said to give you this."

Tresia opened it. Instant tears filled her eyes as she gazed upon an amethyst necklace. She pulled it from its black velvet bed by the gold chain, allowing the pendant to twist and turn. It caught the sunlight shining in from the window and cast pale purple sparkles on the walls. "It's beautiful." She glanced at Avery, who stood before her expectantly. "Did you know about this?"

Avery nodded enthusiastically, her light brown curls dancing around her head. "Me and Daddy picked it out."

"You did?" It was a wonderful surprise. More importantly, it was perhaps the only time in her life that Avery had kept a secret. Tresia wasn't sure if that was a good thing or not. She was used to Avery just blurting everything out. She drew Avery into a hug. "I love it, sweetheart. Thank you!"

"Let me put that on you."

Tresia handed over the necklace to Lucy then turned around, lifting up her hair so Lucy could clasp the gift around her neck. When she was done, she turned around and looked in the mirror, adjusting the necklace so the pendant lay against her skin just above the top of her dress. It was beautiful, something she would treasure, and every time she looked at it, she would remember this day.

"Are you ready?" Lucy asked as she did a last-minute adjustment to her hair and puffed out the sleeves of the dress she wore.

She smiled. "I am."

"Devlin is champing at the bit. He's ready, too. When I went downstairs earlier, he was pacing back and forth in the parlor, barely acknowledging the conversation going on around him." Lucy laughed. "I think he's nervous." She paused and looked into her eyes. "Are you nervous?"

"Not in the least." She left the room and stopped at the top of the stairs to catch her breath. She hadn't lied. She wasn't nervous. She was happy and excited, anxious to begin her married life.

"Don't forget your flowers." Lucy shoved a bouquet of white, yellow, and red roses into her hand, compliments of *Tia* Evie and Jake, who had arrived shortly before Justice Peabody with Hilde and Antonio in tow. All four were in the kitchen, preparing the luncheon that would be served after she and Devlin took their vows. There would be photographs, too, Lucy's wedding gift to them.

"You wait here. I'll get everyone settled in the parlor and I'll let you know when you should come downstairs." Lucy reached out her hand and grabbed Avery's. "Come on, sweetie."

Avery followed along, then leaned toward Lucy as they started down the stairs. "We're gettin' married today!" she exclaimed, barely able to contain her excitement.

Tresia laughed.

She watched them disappear from view, though she could still hear Avery talking and laughing, which made her heart proud. To think, she had spoken very little, only answering questions with a nod, a shake of her head or one word when they'd first met. Now, she was a vibrant and happy little girl.

It only took moments for Lucy and Avery to usher *Tia* Evie, Jake, Hilde and Antonio into the parlor, but it felt like a lifetime before Lucy closed the pocket doors and signaled to her. She fairly flew down the stairs, beyond anxious to show everyone present exactly how much she loved Devlin Goodrich.

"Ready?" Lucy asked, her eyes bright, her smile wide as she met her at the bottom of the stairs.

Tresia nodded. "I—" The words she wanted to say, the expression of gratitude toward Lucy and what she had done—introducing her to the love her life and the little girl who had changed her in so many ways—died in her throat and she couldn't speak at all.

Lucy laid gentle hands on her shoulders and squeezed. "You don't have to say anything. I know." Her own eyes were shiny with tears.

Tresia took a deep breath, her heart brimming with thankfulness, then she gave a quick nod. "I'm ready."

Lucy nodded, turned and opened the pocket doors before walking slowly into the parlor to take her place on the other side of Justice Peabody.

Tresia entered the parlor, her gaze focused on Devlin and Avery, who stood beside him, for once without her ever-present and much beloved Cecily.

Joy bubbled within her, so much so that she could hardly contain it. It was her wedding day. She didn't want to contain it. She wanted everyone to know how happy she was as she took another step closer—to her loves. Her family. Her future.

Devlin returned her gaze, his eyes bright, his confident, trusting smile touching her. He inhaled deeply, his chest puffing out with what she assumed was pride, then, though it wasn't tradition, he strode toward her and took her hand in his, as if he couldn't wait. "You look... beautiful doesn't even begin to describe how lovely you look."

"So do you." And he did, dressed in a coal black suit with a pristine white shirt and silver brocade vest. "Handsome, I mean."

He fingered the amethyst pendant resting on her breastbone. "Do you like it?"

"It's beautiful. Thank you." She looked at him and saw the promise of their future shining in his eyes. Her pulse raced and butterflies danced in her belly. "I'm surprised Avery kept your secret."

Devlin laughed. "She almost told you so many times! I had to keep reminding her that she couldn't tell."

She looked into his face, embracing the love she saw there. "I'm sorry. I have no gift for you."

He leaned forward, his lips brushing her ear. "You love me and Avery. That's the best gift any man could ever ask for. I don't need anything else. Just you."

His statement touched her heart. Tears flooded her eyes and rolled down her cheeks.

Devlin brushed his fingers beneath her eyes, wiping away her tears then smiled gently. "If I thought marrying me would make you cry, I never would have asked."

"Rest assured, my love, these are happy tears." She smiled. "Let's get married."

He turned toward the assembled guests. "We're ready," he announced, then led her toward Justice Peabody, who waited in front of the fireplace. He reached for Avery's hand and drew her forward to stand between them as if the three of them were marrying each other.

And once again, it was perfect.

Oh, she so loved this! Waking up beside Devlin in the morning, watching him as he slept, his face full of peace, despite what had happened with Frances just three days ago. She lifted her hand to gently touch his handsome face but the sight of the ring on her finger stopped her and for a moment, all she could do was stare at it. She turned it this way and that, watching as the sunlight coming in through the window made the plain gold band shine.

She couldn't be happier.

"Good morning, Wife."

She forced her gaze away from the ring and focused on him. A devilish grin spread his lips and heat flashed through her, though she should be exhausted. So should he. Neither one of them had slept very much as they celebrated the beginning of their marriage. "Good morning, Husband."

Devlin rolled onto his side and pulled her closer, his hand sliding up and down her arm, moving the blanket that covered her. "I don't want to get up yet."

She snuggled into him. "Neither do I."

"Let's just stay here all day," he said before he dropped a soft kiss to her lips.

"I don't know if I can do that. I've never spent the entire day in bed, not even when I wasn't feeling well." She smiled, beginning to like the idea, and laid her hand on his cheek. "But maybe you can change my mind."

"I'll see what I can do." He laughed before he started nuzzling her neck and she melted into his arms.

A long time later, Tresia sat across the table from Devlin, the remains of a hastily prepared breakfast littering their plates. She watched him finish the coffee in his cup, still amazed she could call him husband.

He smiled at her as he pushed his plate away. "What are your plans for today?"

"More cleaning at the store. It's a complete and total mess and I'm going to take advantage of Avery staying at Montaña del Trueno for a few days to get everything in order for my grand re-opening."

"Do you need help?"

She shook her head, pleased that he'd offered. "You have more important things to do, like protect this town. I'll be fine. Besides, I'd rather clean by myself because I know exactly how I like things."

"Don't wear yourself out." He gave her a wink as he rose from his seat. "I'm not done celebrating."

Warmth encompassed her face. Indeed, her entire body heated, knowing precisely what he meant. "I'll never be too tired." She laughed and stood as well, then walked straight into his arms.

He dropped a kiss on her lips. "I'll see you later." He broke their embrace and walked to the front door, then just stood there with the door open for the longest time, his gaze roaming over her. "I love you, Mrs. Goodrich," he said before he let himself out.

The heat in his stare as well as his words remained with her while she cleaned the kitchen and left the house shortly after he did. She cut across the town square, spotting Mrs. Dameron weeding the flower bed along one of the walkways.

The woman stuck her gardening spade into the rich dirt of the flower bed and rose from her kneeling pad as she approached. "I hear congratulations are in order, Tresia." She smiled as she removed her heavy work gloves. "You and the marshal."

"Thank you! I didn't realize you knew."

Mrs. Dameron patted her hand. "Everyone knows, dear. The whole town has been buzzing about it since Mr. Peabody stopped in the Silver Spur the other day and told everyone he'd married you and Marshal Goodrich. I understand he got a few free beers out of his announcement." She smiled. "Maybe Lucy Hart can find someone for me."

Tresia laughed. "I'm sure she could. You should go and see her."

The woman winked at her, and in that moment, she became young again, despite the mop of white hair poking out from beneath her bonnet and the wrinkles on her face. "Maybe I will. It's been a long time since Mr. Dameron passed." A look of sadness passed over her features, as if she remembered the good life she'd had with her late husband. "Heard you got your store back, too."

Not much stayed secret in Serenity. "I did. I'm heading there now to get ready for my grand re-opening." She grasped Mrs. Dameron's hand, noticing the strength in her fingers which belied the gentleness of her touch. "Speaking of that, I should get moving. The store isn't going to clean itself."

"Have a good day, dear, and congratulations once again. I hope you and Marshal Goodrich will be as happy as Mr. Dameron and I were."

"Thank you!"

Spirits high, she continued across the town square, then stopped at the edge of the street and just looked at Sullivan's Emporium. Pride rippled through her, as well as a sense of coming home.

Removing the key from her drawstring purse, she headed across the street and let herself into the store. She stood there in the doorway for a few moments, wondering what she should tackle first. The dusting? Sweeping? Mopping? It was all a mess, though not as bad as the apartment had been. "Well, nothing is going to get done with me standing here."

Hours later, she came out of the back storage room with a bucket of clean water to mop the floor one more time. It was her third bucket of water, but the floor had been that filthy. Her back hurt and a blister had formed on her hand from gripping the mop so tightly. But the store looked like it once had. The chandeliers, now dust free, glowed brightly above the displays, which were dust free as well.

She placed the bucket on the floor behind the counter then glanced up at the giant bear who kept watch over the register. The thought of moving him again seemed a little daunting at the moment as she'd already moved him twice—and he was heavy, despite the wheeled platform he rested on. "Too bad you can't move yourself out of the way."

She walked behind him and started to push when the little bell over the door jingled. "I'm sorry, we're closed," she called out.

There was no apology from whomever walked in, nor did she hear the bell jingle again as they left. She moved out from behind the bear. "We're clo—" She stiffened and her breath caught as she came face to face with the last person she thought she'd see. "Frances."

The woman stood close to the door, wearing that smile that wasn't a smile at all. To her left was Seth Humbolt. Devlin had told her about him. Seth was the person Frances relied upon the most to carry out her dirtiest work.

And at this moment, Tresia wasn't sure who scared her more —Frances or Humbolt—but she wasn't about to show either one of them her fear. "What do you want?"

"Did you really think you and that bastard I called my son-in-law could scare me away from my granddaughter? Did you really think I would not come back for her?" Frances took a few steps away from the door then gave a quick nod to the man, who moved in the opposite direction. "Where is she?"

Tresia straightened her shoulders and moved away from the bear to stand directly behind the counter, keeping the glass and wood structure between them, her focus on Frances though from the corner of her eye she watched Humbolt gravitate toward one of the ceramic tea sets on display. "Avery isn't here."

The resounding crash of that tea set being swept off the table onto the floor made her jump, but she never lost focus. Anger flashed through her.

"Get Avery." Frances barked. "She's my blood."

"I will not. She doesn't belong with you. She belongs with her father."

Another cacophony of noise made her flinch as Humbolt pushed a table filled with brand new copper pots and pans to the floor. The sound seemed to echo, and she turned her head for a just a moment, not only to stare at the man, but to try to discern what could be used as a weapon to defend herself.

Frances smiled, a parody of what a real smile should be as she took a few steps closer. Her eyes were wild, so dark they appeared almost black, and held what Tresia could only assume was rage. Or insanity. Perhaps both.

"Humbolt is enjoying himself," Frances said in a voice that confirmed the woman was indeed utterly mad as all the shovels and rakes, brooms and mops leaning against the wall went clattering to the floor. Tresia refused to flinch again.

Was he trying to distract her? Make her take her eyes off Frances? Yes, he was. And he was moving closer to her, step by slow step as each display tumbled or crashed to the floor, which didn't help the fear and anger that made her heart pound and her mouth dry up.

She took a breath to help her remain calm, though it didn't work, and moved slightly, taking a few steps further away from Humbolt, which brought her closer to Frances, though she was still behind the counter.

She had to find a way to reason with the woman but how was that accomplished with someone like her? Reason didn't seem to be something Frances understood.

Another crash resounded as Humbolt swept all the dishes from the shelves where they were—had been—displayed. Her hands curled into fists at the damage. On the outside, she fought to look calm.

"I thought you were going to ruin Devlin."

That made the woman deflate, just a little, as her cheeks reddened. "I've changed my mind." She acted as if it didn't matter, though Tresia could see it plainly did. "It seems that Devlin Goodrich is a true hero. No one on my payroll wants to touch him." She glanced at Humbolt. "Except for him. He has an axe to grind with the marshal, don't you?"

Humbolt grinned and it was even more evil than Frances' smile. "Yes, ma'am."

Tresia stared at the man, unable to take her focus away from him and that wicked grin. She shouldn't have done that. She felt rather than saw Frances take another step toward her. She swung her gaze back to the woman and finally saw her salvation—a way to defend herself.

There, on one of the tables, was a weapon—the hammer she'd used earlier to fix that table. There was a screwdriver, too. They weren't much, but she could reach them. She wished now that she had kept a gun hidden in one of the cubbies behind the counter, but she'd never been a fan of guns. How ironic that she married a man who used guns for a living.

She moved a little closer to the table.

"A little more, Humbolt, if you please. I think we're making Tresia here nervous." The woman cackled, actually cackled, making the hair on the back of Tresia's neck rise, as Humbolt pushed over her display of soaps—the one she'd worked so hard to get right.

And Tresia made her move. She stepped from behind the counter, grabbed the hammer and paused. What could she do with it? There were two of them and only one of her.

"What are you going to do with that?" Frances laughed as she pulled a little derringer from her pocket and aimed it at her. "A hammer is no defense against a bullet."

What she needed was help. Something to draw attention. She glanced at Humbolt. He was closer, almost to the counter.

She hauled back and threw the hammer with all her might toward the plate glass front window. It shattered with a loud crash.

"Well, that was a stupid thing to do. Now you have no weapon." Frances laughed and glanced toward Humbolt, who was much closer now than he had been. He reached for her, wrapping his strong arms tightly around her chest, lifting her off her feet. He squeezed tight, making it difficult to draw a breath. She struggled, trying to get free, but he squeezed a little harder. Not only could she not breathe, but dark spots shadowed her vision. If she kept struggling, Humbolt would likely squeeze the life from her.

"Now where is my granddaughter? She's not at the house.

She's not here and she's not at your friend, Lucy's, either, so where are you hiding her?"

Tresia struggled to speak. "If you kill me, you'll never know."

"You're smarter than I thought, but you won't win against me. Humbolt here has ways of convincing people to talk. By the time he's done with you, you'll tell me everything I want to know." Her eyes narrowed as she focused on her henchman. "Show her."

Devlin finished writing his report and started to close the ledger. He stopped with his hand on the edge of the hardcover journal and just stared out the window, remembering how delicious Tresia had looked earlier this morning.

He rose from his desk and strolled toward the front door but before he could open it, it flew open and banged against the wall.

Paul Jennings, the Ice Man, rushed into the office, breathless, his face perspiring, his movements stiff and jerky in obvious panic. "Something's happening over at Sullivan's!" he blurted out.

Tresia was at the store. Devin placed a hand on the man's arm. "What's happening?"

"I don't know exactly but as Lilibet and I were coming down the street, a hammer came flying through the window!" Paul smoothed his hand over his face as if worried. "I didn't go into the store. I just looked in through the broken window. A man was holding your wife. She wasn't happy about it either. Kept struggling to get free."

"Anyone else in the store?"

"A woman. Dark haired. Thin. Stylish. Agitated. She was pacing back and forth. I can't be certain, but I think she was holding a gun."

Frances. He'd thought she'd left town. Apparently, she had not and just waited for the right time to...do whatever she was going to do. He reached for the Colt revolver in his gun belt. He flicked open the cylinder. It was fully loaded. He put it back and reached for the other. It, too, was fully loaded. He might just need every one of those bullets. "Thank you, Paul. Go on home."

The man shook his head. "I want to help. Tresia has always been kind to me."

He studied the man for a moment, just long enough to make a decision. "All right, but you have to listen to everything I say." He glanced at Sherm, who had joined him and said, "You're with me."

The three of them took off, Devlin in the lead. He stopped them on the edge of the square and turned to Sherm. "I want you to go around back and let yourself into the store through the storeroom. Quietly." The young man started walking away but Devlin stopped him. "And for God's sake, don't shoot anyone if you can help it."

"Yes, sir." Sherm crossed the street, heading toward the back of the building at a run, his long legs eating up the distance until he turned the corner and disappeared.

Devlin glanced at Paul then at the people starting to gather on the sidewalk outside Sullivan's. Obviously, they had either seen or heard the hammer breaking glass. It was the last thing he needed—an innocent bystander getting hurt. "Try not to let anyone come close. And try not to be seen."

The man gave him a sharp salute and went to do his bidding, pushing people further down the sidewalk, away from harm.

Devlin crossed the street at an angle, staying out of sight from the windows lest anyone inside Sullivan's saw him. He edged up to the broken window and looked through, his heart thundering in his chest, fear making his mouth dry.

Tresia was tied to one of the chairs, rope wound tightly around her. Humbolt stood beside her, smirking. Blood trickled from the corner of her mouth and a red splotch marred her cheek.

The bastard had hit her! Rage surged through him, so much

so that he shook. He forced himself to remain calm and assess the situation.

How to get into Sullivan's without being seen or heard? Noise. He needed a distraction.

Focus turning on him rather than Tresia.

He glanced at the people gathering in the street, though Paul was doing his best to keep everyone back.

He drew his gun and barged into the store, just as Humbolt drew back his fist to hit Tresia again. He pulled back the hammer of his revolver—the click loud in the silence—and settled his finger on the trigger. "I wouldn't, if I were you."

The look in Tresia's eyes was one of pure confidence. Her body seemed to sag with relief, pulling the ropes a little tighter.

Aiming for Humbolt's arm, he pulled the trigger.

Humbolt cried out and clamped his hand over the bullet hole to staunch the bleeding, his face a mixture of rage, pain, and incredulity. He took a step away from Tresia, but not far enough.

Frances turned toward him immediately, the little derringer pointing at him. Her hand shook just a bit. "Good. You're here."

"What are you doing, Frances?" He kept his voice calm, though it was an effort.

"I want my granddaughter."

"You can't have her."

Frances laughed, though the sound was without humor. "I'll make a fair trade. Avery for your wife."

"I'm not willing to lose either one of them." From the corner of his eye, he saw movement. Sherm. He kept his focus on his former mother-in-law. "Drop the gun, Frances. You won't win this." He took a step closer to her then stopped. She could just as easily shoot him. He was standing not less than three feet from her, but he didn't think she would. No, Frances wanted him to suffer, more than he already had.

"Then I'm going to take from you what you took from me." She said the words calmly, then turned slowly, as if making sure he saw her every move, and aimed the derringer directly at Tresia.

He moved quickly, grabbing Frances around the waist, reaching for the derringer in her hand, just as she fired. His heart stopped for a brief moment as he forced the gun from her hand then risked a quick glance toward Tresia. Blood blossomed on her shoulder, staining her white blouse. He saw Humbolt move, whether to reach for the pistol he carried or to get to Tresia, he didn't know, but he never had the chance as Sherm raised his own gun and shoved it against the man's head.

"I wouldn't," his deputy warned, his voice low and threatening. Humbolt froze. Sherm brought the butt of his pistol down on the man's head in the next instant and Frances' henchman crumpled to the ground.

Frances screamed, a guttural cry that sounded half human, half cornered animal. She renewed her struggle against him, driven by madness or revenge or whatever emotion a woman like Frances could feel. She punched and kicked at him, twisting in his arms. He squeezed a little tighter then nodded toward Sherm.

The deputy ran to his side and he shoved the struggling woman into his arms. "Cuff her." He nodded toward Humbolt, who remained on the floor, unmoving. "You better cuff him, too, before he wakes up."

The young man smiled. "My pleasure."

Devlin moved toward Tresia, quickly untied her and helped her to her feet, resisting the urge to draw her into his arms as he didn't want to hurt her more than she'd already been hurt.

Tresia raised her gaze to him, tears filling her eyes, her body trembling. "I knew you'd come." She pulled in her breath as the reality hit her. "She was going to kill me."

"I know. Let me see that wound." He ripped away the sleeve of her blouse carefully. "Looks like the bullet is still in there." He pulled a handkerchief from his pocket then looked at her. "I'm sorry. This is going to hurt."

She nodded then stiffened, as if preparing herself for the worst. She let out a groan as he pressed the handkerchief to her shoulder.

"Hold that there," he instructed her.

Tresia held the handkerchief in place as she looked at him, the color draining from her face. He wasn't sure if that was from the pain or the strain of what she'd been through but her entire body began shaking. "Thank God Avery wasn't here."

He took her hand and brought it to his lips. "Genius idea to throw something through the window."

She shrugged then winced as the movement brought her more pain. "I needed help and smashing the window seemed to be the best way to get attention."

"Let's get you to Doc Hart to remove that bullet." He lifted her in his arms and strode toward the door, passing Frances, who now sat in one of the chairs with her hands cuffed behind her.

"Bastard!" she screamed, her face white except for the two spots of color on her cheeks. "This isn't over."

"Yes, it is." He fought to get his anger under control. Frances, as he now realized, was not a well woman. Perhaps, the loss of Hannah had done something to her mind. Still, he could not continue to have her be a threat to Avery and Tresia. He glanced at Sherm. "Lock her up. Humbolt, too."

Frances spit at him though he was too far away for her to do much damage. "You can't arrest me! You know who I am!"

"I'm well aware of who you are, Frances. You are the person who just tried to kill my wife." He stared at her. "Hear me well. You will never hurt anyone again."

He turned away from her then with Tresia held more closely in his arms, he walked outside to face the growing crowd of people standing on the sidewalk and the street in both directions, blocking his way. "Get out of the way," he shouted. "She's been shot."

He glanced up and recognized Merrill. "Help Sherm. He's inside." The crowd began to part, opening a path for him.

He glanced at Tresia. Her eyes were closed, her face pale. Had she passed out? From the pain? From the loss of blood? He ran toward Doctor Ben's on the next street over. "Don't you dare die on me, Tresia Goodrich! I love you too much to lose you."

She opened her eyes and smiled softly, despite having a bullet in her shoulder. "I'm not going to die, Devlin. You're stuck with me." She reached up and smoothed her hand along his cheek. "For the rest of our lives."

EPILOGUE

AUTUMN 1893

"It's a good letter, Lucy." Tresia folded the thick sheaf of paper and handed it to Lucy. The action made her wince, just a little. Every once in a while, the shoulder where Frances shot her reminded her of how close she'd come to dying. "I wouldn't change a thing." She watched her friend wander over to the stove and pick up the coffeepot. "It must have been hard, letting Josie's daughter know what happened to her."

"It wasn't easy, I will admit. I struggled a bit." Lucy patted the pocket where she had placed the letter then poured the rich brew into cups and slid one across the table to her. "This is my fourth attempt."

"Why did Mr. Applebaum ask you to write it? He's a lawyer. A good one. He should know how to compose a letter."

Lucy laughed, her face turning a lovely shade of pink as she put the coffeepot back on the stove and slid into her seat. "Because, while he's an excellent lawyer, he has all the finesse of a bull in a China shop and the situation required a little more delicacy than he can handle. We didn't know what Sheridan—that's her name—knew of Josie's life. We didn't even know Josie had a daughter until Mr. Applebaum opened probate, so the situation required a little more diplomacy than Mr. Applebaum possesses."

"Well, you did a good job. I'm sure Mr. Applebaum will appreciate it. Sheridan, too."

"He's helping you as well, isn't he?"

She nodded, grateful that the good lawyer was, indeed, helping. "And there's a lot to do. As you know, Frances never stood trial for what she tried to do to me. Her mind...isn't what it should be. The loss of Hannah was finally too much for her. She will be locked up in the sanitarium for a long time." Tresia stirred the coffee though she hadn't added any sugar or cream to it. "Devlin's old friend and his wife are taking care of the ranch until Avery comes into her majority at twenty-one. Mr. Applebaum is working on all the legalities of that as well as keeping Frances where she is so the doctors at the sanitarium can continue to help her. I doubt she'll ever leave, but she'll be well taken care of."

Tresia sighed and pushed her coffee cup away, unable to tolerate the aroma. In fact, it was making her stomach roil, and if she wasn't careful, she'd been running for the chamber pot, as she'd done several times this past week. Funny that it only happened in the morning and early afternoon—by evening, she was craving the rich brew. She glanced up to see Lucy staring at her with the most peculiar look on her face.

"Everything all right? Is the coffee too strong?"

"I don't know. I can't get past the smell, which is so strange. That's never happened to me before. Lately, when I'm brewing coffee in the morning, the smell is enough to make me nauseous."

"Nauseous? Well, that's odd." Lucy's brows rose as a smile lifted the corners of her mouth. "How long has this been happening?"

"Just the past few weeks or so."

Lucy's smile grew. "Anything else unusual?"

"I'm tired." She let out a sigh. "Which is also unlike me. Some days, it feels like I can't get enough sleep. Other days, I have so much energy, I don't know what to do with myself. Teaching Corianna how to run Sullivan's must be more exhausting than I thought, even though she's catching on quickly." She was still happy with her decision to help Corianna leave Josie's Parlor House and come to work for her at the store.

"She's smarter than she ever gave herself credit for. She loves the store almost as much as I do and she has some great ideas to make it better." Tresia reached for a slice of cake then changed her mind. Just the thought of eating that sweet treat made her stomach turn. She looked at Lucy across the table. "Why are you smiling like that?"

"Oh, no reason, but I think you should see my husband—in his professional capacity."

"It's nothing, Lucy. I'm not sick. I don't even have a fever."

"No, you're not sick. You're just…I think…maybe…." She clamped her mouth shut, but there was a glimmer of mischief in her eyes. "I'm not going to say anything. Let's see what Ben has to say. He's here now. I don't think he has any patients at the moment. Why don't you go see him?"

"Lucy, you're being ridiculous. I'm just tired."

"For me? Please?" Lucy asked then rose from her chair and grabbed her hand, forcing her to rise as well. It didn't look like she had much choice.

"All right. Just to prove to you there's nothing wrong with me."

A few moments later, she was ushered into Ben's office through the separate entrance and looking at him. "I'm not even sure why I'm here. I'm not sick, but Lucy insisted."

"That's fine." He laughed. "You don't have to be sick to see me. In fact, you're one of the healthiest people I know, but it couldn't hurt. You're here. I'm here. Let's just examine you." He led her into the examining room and helped her up onto the table. "There's a reason why Lucy wanted me to look at you. What did you tell her?"

Tresia shook her head and played with the strings of her drawstring purse, a little nervous. "Just that I'm tired. And the smell of coffee makes me nauseous."

He smiled as he fitted the earpieces of his stethoscope into his ears and pressed the chest piece to her heart. He listened quietly for a few minutes. "Your heart is good, beating normally." He moved behind her and pressed the chest piece to her back. "Breathe in."

She did as she was told, although this seemed pretty ridiculous. She was just tired, that's all.

"Again."

She pulled air into her lungs and let it out slowly.

"Very good," Ben said as he came around so he could look at her, the stethoscope now around his neck. He looked at her eyes, then felt along her jawbone with the pads of his fingers and lower still to her throat. "I detect no swelling and your eyes are clear." His smile was reassuring, as it always was. He was a great doctor—kind, compassionate, and truly knowledgeable. "Is there anything else besides being tired and the smell of coffee making you nauseated? Is coffee the only thing? Any other changes that are different than before? Differences in your body?" He hit her with rapid fire questions, almost too fast to respond to, then took her hand and pressed two fingers to her wrist where her pulse beat. "Hmmm, nice and steady."

Her face warmed with embarrassment as she thought about what he asked though she should be able to tell Ben anything. He was her doctor and had been treating her professionally for quite some time. "Well, my clothes have been feeling a little tight." She gestured to her chest. "Especially here. And my breasts are tender. Tightening up my corset is sometimes...uncomfortable. Taking it off is worse."

He said nothing, but his smile grew and his eyes danced with mischief like Lucy's had just a short time ago. "When was your last monthly flow?" he asked, rather bluntly in her opinion.

And surprisingly, she really had to think about that. Truthfully, she hadn't been paying attention. Married life, plus making sure Avery was happy and healthy, while teaching Corianna how to run Sullivan's had kept her so busy, she hadn't noticed. "I don't know," she admitted finally, a little embarrassed by that, too. She'd always been as regular as clockwork and knew her schedule down to within a three-day window. "It's been at least two months."

"You're right. There is nothing wrong with you." He smiled in that reassuring way he had then took her hand in his. "I believe you're going to have a baby."

It was the last thing she expected to hear. "What?"

"You're going to have a baby," he repeated. "Are you surprised?"

Surprised didn't even begin to describe what she was feeling at the moment. "Well, yes! I never thought I would become pregnant. I didn't think I could."

"Why not? You're young and healthy."

"But Brett and I tried for a long time."

He removed the stethoscope from around his neck and laid it on the desk in the corner then came to stand in front of her, his hands on the examining table on either side of her hips. "Did you ever think it was Brett's condition that prevented you from becoming pregnant?"

"No, I never did. I always figured it would happen if it happened and then, when it didn't, I just thought…that I wasn't meant to be a mother."

"Well, you are now—" he gestured to her belly "—not only to this little one, but to Avery, too."

He took her hand and helped her slide from the table. "Congratulations, Tresia."

Stunned by the news, she left Ben's office then let herself into Lucy's kitchen. She was waiting, hands on her hips, a look of expectancy on her face.

"I'm going to have a baby," she announced, still reeling then shook her head, not sure if she should laugh or cry. "How did you know?"

Lucy chuckled. "I've been a doctor's wife for a few years now, plus I have three sisters-in-law. I know some of the signs." She handed her a glass of lemonade and gestured to a chair. "What's wrong? Aren't you happy? Haven't you always wanted a baby?"

"I did. I do. I didn't think I could." She let out a sigh as a thought occurred to her, dampening her happiness. "I'm worried about how Devlin is going to react. You know he lost Hannah in childbirth."

Lucy's face paled a bit and she lost a little of her enthusiasm. "No, I didn't know, but it's going to be all right. You're not Hannah. He knows that."

Tresia took a deep breath. "How am I going to tell him that I'm pregnant?"

"What's pregnant?" A small voice asked from the doorway.

Tresia turned in her chair quickly to see Avery and Savannah, the both of them wearing the efforts of their goal to dig a hole all the way to China.

Before she could compose herself, Savannah rolled her eyes like Avery was the dumbest person on earth. "She's going to have a baby, silly," she said. "That's what pregnant means. You're going to be a big sister."

Avery's eyes widened in surprise as she looked at her friend. "I am?"

"Don't get so excited." Savannah let out an exaggerated groan. "Babies cry all the time!" She jerked her thumb toward her chest. "I know. I'm big sister to three brothers, and they're all a pain!"

Lucy let out a sudden peal of laughter then slapped her hand over her mouth. When she recovered from her apparent shock, she admonished the girl. "Savannah! That's not nice to say. I have three brothers, too, and they're not all bad."

Savannah shrugged. "But it's the truth. They are a pain... sometimes. I still love them though."

Tresia held out her hand for Avery, who hadn't moved from the doorway, still apparently surprised. She moved forward and Tresia pulled her onto her lap, despite the mud on her clothes, hands, and face. Even Cecily, who she clutched in her arms, was covered in mud. There was a bath in Avery's future...as soon as they got home. She pushed Avery's curls, which were getting long, away from her face then grasped her little chin between her fingers. "Is that all right with you, sweet pea?"

Avery nodded eagerly, no fear or apprehension in her expression. She may have been too young to remember what happened with her mother, or had been shielded from the truth, which was a blessing in many ways. "Let's go home and tell your father." She rose from her seat, Avery still in her arms, then leaned in for a quick hug for Lucy. "I'll see you tomorrow. And thank you, Lucy. This is kind of wonderful!"

As they walked home, Avery clutching her hand and skipping beside her, Tresia wrestled with exactly how she was going to tell Devlin the news. The words just wouldn't come to her, no matter how hard she tried.

She was saved from having to find the right words at all. Avery ran through the front door and saw Devlin. "I'm going to be a big sister!"

The words evidently stunned him as well because he released the vase of fresh flowers he'd set on the fireplace mantle, and just stood there, his mouth open even as Avery launched herself into his arms. "Mama's gonna have a baby!"

The expression on his face made her hesitate. She couldn't tell if he was happy or sad or concerned or all three.

"Is it true? Are you...?" He lowered Avery to the floor then took a step away from the fireplace, a slew of emotions passing over his face.

Tresia nodded, still unsure, as she closed the door and just stood there, waiting to see what he would do or say.

It only took a moment for a big smile to lift the corners of his mouth and then she was in his arms and he was dropping kisses all over her face and laughing.

"Does this mean you're happy?"

"I am. Incredibly so."

She laughed as he picked her up and whirled her around, then quickly realizing what he was doing in her condition, set her down. "I shouldn't have done that. Are you all right?"

"I'm all right, Devlin. I'm not made of porcelain. I won't break though I am a little nauseated."

"I'm sorry." He led her to a chair, the most comfortable one in the parlor, and made her sit, then knelt in front of her. Avery took advantage of the situation and crawled into her lap.

She ran her fingers through Avery's curls, then reached out to cup Devlin's cheek. "No need to be sorry." Her gaze roamed over his face and she saw his concern. Was he thinking of Hannah? "Dr. Ben says I'm young and healthy and should have no problems."

He nodded, as if understanding all the words she didn't say. "Are you happy?" he asked finally.

"I am." She smiled as he took her hand from his cheek and kissed the palm. "Very much so."

And she was. Who'd have thought she'd have everything she'd ever wanted—the store, a husband who adored her, and children to love, and it was all because of Lucy Hart and her matchmaker mischief. She'd have to remember to thank her...but not too soon!

ACKNOWLEDGMENTS

The Marshal & Mrs. Morgan is my own story; however, I couldn't have written it without the people who helped me along the way—

Lexi Post, critique partner and dear, dear friend, who tells me all the time to "give me less here" as I tend to get a little wordy;

To Jan Walkosz and Paige Wood, beta readers extraordinaire, who are able to find things I don't even see;

To my son and his lovely wife, who continue to show me the beauty of love;

To my editor, Jill, who is still showing me so many things I didn't know I didn't know;

And finally, to my husband, my very own hero, who bought me my very first electric typewriter so many years ago—you believed in me then...you still do!

Thank you all!

ALSO BY MARIE PATRICK

Matchmaker Mischief

The Maverick & Miss Miller

The Marshal & Mrs. Morgan

Wives of Bravado County

Wife for Hire

Wife Wanted

MacDermott Brothers

A Kiss in the Shadows

A Kiss in the Morning Mist

A Kiss in the Sunlight

Standalone Novels

Mischief and Magnolias

A Treasure Worth Keeping

A Scandalous Woman

Touch the Flame

Angel in the Moonlight

ABOUT THE AUTHOR

Marie Patrick has always had a love affair with words and books but it wasn't until a trip to Arizona, where she now makes her home with her husband, that she became inspired to write about the sometimes desolate, yet beautiful west. Her inspiration doesn't just come from the Wild West though. It comes from history itself. She is fascinated with pirates and men in uniform and lawmen with shiny badges. When not writing or researching her favorite topics, she can usually be found curled up with a good book. Marie loves to hear from her readers. Drop her a note at Akamariep@aol.com or visit her website at www.mariepatrick.com.

www.ingramcontent.com/pod-product-compliance
Lightning Source LLC
Chambersburg PA
CBHW020402110726
47899CB00006B/1827